VANITAS

VANITAS

JOSEPH OLSHAN

BLOOMSBURY

First published in Great Britain 1998
This paperback edition published 1999

Copyright © 1998 by Joseph Olshan

The moral right of the author has been asserted

Bloomsbury Publishing Plc, 38 Soho Square, London W1V 5DF

A CIP catalogue record for this book is available from the British Library

ISBN 0 7475 4425 5

10 9 8 7 6 5 4 3 2 1

Printed in Great Britain by Clays Limited, St Ives plc

For Barry Raine

ACKNOWLEDGMENTS

I feel lucky to have had astute guidance while writing this novel and would like to acknowledge the splendid efforts of all the people who were helpful to me.

George Shackelford, the curator of European Painting at The Museum of Fine Arts in Boston, gave me a very careful reading of the manuscript as well as many important suggestions toward developing the narrative line. In so doing, he introduced me to the painting conservator Alain Goldrach, who allowed me to visit his studio and kindly demonstrated his art.

The writings of the art scholar Lorenz Eitner were inspirational to me, as was his extraordinary passion for Géricault's work.

I am also indebted to Wheelock Whitney for sharing with me his intimate knowledge of Géricault's life.

Margaret Edwards helped me refine many of my ideas and, in several careful readings of the manuscript, gave great suggestions and advice.

Elisabeth Jakab gave a detailed and comprehensive reading of the manuscript and was most helpful.

I would like to thank my agent, Mary Evans, for her honesty, her great and unflagging support, and her many accurate editorial comments.

I would like to thank Liz Calder of Bloomsbury, Ltd, in London for her honesty and her editorial help.

At Simon & Schuster, I would like to thank my editor, Dominick Anfuso for his early and continuing enthusiasm in the novel; Ana DeBevoise for her patience and dedication; and Michael Selleck for his belief in my work and for his many efforts on my behalf.

And lastly I would like to acknowledge the late Robert Woolley, who urged me to find in a novel a place for his memory.

No insect hangs its nest on threads as frail as those which will sustain the weight of human vanity.

— EDITH WHARTON, *The House of Mirth*

One

1 Thousands of miles behind him was the continent of America, and hours ahead lay the British Isles, somewhere in the vaporous dawn. Leaning his forehead against the airplane window, Sam Solomon told himself: I am forty, I am nowhere. So many lost opportunities, lost lovers, he thought as he looked down on the dark plain of the Atlantic, wondering what would happen if there weren't some major shift, some turnaround in his life.

Just then the plane lurched. Next to him a sleeping Indian woman jerked awake with a chorus of silver arm bangles. A drowsy flight attendant ambling down the aisle with an empty coffeepot dangling from her fingers stiffened where she stood, grabbing the back of the nearest seat. The aircraft almost seemed to rear up before it began plummeting.

It happened so quickly, the most anyone could do was gasp. Gravity was lost, and Sam was thrown up out of his seat, as far as the seat belt would allow him. The book he was reading levitated out of his hands, separating from its wrapper. A loose strand of pearls was floating in front of the Indian woman's stricken face. As the interminable plunge continued, he grew more and more convinced that he was going to die.

But then, miraculously, the plane leveled out, triggering a round of shrieking passengers as pocketbooks and paper cups and loose liquids rained. Gravity had returned, but for only an interval, only until the plane began another dive. This time the flight attendant standing in the aisle was reeled up to the ceiling and stayed there until the plane leveled out again, and she clumped down to the floor, screaming, quickly followed by her shoes. The journey had gone wild.

Finally, the British captain came on the public address system. "Please, ladies and gentlemen, try to remain calm. We are experiencing severe turbulence. *Nothing* is wrong with our aircraft." Explaining that the disturbances were being caused by a severe updraft from the Atlantic, he promised to find higher altitude.

As the plane began climbing through the clouds, Sam, only somewhat relieved by the pilot's reassurance, turned toward the window. There was a face outside its darkened screen. A face of liquid light, a face of incomparable beauty, vaguely recognizable at first, was staring back at him. Then he remembered. It was the man he used to call "the angel."

How vivid he was after so many years: the flaxen hair, and the pale, importunate eyes—for so long Sam had hoped to encounter him again. Now, looking closer, he saw something deformed in the midst of the man's beauty and shut his eyes. But even from behind closed eyelids, Sam could perceive the shining image, one more lost opportunity in his life, and with that, he panicked.

Between one country and another, between day and night, perhaps even between life and death, why would the little-known face of a dead man come to him miles above the earth? The pilot came on again to say, "Ladies and gentlemen, we are expecting a smoother ride at this altitude," but Sam's heart continued to bang. Finally, he reminded himself there was a painting in the cargo hold, an artist to track down; this trip to England had to be completed. When he opened his eyes again, he was relieved to find the angel had fled, the face replaced by the first traces of the morning finally catching up to the plane.

From Heathrow, the empty train slowly filled up with dazed, early-morning commuters heading into central London; they seemed more docile and self-contained than their counterparts in New York City, their perfumes and colognes more citrus in fragrance. He rode directly to King's Cross, then hailed a cab to a terrace of late-eighteenth-century Georgian homes that were within walking distance of Highgate Cemetery. His arrival had been timed to coincide with Jessie's thirty-eighth birthday party, which was being held six weeks late due to the fact that when the actual date fell, she had been too busy working on an ad campaign.

Jessie Every's house was blooming with wisteria. Near her front gate was an enormous lavender bush, whose sprigs Sam always picked whenever he visited. He'd stow the cuttings in his coat pocket and forget about them until months later when he was back in Manhattan and suddenly his fingers would encounter foreign powdery matter in his jacket. He'd pull out tiny scented twigs. "Smell this," he'd say to anybody who might be with him. "This is authentic English lavender."

He climbed out of the cab, extricated his bags, staggered up the front stone stairs and glanced at his watch—it was just after nine-thirty. He had to bang the door knocker for a few minutes before he heard any movements inside.

Jessie finally opened the door. Even swaddled in a faded paisley silk dressing gown, she seemed to have shed some weight since his last visit, and her broad, slightly freckled face looked almost gaunt. Her luxuriant auburn hair was piled into a soft swirl on top of her head, stray tendrils mobile. "Sam!" She gave him a great squeezing hug through which he could feel her bones. And when she held her face a few inches from his, he could see a puffiness around her eyes. "You're looking really well," she said. "But your hair is so short."

"You like it?"

"Yes, but no shorter, okay? It'll make you look too severe."

Jessie's manner of speaking was a hybrid of British and American expressions. Her accent sounded British to most Americans, whereas, to the British, she sounded like an American.

She tried to take one of his bags, but Sam gently prevented her. He brought them in himself and leaned them against the staircase. The house was steeped in an unnatural quiet. By now Jessie's five-year-old daughter should have been scampering up to greet him. "Where's Eva?" he asked.

Eva had gone to be with one of her friends for the day and evening. "She was very understanding when I told her about the party." Eva was quite used to her entertaining, Jessie explained. "She's so adaptable."

They heard somebody shuffling up the front steps and then a knock at the door. Sam thought it might be Rudy, Jessie's most recent boyfriend, but it was an Indian man with glossy hair, diffidently announcing the arrival of an order of wine. At the bottom of the steps was a hand truck piled up with ten cardboard cases. "Must be some shindig," Sam said. Then he and the man began to ferry the load of bottles up the stone steps into the house.

"Sixty people," Jessie admitted, standing to one side, hands on her hips. After directing the placement of the boxes, she paid the deliveryman and shut the front door behind him, looking relieved. "I've put on the tea," she told Sam as she led the way deeper into the house.

Sam followed her down the front hallway, past the sitting room that was painted a mossy green and where, in one corner, stood a battered-looking upright piano. There was a scent of spice in the air, perhaps from one of Jessie's stir-fried vegetable curries. How different this house was, thought Sam, how dusty and cozily threadbare, in contrast to the opulent apartment where he had been spending much of his time. Over the last few months, Sam had been helping a dying art dealer write his memoirs. A pile of morning mail was lying on one of the steps that led to the upstairs, to Jessie's bedroom. Wondering if she were alone, Sam managed to catch her eye before she turned down the flight of thinly carpeted stairs to the kitchen. He pointed his finger upward.

"Oh, yeah, he's here," she said. "When I came home last night, he was conked out on my doorstep. We had ended up at different parties. Because his wife decided at the last minute that she had to go with him."

Though Sam had twice been over to London during Jessie's affair with Rudy, this was the first time that Rudy was actually in Jessie's bed when he arrived.

"Doesn't he have to be at work?" Sam asked. Rudy was a British-educated Dutch citizen who worked as a roving correspondent for a major Dutch television station.

Jessie shrugged and said she had no idea.

"Well, what does his wife do, when he goes off like he does?" Apparently, Rudy's wife knew about and tolerated his affair with Jessie.

"If she allows him out overnight, it's her problem, don't you think? I could never put up with that kind of behavior myself."

Sam couldn't decide which was worse: being honest about sexual indiscretions, and carrying on openly, or lying to "protect" the spouse who was being betrayed.

He loved Jessie's kitchen, paved with terra-cotta tiles. Several hanging planters spilled translucent manes of spider ferns. At the far end was the glass lozenge of a back door that looked out on a deep, verdant garden, a long, beautifully cultivated strip of property that ended at an octagonal potting shed.

Their ritual, whenever Sam visited England during the warmer months, was to have tea in Jessie's garden. Tea in the garden had been the very first ceremony of Sam's affair with her. Perhaps the whole affair—between a maverick young woman and a bisexual man—was ceremonious. Ten years ago, when Sam was thirty, the ad agency that employed them both had sent him to its London office for six months, during which they began an unconventional relationship. However, Jessie severed that six months after Sam returned to America, claiming the distance between them was too great.

From the vantage point of where Sam now stood, he could spy the nineteenth-century teapot and the large, white embossed teacups resting on a wrought-iron table. They were larger than normal teacups, and something about their warm amplitude made them extremely comforting to hold. For a while he had tried to find replicas of them all over London, only to learn that they had been cast from a mold that had since become unavailable. The style was extinct.

So much of what Jessie owned was rare. The house had always struck Sam as one great comfort zone: wall-to-wall bookshelves, Victorian sofas covered with woolen blankets, African tribal masks, old tea tins that held polished stones. Because he himself had grown up among serviceable dinette sets and department store drapes, this place had understandably taken on mythological proportions, pointing out a new direction for his life.

"I'm just getting the biscuits." Jessie had crossed the kitchen and was reaching for a tin on a shelf crammed with home-decanted spices she'd collected from all over the Mediterranean. She carried a tray of tea, toast, jam, and almond cookies out into the garden, saying, "Oh, and thanks for bringing the beautiful weather once again."

Sam followed her. "Has it been otherwise?"

"Horrible. Horrible summer. Horrible like always. Just rain and more rain."

He heard her set down the tray with a bony clatter of crockery as he looked up at the presently blameless sky. "You'd never know it."

"You *always* say that, Sam! Every year you manage to miss the worst. The next time we're having a bad patch of weather I'm going to send you a plane ticket. By the way, how was the flight?"

The terrifying feeling of plummeting seized him once again. He described how the plane had hit an air pocket and plunged a great distance.

"How awful."

"For a few seconds everybody thought that was it."

"God!"

"I've been feeling light-headed ever since." Sam heard the toilet flushing and looked at the upstairs windows. He hoped Rudy would remain upstairs but knew there was a slim chance of that.

Jessie reached out and touched Sam's arm. "Have lots of toast. You'll feel better. . . . So now, you've come over to interview some people?"

"Two people."

"And it's for a book that you're . . . *ghostwriting?*"

He nodded.

"How does that affect your byline?"

He could tell her look was skeptical. Jessie had often expressed her pride in Sam's accomplishments as a failed poet. He'd shown her the start of his never-finished novel as well. She'd praised his creativity and wanted him to believe in it, too. Ghostwriting would seem too practical for Jessie.

"I'll be completely invisible."

She took a long draught of tea before saying, "And that's perfectly fine with you?"

Sam explained that it was all part of the job description.

Although Sam's employer/subject was quite famous in America, Jessie had never heard of him. "I don't know what's going on there anymore," she said wistfully.

"You should come over more often."

"The more I come over, the more I want to live there."

And yet Sam knew that despite a certain amount of lament, Jessie would spend the rest of her life in London. She'd paid a song for the house's ninety-nine-year lease; they both knew that she could never live in a major American city in such comfort for a price anywhere near as reasonable. Then he saw movement in the kitchen and knew Rudy was probably about to emerge into the garden. "Here he comes," Sam warned her.

Jessie pivoted around to bid good morning to her lover, her teacup held aloft in greeting. Quickly turning back, she said in a low voice, "Before he gets here, just tell me one thing. Is it still over between you and Matthew?"

He nodded.

A year before, when that relationship was first ending, he had retreated here, to this house of oversized teacups and voluminous bookshelves, losing himself in its comforts. Jessie was the person he turned to when he needed to tend his battle wounds.

"He was way too young for you, Sam," she said gently. "Everybody thought so."

"I don't give a shit what everybody thought—or thinks," he said.

She flinched. "Now, don't get upset. You've just arrived."

"I'm not upset."

"Hello there, Sam," Rudy called from across the garden.

Sam waved and under his breath said to Jessie, "You know, I could say the same thing, about somebody being way too young for you." There was a five-year age difference between Jessie and Rudy.

"You could, darling, but, as you know, this is a whole different situation."

"How so?"

"Simply because he's already married."

2   Sam, in his lackluster career as a journalist, had never even considered writing anyone else's material until a publisher had contacted him. A renowned art dealer who was dying needed someone to ghostwrite his memoirs and was in the process of interviewing.

Sam's noon appointment with Elliot Garland happened to coincide with a blizzard that stopped traffic in Manhattan. Just as he was leaving his apartment, the book's editor phoned. "Hello, Sam, it's Jonathan Wade . . . assuming you're on your way—"

"Just out the door."

"Well, the city is pretty dead. And Mr. Garland's favorite delicatessen can't deliver his lunch. Would you mind picking it up for him?" The editor gave the name of a fancy food shop whose ridiculous prices were legend.

How nervy, thought Sam. Glancing at his watch, he knew that the unexpected stop would probably make him late for his appointment. Afraid that subway service might be delayed, he decided to brave the storm on cross-country skis that he'd brought down from Vermont when he first moved to New York fifteen years before. Soon, he was pushing away from his apartment on Twenty-fourth Street, effortlessly gliding up Madison Avenue, passing New Yorkers who hadn't ventured belowground in years, forced to make their way down into the subway system, wearing expensive furs and camel-hair coats. The muffled midday quiet that greeted him was reminiscent of the wee morning hours, and every car and bus was stranded.

Once he reached his final destination (one of those very grand Upper Fifth Avenue apartment buildings), it took a bit of arguing with the doorman before he was permitted to park his skis in the lobby. This was the sort of prewar building that featured original art as well as porcelain umbrella stands in the hallways outside the apartments. Standing outside Elliot Garland's door, Sam was hit with the strong fragrance of vetiver.

The moment he rang the bell, two yipping dogs began scrabbling at the floor. The commotion continued for a minute, and eventually a voice yelled, "Shut up!" The door finally swung open and there stood a thin, middle-aged man wearing a black silk shirt tucked into a pair of tailored jeans. The gaunt yet somehow still cherubic face was made serious by reading glasses and a closely cropped beard. The dogs were a Labrador as black and sleek as an otter and a small gray schnauzer. They began to wriggle themselves in between Sam's legs. "Come on in, they don't bite," said the man while, in an immediate paternal gesture, he brushed plumes of snow off Sam's jacket.

Elliot Garland then relieved Sam of the white paper shopping bag full of sandwiches and headed toward his kitchen, directing his guest to a sitting room that faced Fifth Avenue. Alone for a moment in the cavernous apartment, Sam peered around. It was almost too much to take in: walls crammed with paintings and tapestries, rooms and hallways lined with jewel-encrusted clocks and gilded eggs and small gatherings of old leather-bound books. The doors on several of the closets and rooms seemed to be inlaid with exotic wood of a beautiful grain. And the sitting room Sam had entered was covered floor to ceiling in a bird motif: bird paintings and figurines, bird plates and even bird taxidermy. It was clear that for Garland collecting was a devout vocation, and in the presence of such acquisitions, Sam (whose own apartment was relatively barren) began to feel somewhat unsophisticated and provincial.

"Why do you think it is that we've never met before?" Garland said, holding Sam's gaze as he came into the room bearing two black plates with the elegant, foil- wrapped sandwich squares that Sam had bought at the delicatessen. Garland's eyes were small and shrewd, the color of flint. "In one way or another, I happen to have previously met every single other person who wants to write this book." He sat down at a round lacquer table next to a bank of windows and invited Sam to join him.

"Well, maybe we *have* met and we just don't remember each other."

"Oh, no, I'd remember you," Garland said.

"I guess I should take that as a compliment."

"That's up to you. Do go ahead and eat." The elegant little man did not even bother to unwrap his own sandwich. Sam peeled away the tinfoil to find turkey with cranberry relish and couldn't believe how meager it was: the sandwich was gone in five bites. The small eyes watched him.

It occurred to Sam that the one photograph that he had seen of Elliot Garland in *Vanity Fair* revealed a rather overweight man with an insolent gaze, posing with a group of other collectors, whose names Sam perhaps should have recognized but did not. But the Elliot Garland now seated before him, cross-legged, with the upper leg draped over the lower one in a limp, limber manner, was not just thin, he was pretzel-thin.

The book's publisher had sent a few of Sam's articles in a packet of work samples belonging to the rest of the applicants. However, Garland confessed he had yet to read anything by any of them.

"Well, then how can you expect to know who's right for you?"

"Instinct," Garland said. "When I interview each person, I can get a sense of what the chemistry would be like. But let me ask, are you eager to do this?"

"Do I want the job, is that what you're asking? Sure I do, but I also know that a lot of people have come to see you about writing your book."

"Do you know very much about my life?"

"Just what I've read in the magazines." Sam went on to confess to knowing little about the art world, much less the decorative arts, Garland's particular specialty.

"So you're telling me that collecting is not something that interests you normally?"

Sam was aware that anything less than the strict truth would be instantly apparent to this shrewd dealer. "I'm no connoisseur. And I'm certainly not knowledgeable. Then again, I suppose I could do some reading—"

"That's not necessary," Garland interrupted. "Why do you want to write this book?"

Sam hesitated, afraid to mention that actually he needed the money.

"Everybody's got to make a living, I guess." Garland nodded, glancing at his watch. Then, keeping his eyes averted, "And now I'm afraid I'm going to have to conclude this meeting. Somebody from my gallery is coming over with some papers."

Sam observed how the ailing man made a feeble effort to stand up, but suddenly lost his energy or his inclination and opted to remain seated. Garland apologized for not seeing Sam out, and Sam, getting up to leave, couldn't help but point out that his host had forgotten to eat his sandwich.

"I'm not hungry," Garland said with resignation and then fixed his flinty eyes on Sam. "Why, do you want it?"

Of course Sam wanted it. "No, no. I'm fine. Thank you."

"Well, then, I guess it's goodbye." Garland continued to sit there, waiting for Sam to leave. He did not offer to reimburse Sam for the sandwiches and Sam wondered if his gracefully absorbing the cost was part of his test. As far as he was concerned, the interview had gone poorly.

And so he was shocked when Jonathan Wade called later on that night to say that he had the job, so shocked that he asked outright if the editor was positively sure Mr. Garland had wanted *him*. The editor laughed at him and said, "Why, what happened during the interview?"

"He seemed pretty dismissive."

"Probably didn't want to give you any false hopes."

A little more than a week later, Elliot Garland and Sam Solomon reconvened—this time as memoirist and ghostwriter. The dogs made their usual commotion and then settled down into doughnut formations on either side of their master in the sitting room.

"I understand you were surprised to get the job," Garland said with a smirk.

Sam was annoyed that the editor had relayed this bit of information. Noticing that a small black porcelain bowl near him was filled with Jordan almonds, he said, "I didn't think I had a prayer," and impulsively reached for one.

"You also like to eat, don't you?" Garland remarked.

Embarrassed, Sam admitted, "I *do*."

"You probably eat like an adolescent." Garland suddenly

clapped his hands, applauding, and startling the Labrador, who let loose a muffled yip. "Anyway, in case you're wondering why I chose *you*—"

"I'm assuming you never got around to reading my clips," Sam interjected.

"I never did, that's correct. However, I liked the fact that you were honest about your lack of knowledge. And you didn't seem overly eager."

Garland went on to say it might actually be an advantage that Sam didn't know anything about him, or any of the people involved in his life. Therefore, Sam wouldn't make any assumptions. Garland added, "I also chose you because I like your name. Sam Solomon. It's rather euphonious."

"If you like alliteration, I suppose it is."

Garland smiled. "But you actually cinched the job when I heard you arrived here on a pair of cross-country skis." Garland scrutinized him. "You seem rather densely built. Did you play Rugby or some such thing?"

"Water polo, actually."

"I've never seen water polo." Garland pronounced the word as if it were anathema. "But I'll have to look out for it. . . . Anyway, shall we start with my childhood?"

As Sam took out the pocket-sized tape player with its voice-activated recorder, he said, "I'll need to read the book proposal. Just to get a sense of what the publisher is going to be expecting."

Garland stiffened ever so slightly. "That's not really necessary. It's very sketchy. Basically offering to tell about my life, and my work. Before I wrote it I had a meeting with the publishers and that's when they decided to buy the book. The proposal was mere formality."

"Okay, then there's just one more request I have to make before we begin."

"And what's that?"

"That everything I write be the truth."

Garland frowned. "Do you think I'm going to sit here and make up lies?"

"People do sometimes to 'protect the innocent,' or to keep from revealing some part of themselves that they'd prefer to keep hidden."

"Don't they always say that 'fact can be stranger than fiction'?" Garland sounded flippant.

Sam agreed. And yet people he knew who had experience with ghostwriting had all warned him that there would be certain important facts, crucial to the memoir, that his subject undoubtedly would want to avoid. "It's going to be the chronicle of your life," said Sam. "The thing read years from now by people who never knew you."

Garland gaped at him, as if surprised at even an oblique reference to his impending death. Sam could tell this was a powerful man who probably resented being told how he should proceed in any new venture—who *wasn't* used to being told, either. And, yet, because Sam's request was reasonable, how could it possibly be refused? "Okay," Garland said finally, looking away, out the window toward the tree line of Central Park.

The thrust of the collaboration was that Garland would be interviewed and the book written within six months, to insure that publication would occur during the same year as the manuscript's completion. Obviously, the rush was due to Garland's illness, to the fact that he didn't want to die without at least having had the intense though fleeting pleasure of holding the book in his hands.

And, so, they began their work. Sam would arrive at Garland's apartment nearly every weekday afternoon at around two and interview his subject for no more than a few hours—for that was all Garland could manage. The only days they didn't work were those when Garland wasn't even feeling well enough to sit up in bed, in which case Sam would get a peremptory phone call from a man named Pablo, Garland's personal assistant at the gallery, telling him not to come that day. Depending upon how Garland was feeling, they'd either work in his bedroom (Sam would sit in a chair by his bedside) or in the Fifth Avenue sitting room (Garland called it "the aviary") where Sam's job interview had taken place.

At night back in his apartment, Sam would transcribe the tapes; and each morning he attempted to convert these transcriptions into a first-person narrative. It told the story of the only son of concert musicians who had moved around quite a bit, but who had otherwise had a rather unremarkable childhood, neither lonely nor particularly eventful. During his early twenties Garland had stumbled into the art world through a series of clerical jobs in galleries. These jobs had eventually led him to a guest curatorship of an exhibition of Fabergé eggs, which had attracted a lot of media attention. Basking in the glow of his first success, he was recruited by a New York auction house, and though he had an innate sense of good taste and style, he showed an even greater aptitude for marketing, for organizing art auctions around themes and trends rather than by period or locale. He ended up spending the major part of his fifty-six years traveling around the world on buying expeditions for wealthy and celebrity collectors.

However, just as Sam expected, Garland turned out to be more reticent about subjects closer to the bone, about his relationships—particularly with other men. Sam tried to explain that intimate revelations were what people wanted to read about in a memoir. "This isn't going to be brought out by a vanity publisher. You'll have a real audience." But Garland kept hedging.

"Let me ask *you* something?" said Garland, turning the tables one afternoon. "I've never seen you around New York. . . ." His voice trailed off meaningfully.

"Well, what exactly do you want to know?"

"The most obvious thing—let's start with your sexual preference. What are you, anyway? Are you straight or are you queer?"

Sam threw back his head and let out a hacking, honking laugh.

"You certainly don't laugh like a queer," Garland said.

"Are you being self-deprecating now?"

"Hardly." Garland tittered. "I like to use the word *queer*. I've asked everybody I know and *nobody* knows who you are. Obviously, when I hired you I *assumed* you were homosexual, but lately I've been wondering."

Sam reached over and turned off his tape recorder and stowed his pad and pen on a nearby round marble-and-mahogany stand. "So, if you didn't think I was *gay* you wouldn't have hired me. Is that what you're saying?"

"It would've been even more difficult to talk about the men in my life."

"*Even more* difficult? Why is it difficult at all?"

Garland shook his head and then his unsettling gaze bore down again. He was intent on an answer. "You certainly don't strike me as asexual . . . rest assured, if I thought you were asexual I *never* would have hired you. Straight or gay?"

"Well, if my history talks, then I guess it depends on the person. But there have been more men than women in my life."

Garland rolled his eyes. "That's what a twenty-two-year-old says when he still hasn't come to terms. Anybody who tells me that he likes both I assume is lying."

"You don't think it's possible to be bisexual?"

"No, I don't. Bisexual to me means only halfway out of the closet."

"Well, my parents know about my various relationships—male and female. So do my close friends."

"Was the most recent relationship with a man?"

"It was. However, my most *important* relationship was with a woman."

Garland dismissed this with "In my book you're as queer as your last relationship."

"Speaking of books, would you please tell me about *your* last relationship?"

The word "last" hung in the air. Inadvertent, inescapable. Garland winced and said that it was too painful to discuss. Sam gave him a look that said, *So then why are we here?* Garland's face darkened and then he complained, "Do you really think that all these memoirs coming out aren't embellishing some things and glossing over others? Sam, come on. Most of these people have given their lives a thorough cleaning and restoration. Why shouldn't I?"

Sam stared at Garland. "You promised to be truthful."

The thin lips grinned. "I was humoring you, because I couldn't believe your naïveté." He glanced down at his slippered feet and a few moments of silence passed. Finally, he looked up. "I'm feeling rather tired. Would you mind if we stopped here?"

"I suppose we can."

"Tomorrow we can start at an even earlier hour if you'd like."

Sam left the meeting and rode the elevator feeling depressed and frustrated. In his labor of spooling onto tape and then setting down on paper the story of a man who was dying before his time, Sam often imagined that he, too, was dying. After all, Garland was only fifty-six, a mere sixteen years older. Sometimes Sam would look at the skull under the papery skin and be petrified. Garland's appearance, the wasting look, the slurred movements, the spells of mental fuzziness, were reminiscent of the demise of a close friend. It was an ex-lover, actually, someone with whom Sam had been involved prior to Jessie. The man, whose name was James, had fallen ill several years ago, and one afternoon developed a high fever of 107. Sam rushed his friend to the hospital, where he was first admitted to a room and then discharged into a corridor where he lay for six hours because the initial admission procedures had been improperly performed. It was a terrible ordeal, and Sam had had to scream at the nurses to get proper medication to reduce the fever. Finally ordered to leave at two-thirty in the morning, Sam only agreed because James was calm and seemed to be resting peacefully. "I'll be here bright and early tomorrow," Sam remembered saying as he left. But James died ten minutes later. Apparently, his lungs filled with fluid and he asphyxiated in the hospital hallway, completely alone, his death too horrible to even imagine. And Sam would forever feel guilty for being persuaded to leave him.

As Sam left Garland's building, he prayed for the twin blessings of health and longevity. However, the moment he stepped out onto the cold, windy sidewalk of Fifth Avenue, he felt a sense of life again, the euphoria of being in a city and having so many choices of what and what not to do. Drinking in a deep breath of cold winter air, he began strolling down the windy avenue, reminding himself again and again that he was fit and strong. When he reached Ninety-sixth Street, he impulsively made a dangerous beeline across the wide, two-way road, right smack in the middle of the rush-hour traffic. Death was not ready for him, nor he for death.

He grew aware of the smells of night life, of prime meat being grilled in an Upper East Side restaurant, the fetid scent of steam spiraling up through the subway grating, the sweet burning of the toffee cashews and peanuts sold by street corner vendors. Suddenly hungry, he darted into a small French delicatessen he'd recently discovered and bought a cardboard cup of white bean soup and a *ficelle*. Outside again, he began slurping the delicious soup and gnawing the crusty bread, the world suddenly holy as a shrine.

As he walked on he replayed in his mind the conversation about sexuality—*his* sexuality, rather. He was bored by Garland's skepticism, a skepticism similar to that of his most recent lover, Matthew. Sam never fooled himself. He was primarily attracted to men. However, one of the most difficult lessons that he'd ever had to learn in every gay relationship was that sexual attraction seemed to substantially die down within a few years. He felt this was the reason why so many men kept changing lovers, ignorant of the fact that a relationship had to be held together by many more virtues than just sex.

The *virtue* of sex? Well, it *was* in his mind a virtue—but no more important than loyalty, which he highly valued. And honesty, which Garland mocked.

But Sam was genuinely drawn to women. He found most women generally easier to talk to, more sympathetic, and far more complex and interesting than most men he knew. Many women he'd grown up with had managed to find careers as well as be married and raise children.

Sam himself came from an offbeat family. His mother had been a nurse, his father had given up a career as a psychiatrist at a Boston hospital to move to Vermont, where he not only saw patients in private practice, but also milked a small herd of Holstein cows and grew lots of hay, which he tried to sell to the locals. Sam's parents were liberal. They hadn't been so upset to learn their son was gay as much as they were disappointed that their only child might never give them grandchildren. This disappointment he could well understand; indeed, it was difficult for him to face the idea that eventually settling down with another man would probably mean that he would never be a father. And he'd always wanted to be a father. It was this desire that, at one time, made him try to have a relationship with Jessie.

Wanting a child not only defined him, it made him feel isolated in a city where, it seemed to him, the majority of gay men were content to build lives geared toward gaining affluence, toward acquisitions—where, outside of their jobs, they lived in a perpetual adolescence of circuit parties. In this kind of life, any desire for children was sublimated into the adoption of pets. Pets could be boarded easily when their owners went on exotic, far-flung holidays. Pets—he thought of Garland's dogs—settled on either side of "Dad" and listened to tales of youth respectfully.

The following afternoon Sam arrived at Garland's apartment to find the door ajar. Figuring it was his signal to enter without being met, he was greeted by the usual yipping of the dogs as he made his way to the "aviary" room. There he found Garland huddled over some papers, dutifully attended to by a young, fashionably dressed man with a swarthy complexion whose jet hair looked fastidiously cut and styled. "Sam, this is Pablo Fortes, my assistant," Garland said, looking at Sam over his half-moon reading glasses. "Go help yourself to a drink and give us another minute, will you?"

Feeling a bit brusquely dismissed, Sam ambled down the hallway that led to the kitchen, glancing at a trio of landscape paintings. There was always something new to see. The kitchen was hung with a startling number of gleaming copper pans. When he came to a small bathroom off the kitchen, he took the opportunity to relieve himself.

He'd shut the door, turned on the light, and was half unzipped when he glimpsed a stunning drawing hanging over the toilet. It was a study in fine charcoal pencil of a male nude lying in bed, the torso impeccably drawn with shadows that suggested the ridges of musculature, as well as the hollows of armpits and pubic hair. The head of the nude was half-hidden by the wreath of arms crossed above like a dancer's port de bras. The right leg bent at the knees, and the left leg, massive and muscled, splayed outward. The figure itself was cradling a skull that was half-swathed in a rich-looking fabric.

Looking at the drawing, Sam was deeply stirred. Such an eerie juxtaposition, the languid body and the skull, suggested the alignment of two great mysteries: sex and death. Of everything he'd seen in Garland's apartment, the drawing was the only work of art that Sam wished he owned.

When he emerged from the bathroom and went back to the front of the apartment, Pablo was being ushered out the door. Garland peered at him and said, "You look as if you've seen a dead rat."

"That drawing," Sam said. "In the bathroom. It's so beautiful."

"Nice, isn't it?" Garland turned away.

As they were walking back toward the room where they always worked, Garland explained, "It's done in the tradition of *Vanitas*. Do you know what I'm talking about?"

"Vanity?"

Garland sat down at the round black lacquer table and, crossing his skinny legs, looked pleased as he quoted the Bible: "'Vanity, vanity, all is Vanity.'" He went on to explain, "Vanitas is a theme in painting that was particularly popular in seventeenth-century Holland. In those days, painters would place such things as clocks and dying flowers and skulls in the midst of vibrant scenes of village life to remind us that the everyday, secular world was mortal, whereas the world of the spirit was everlasting."

"So, the drawing is Dutch?" Sam had sat down facing his subject.

Garland frowned. "No, contemporary." But Garland's frown deepened as he added gloomily, "It's the work of a young artist who now lives in England but who used to live in New York."

"I see."

From his backpack, Sam removed his voice-activated tape recorder and his legal pads and pens. He found himself fantasizing about the drawing as if it were alive. Without even thinking, he said, "Do you know if this artist did any more like it?"

"No idea," Garland replied.

"Well, if you ever think of selling it, would you let me know?"

Garland's astonished glare made Sam aware that his question had been very inappropriate. "It's not for sale. Ever!" Garland snapped. "And if there's anything else of mine that you want, kindly have the decency to wait until after I'm dead. Then you can approach my estate."

"Oh, my God, I'm sorry, I didn't mean—"

"Let's just forget this little episode and get to work."

It was a tense moment between the two men, but it was quickly over.

Despite a few minor infections and a nasty bout of bronchitis, Garland's health remained fairly stable throughout the rest of the winter. The only noticeable change was his weight's slow decline. His emaciation grew more apparent. He complained that he never had an appetite and that whatever food and nutritional supplements he managed to get down went right through him. Toward the end of March, his doctors prescribed Marinol, the marijuana-based substance that was a strong appetite stimulant. The drug, however, hardly affected Garland's desire for food. He continued to waste. In early April he was put on a daily dose of human growth hormone, a very expensive, experimental treatment made of extracts from cadavers that cost fifty dollars per day. There was some progress but not as much as the doctors had hoped.

Sometimes, during the first months of their collaboration, Garland would send Sam to interview other dealers and collectors, as well as key players at auction houses, people whose versions of Garland's life were necessary to the book. Most of the interviews took place in New York, often a simple cab ride away. Then on one unseasonably warm day in May, when the book was more than half-written, Garland asked Sam to go to London to interview a curator at Sotheby's as well as an art dealer on New Bond Street. "And I'm going to ask you to do me a favor while you're there." Garland seemed to be consciously fixing his face in an expressionless mask. "I want you to track down the artist who did that drawing you've been shamelessly lusting after. The *Vanitas*. As I mentioned to you, he lives in London. But we've been out of touch for a few years."

Garland explained that the artist had once earned a substantial living in New York doing art restoration. He had opened a small gallery in which he sold nineteenth-century French and English paintings he bought at auction and restored himself. "Everything was going well for him, but then he did something a little bit naughty," Garland said primly, "and had to leave America."

"How long ago was this?"

"Around five years."

"What's his name?"

"Bobby LaCour."

"He sounds like the hero of a romance novel," Sam commented.

Garland looked displeased as he said, "It's a Cajun name. He's from New Orleans."

After Bobby left America, he'd kept in touch with Garland. Then, one day, he disconnected his phone and had not been heard from since.

Sam was intrigued with the notion of finding someone who'd gone missing. "Do you have an address?"

"I do. But in all likelihood he's probably moved. So it may take a bit of sleuthing." Garland paused portentously. "If you *do* manage to find him, I want you to give him something I'm sending him. It's a piece of artwork. I don't know if you've noticed, but over the last few months, I've given away quite a few of my possessions."

Sam immediately began looking around, but such was the magnificent crowd of bibelots and artifacts that he could see nothing missing. Then he recalled that he'd noticed that a bright pastel portrait of a cockatoo had suddenly vanished. Sam had assumed Garland moved the stuff around—like a museum director. A Tang horse that used to reside in the front foyer—it, too, was gone.

"What am I taking him?" Sam asked.

Garland snapped, "A drawing. You haven't seen it. It's at the gallery."

Sam shrugged to show his indifference. He wondered if Garland's medications were beginning to affect his temper. The pale, gaunt face was visibly flushed. The eyes were fierce.

"Okay," Sam said blandly.

Garland looked out the window as he added, "I'll have it delivered directly to the airport. I want you to take it to him. And tell him that it's a gift from me."

"Should I tell him anything else?" Sam now felt hesitant to speak too directly. But he thought a friend should be told of Garland's condition.

"Oh, he'll know why I'm sending it!" Garland laughed grimly. "He'll know at once."

3 Sam leaned back in his chair and watched Rudy enter the garden barefoot, holding a cup of tea. Rudy was wearing a tattered black silk bathrobe that Sam recognized as one he used to wear himself, which had been left behind by one of their predecessors, a married Italian. Sam remembered how the fabric had fallen away from his body with a seductive shimmer when he and Jessie would make love. Unfortunately, the robe was a bit too tight on Rudy and showed a large *V* of soft, powdery flesh down to his navel. Sam found it curious that Jessie encouraged her lovers to wear the robe, almost like a coronation garment.

One thing was certain: Jessie preferred unavailable men. Sam was virtually her only lover who hadn't been a married man—and, of course, Sam, conveniently, was gay. Jessie liked it that her men had "other lives," because she reserved large blocks of time for her own work, which was in advertising.

Jessie had once told Sam how much she relied on the fact that a married man took it for granted that his mistresses would accept various constraints. Rudy's wife tolerated this affair probably because Jessie discouraged Rudy from visiting her whenever Eva was at home, and Eva was at home a good deal of the time. Jessie admitted to being afraid that Eva might misconstrue Rudy as a father figure. And why *should* Eva attach herself to a man who was only her mother's part-time lover? Rudy's visits were rigorously scheduled to the early evenings, when Jessie could meet him after work, before Eva had yet returned from another child's house where she'd spend afternoons sharing a baby-sitter.

Looking bed-rumpled and complacent, Rudy sat down beside Sam and asked, "So what brings you to London?" After Sam explained about the memoir, Rudy responded expansively, "I must say it's fascinating how all these young Americans are writing their memoirs. In Holland the idea of a man in his fifties telling his life's story would be considered"—he smiled—"*premature.*" Rudy got a little tangled up pronouncing the last two words; indeed, his Dutch accent became more evident when he inadvertently rolled his *r*'s. Rudy's eyes were large and dark and, to Sam, looked bovine.

Jessie disagreed with her lover and said, "A man in his fifties can write a fascinating memoir as long as he's had a fascinating life."

Sam explained that Garland didn't have much more time. "But Rudy does have a point," he said. "Even some thirty-somethings I know are already peddling their life stories."

Jessie was skeptical. "Who?"

"Ordinary, run-of-the mill people."

"Ordinary, run-of-the-mill solipsists, you mean," she said.

Rudy blew on the surface of his tea. "So this man has had an interesting life?"

"If you're interested in stories of auctions and acquisitions," said Sam. "That's mostly what he likes to talk about."

"Well, didn't a publisher buy the idea?" Jessie asked.

"Yes, but no doubt they're expecting juicy personal stuff. He's certainly known to have a wonderful eye. But, so far, he's told me almost nothing about his personal life."

"Have you insisted?" Jessie asked.

"I've begged."

"Maybe you should tell the publisher and get them on your side."

"That might only make him furious and then where would I be? Also, the publishers might try to back out of the deal."

Rudy raised an eyebrow. "Then you'll just have to do some of your own digging."

This wasn't so easy, Sam pointed out. Everybody he interviewed seemed to be a good friend of Garland's, and Garland had probably left instructions about what they could speak of and what they could not.

Sam was feeling irked that Jessie's current lover was prepared to "like" him and be nice. The easy conviviality of this morning seemed to negate all the passion Sam once lavished on this woman, in this place. And Rudy was feeling evidently superior to his mistress's "gay friend."

Jessie said, "By the way, what's in that package you brought?"

Sam explained the gift for the lost friend.

"Now *that* could be somebody interesting to interview," Rudy suggested. He laid a proprietary hand on Jessie's shoulder. That was a sign, as far as Sam was concerned, that Rudy was feeling a bit insecure.

A short while later, when the jet lag hit him at last, Sam excused himself to catch up on sleep. "Your room is all ready," Jessie told him, meaning the guest bedroom next to hers. He had a sud-

den vision of *her* room, of the bed where he had once been welcome—its sandalwood smell, its high, carved headboard. And as
he loped back toward the house, he could feel the morning sunlight striking the balding spot on the back of his head. Imagining
them noticing it, he automatically covered it with his right hand.
Jessie liked to tease Sam about how much he hated losing his hair,
which had begun falling out during his late twenties. She used to
tell him—still told him, in fact—that his angular features and
deep-set eyes were only enhanced by hair loss, and that she never
thought of him as balding, even though he clearly was.

Ten years ago, during his six-month working stint in London, Jessie had been a wonderful companion. Sam didn't think
the word *mistress*, not at all. They had taken long walks to Hampstead Heath and Highgate Cemetery. They had patronized the
fringe theater and made excursions to the sea, particularly to Som-
erset and Devon. He remembered how well they had slept together.
The bed had made a lot of noise—Jessie claimed it was due to the
fact Sam was so massively built. She'd told him that he was the
first muscular man she'd ever made love to. It took her a while to
get used to his body. In the beginning, she'd complain that he was
crushing her. Later on, she'd smooth his shoulders and legs with
her hands, murmuring appreciatively.

Once his working stint in London was through, Sam had been
eager to continue a relationship long-distance. But Jessie claimed
to have had other long-distance liaisons. She insisted she knew
from experience how impractical and painful they could be. And
so she had nipped their romance in the bud. Her real reason, or
course, which took her years to admit, was that no matter how
much Sam claimed to love her, and enjoy her, she had never quite
believed it because she'd never believed in his physical attraction to her. She feared his being with her was his attempt to prove
to the world—and to himself—that he wasn't really gay. There
it was, like Garland's—the distrust of bisexuality.

So what if Sam's attraction for her wasn't nearly as deep as his attraction for men? He'd still become extremely dependent on the relationship and on her. He knew this because the year following her decision had been one of the most difficult periods of his life. After she broke it off, he missed her terribly. He had trouble sleeping, was constantly depressed. And although he had started dating men again right away, they hardly distracted Sam from missing the comfort of his conversations and the ease of his physical intimacy with Jessie. But, most of all, giving up Jessie had meant giving up, at least for the time being, his dream of having a child.

They both decided to wait six months before seeing one another again. Sam reasoned to himself that it was only natural Jessie might want to hold out for a conventional "hetero" marriage. And when they finally did see each other, and she suggested that it would be "healthier" if he stayed in the guest room, it had been a night or two of pure hell to sleep on the other side of a wall from where she was. Then the situation relaxed somewhat. That first visit had been incredibly awkward, but by talking, and by taking long walks and going for drives in the English countryside, they somehow managed to get through that difficult time. And on each subsequent visit Sam made to London, things relaxed more and more until, after several years, they were able to forge a long-term friendship out of their short-term love affair.

Nowadays, the upstairs guest room, which once had meant exile, was a place of retreat. Entering it now, he saw that she'd recently painted the walls turquoise with a magenta trim. It reminded him of a Greek garret. He hoisted his carry bag onto a rocking chair and began to take off his clothes, watching the translucent lace curtains billowing in the slight breeze. Naked, he peered down into the garden and saw Jessie and Rudy still at the table sharing sections of the *Guardian*. He heard the rustle of the newspaper pages as he climbed into bed. As he closed his eyes and was sinking into the delicious, treacly slumber of jet lag, he saw himself once again inside the diving airplane, the strand of pearls floating up in front of the Indian woman sitting next to him, and bolted awake.

He must've fallen asleep finally, because he was suddenly very groggy and hearing voices, no words, but sharp, shrill tones. And they were coming from behind his closed door, coming from downstairs. Then an intelligible shout from Jessie, "For fuck's sake, Rudy!"

Sam jumped out of bed, threw on a pair of track shorts and a T-shirt, opened the door, and quietly stood at the top of the staircase.

He could now hear them clearly. They were in the kitchen. "You don't realize what a difficult situation coming here tonight puts me in!" Rudy was saying, his Dutch accent conspicuously thick.

"Of course I do. If I were Carolyn, I would never let you come at all. But I have to go on with my life. I always give a party at this time every year. My friends expect it.

I mean, if you were intent on coming, you could've told a white lie and said you were going on assignment somewhere."

"You know I don't lie to her about you. That's how I'm able to carry this whole thing off."

"You did when we went to France."

"No, I didn't have to explain anything."

"Well, then, I suppose you're going have to stick at home tonight."

"Easy for you to say."

"Rudy, we can't go into this now. I have too much to do."

There was a long pause. Then Rudy sounded plaintive. "You're showing me up because he's here. I can't believe it. This is all because of Sam, isn't it?"

Sam was incredulous. Could Rudy really be so jealous? *"Ssh,"* he heard Jessie say. "Would you please lower your voice? He's sleeping. Of course Sam has nothing at all to do with it. I'm determined to have myself a good time tonight, that's all. Sod the rest of it! Sod the rest of the complications!"

"Well, you don't seem too upset that I might not come."

"I'm *resigned,* not upset, Rudy. I've been resigned for a long time. You're married. Sometimes, insane as it might sound, you're the one who seems to forget that."

"But our relationship should be as important to you as it is to me."

"Oh, come off it!"

Then there was a clatter, the sound of dishes being wrecked.

"Look what you've done, you asshole!"

"When you get angry you sound so *American.*"

"Those teacups . . . are valuable. Goddammit." Jessie's voice became deeper, ragged with rage. "Time to leave, now, Rudy. Time to go. You've worn out your welcome!"

The teacups? Could Rudy have broken them? The next thing Sam knew, footsteps were running for the stairs and he quickly retreated back into his room and shut the door. He heard a loud thump on the landing and then Rudy's voice muttering a few emphatic-sounding exclamations that were probably Dutch expletives. Soon Rudy was running down the stairs again. Jessie's voice (which sounded as if it came from near the front door) shouted, "You're so *paranoid!* Just go home and, for God's sake, don't drink anything."

The front door slammed, and Sam simultaneously heard another noise, outside. A woman pleasantly commanded, "Over here." Peering down into the garden, he could see that a banquet table had been set up on the electric-green lawn, the table spread with a starched, bone-white tablecloth whose panels fluttered like skirts in the brisk wind. Two women wearing belted tunic tops and black leggings were bustling around, carrying bottles of wine and empty stainless-steel platters. How odd that they had been carrying on their activities in the midst of Jessie and Rudy's loud altercation.

Sam counted to sixty, then ventured downstairs to find Jessie sitting at a varnished wooden trestle table. Back issues of the *Ob-*

server and the *Times Literary Supplement* tended to pile up here, and Sam sat among them.

"I'm awake now," he said. "Heard the two of you screaming."

Jessie remained momentarily silent and looked chastened with embarrassment.

"How many teacups got wasted?" he said.

"Just one."

"Jesus." He went over to the sink and surveyed the debris: the antique porcelain vessel smashed into shards, clearly beyond repair. He felt inordinate despair.

Jessie was explaining that Rudy's wife had put her foot down, insisting Rudy couldn't come to the party.

"Is that so out of character?"

"Well, up until now she hasn't stood in the way of his seeing me."

"Does she have any self-respect at all?"

"Sam, she doesn't want to lose him."

"Any chance of that?"

"What do you think?"

Sam sat down next to her. "I think you're more caught up with him than you're admitting."

"I'm *somewhat* caught up," Jessie corrected him. "Though I'm sure she thinks I'm out to steal him from her. Little does she know."

Sam placed in Jessie's hand the largest of the white pottery shards.

Jessie nodded. "I don't know how she puts up with him on a daily basis. I know I couldn't."

In fact, Sam couldn't fathom how Jessie could even find Rudy sexy. To Sam, Rudy's puffy body and stubby hands and flat feet were a joke. Sam touched Jessie's shoulder gently. "So is he really jealous of my being here?"

"Of course he is."

"Even though there's nothing for him to feel jealous about?"

Jessie frowned. "Come on, Sam, now don't be naïve. After all, you and I *were* together once." Sam felt gratified to hear her state it outright. The words were what he'd been angling to hear. She went on, saying, "Whenever you or I get involved with anybody and they get a sense of how we feel about each other, it's . . . I mean, wasn't Matthew threatened?"

"No, he just discounted us."

"So as not to feel threatened."

"Maybe." Sam took his hand away from her and consciously began flipping through back issues of the *TLS*. Finally, he said, "The right person for you would feel secure enough not to worry about being eclipsed." Even as he said this, Sam knew he hoped in some part of himself that she'd never find that "right person," that somehow he'd be the primary one.

Jessie shook her head and said resolutely, "I don't know about you, Sam, but I think my chances of meeting Mr. Right Person are slim and getting slimmer."

He put his arm around her. "What makes you say that?"

"Just the reality of my being a thirty-eight-year-old woman. Men my age and older want women in their twenties."

"Rudy's younger."

"His wife's only thirty."

"So won't you ever settle down?"

"I *am* settled down, but without a partner. After all, I have Eva now."

Sam winced and looked away. Yes, she'd had Eva—and with a man other than himself, some effete literary editor of one of the Sunday papers. Years ago, when she began speaking about having a child as a single parent, Sam had eagerly volunteered to be the father. Jessie had seemed to truly appreciate his interest, but in those days she was imagining having a romantic connection with the hypothetical father of the hoped-for child. The editor was actually single—for once—albeit twice divorced and without children. The pregnancy itself was not planned, and when Jessie first told the man about it, he seemed keen about her having his child.

But, shortly thereafter, he ran off with a performance artist, whom he even married. Jessie decided to have the baby anyway—much to Eva's father's chagrin.

Sam had been so grieved it was not *his* child inside her that it had taken all his reserves of friendship to follow her pregnancy with interest and declare himself joyful at the birth. "Well, I still think about having a child . . . I can't help it," Sam resumed. "I'm allowed that fantasy, aren't I?"

"I understand." She patted his arm.

"And just like you say your chances of Mr. Right are slim and getting slimmer, I feel the same about my prospects of having a son or a daughter. He also felt that way about meeting "Mr. Right" but had more trouble admitting it than she did.

Since Eva's birth Jessie had told Sam repeatedly that one child was enough and that she didn't want any more. "You could adopt—"

"Single fathers have a hard time doing that."

"Then with a lover?"

He looked at her meaningfully. "If I ever find a relationship that lasts long enough."

There followed an uncomfortable silence. Jessie finally broke it. "There's just one thing I ask of you. Please don't start judging Rudy on the basis of the row we just had." Their fight, she was sure, had happened basically because Rudy was worried about Sam's being there.

"Rather ironic when you consider that *he's* the one who's involved with two people."

Jessie held up her hands. "Believe me, I know it's crazy. But that's men for you."

"Not all men," Sam said defensively.

One of the catering women summoned "Hello?" from the garden, and Jessie was just about to go outside when the phone rang. She went into the study to answer it. Sam listened and heard her saying, "Hello, darling. What's that noise?" He hoped her "darling" wasn't aimed at Rudy. "Is somebody making something over there?" she asked and paused. "Oh, how lovely!" she exclaimed. "Yes, I am, why do you ask?" Sam felt relieved. It had to be Eva calling. "Would you?" Jessie said. "Well, I thought you wanted to stay over with Alex. Now guess what—your Uncle Sam has just arrived." Sam inwardly groaned at being called America's nickname. "Remember I told you he was coming from America?" Sam looked intently at the doorway of the study, thinking he might be summoned to the phone. But, no, Jessie said only, "And I'd love it if tomorrow you brought me home a piece of Claire's cake. . . .

"She's being a perfect angel," Jessie exclaimed as she came back into the kitchen. She was headed out to talk to the caterers in the garden but first wanted to know what Sam's plans were for the rest of the afternoon.

He explained about having to go to Kingsland Road in Dalston to try and track down the lost artist. He asked to borrow her London A to Z.

"Darling," she said, smiling and shaking her head. "It's not direct from here. Going by public transport, especially with a piece of artwork, might be tricky. You're better off springing for a minicab. Won't your man pay for it? After all, it *is* a business expense."

Not waiting for an answer, Jessie went back into the study, grabbed the phone again, and dialed her favorite minicab company. "Five minutes they'll be here," she called out to Sam. "They're very punctual, so you better hurry up and put something decent on." She waved her hands at him, as if to shoo him at once upstairs.

4 The moment the minicab turned onto the High Street, Sam realized that this rougher area of London was familiar to him from ten years ago when he'd first come to stay with Jessie. One of her friends, a former boxer, had brought Sam to a gym where he'd been able to work out. Yes, there it was, King's Gym, the same paint-peeling marquee half hanging from a warehouse building. The place had been a run-down establishment occupying several floors of what was once an old textiles mill. It looked exactly the same.

The cabdriver explained that Sam's destination, Ridley Road, was two blocks from the gym and couldn't be reached by car. It was the site of an African/West Indian outdoor market. Paying his cab fare, Sam grabbed Garland's gift and began walking. The package, about two by three feet, was relatively light.

Though the African market appeared to be largely managed by white East Enders, the place was mobbed with streetwise black women, who looked barely teenaged, with overdressed small children in tow. Piles of mangoes and papayas gleamed in wooden bins next to stalls selling posters that ranged from pictures of Bob Marley to African desert scenes and soft-porn sepia prints of dark couples in various stages of undress. The air was thick with the sounds of different languages, and flavored with the scent of burning joss sticks sold in red- and silver-wrapped bunches. Adjacent to the market was a twenty-four-hour bagel bakery and delicatessen that, Sam remembered, used to be a great place to go after the Tube stopped running and the clubs closed down. He finally found LaCour's house number on yet another industrial-looking building that overlooked the market. Peering up at the windows of the flats, he wondered how anybody could possibly live in the midst of such a noisy attraction.

Sam inspected the names on the various buzzers. There it was—Robert LaCour, printed on a slip of paper and clumsily inserted in the appropriate slot, as though the guy had only just moved in. Sam rang the bell several times, but no one answered. Before leaving Jessie's, in anticipation of finding no one, he'd written a note with his name and phone number and had borrowed a cartridge of cellophane adhesive. After affixing his message to the door of the building, Sam decided to stop in at his old haunt, King's Gym.

Sitting at the front desk was a man Sam recognized as one of the owners. In more than a decade, an American gym probably would have changed ownership several times. But, after all, this was England. Sam presented himself to the middle-aged, well-proportioned Scotsman with white hair and twinkling eyes, who surprisingly looked no different than he had ten years before, and the man squinted, as though trying to place him, then pointed a crooked finger. "You! I remember you from . . . Must've been eight years ago."

Sam grinned. "More like ten."

"You lost some hair, mate. But you look pretty good."

Sam shrugged and patted his thinning pate and muttered something about getting older.

"So you back in London?"

"For a short time."

"Well, come and work out. Whenever you'd like. I'll charge you the flat rate."

That would be difficult, Sam said, because he was staying pretty far away in Hampstead. Quite naturally, the man then asked what had brought Sam back to the neighborhood. Sam told him.

"Artist, huh? You said he was American, right?"

"Yeah, he's American. But so—"

"Sort of olive skin, dark hair, dark eyes? Looks almost a little bit Indian? Or American Indian?"

"I've actually never seen him."

"Well, if it's the same one, he comes in here all the time." As if perceiving this doubt in Sam's face, the gym owner added, "Been coming here for a few years. Not a big guy, but religious."

Sam explained about the disconnected phone and the man said he wasn't surprised to hear it. "Bit of a recluse, that one."

Sam wondered aloud if it actually might be the same person.

"What's today?" The man gazed up at the moldering ceiling as if it had the answer written there. "Wednesday . . . matter of fact, I believe you just might be in luck. He tends to come in a bit later on. You could stay and get your workout, wait to see if it's the same bloke."

"I'm actually feeling a bit jet-lagged. Do you mind if I look around? I mean, I practically used to live in this place."

"That's why I remember you," said the proprietor.

Sam hiked up two more levels and entered a room that was

floor-to-floor red mats covered with a patina of white chalk dust. There was no one there at this time of day. The air smelled dank and metallic from the old free weights and from the antiquated machines that (some of the guys used to joke) dated back to the turn of the century. Rusted, skeletal-looking equipment, some of which was operated by ropes and pulleys, foamed over with rust as though dredged up from the bottom of the sea. The first time Sam had come to King's he had dismissed the place as being "bush league"—until he saw the magnificent men who flocked there from all over sprawling London, legions of athletes and weight lifters of all races and nationalities burnishing their magnificence on this antediluvian gym equipment. He remembered the room, the pack of bodies straining against weight and metal, and re-membered gazing out of its huge, mullioned windows at . . . It was still there, a junkyard filled with caved-in, rusted automobile car-casses. Beyond the junkyard lay the cement banks of an intercity canal. He remembered that one of the patrons of King's Gym had great taste in hard rock music, and would play groups like ACDC. The sex beat blared out until all the men working their bodies un-consciously took on the rhythm of the song. Sam had been stirred up by all the male movement; to him, the atmosphere in the room was erotic yet obviously chaste. During winter the underheated building would warm up from all the chafing muscle.

Ten years ago, when he'd been involved with Jessie, she had been troubled by his compulsion to weight-train several times a week. She was no fool: she sensed that the atmosphere of King's Gym turned him on. And this became somewhat of an issue. To her, the gym represented the fact that she wasn't enough for him, that she would never move him as deeply as would another man. And, yet, so many of these men with whom he'd worked out and who went home to their women got the same voltage out of the gym as Sam. He knew they thought about his body as much as he thought about theirs, like a union of two powerful gods. The urge was there, and because of it, the flirtation was intense. The pats of encouragement, the arms thrown around his shoulder—these were the furtive attempts at seduction. In his own life, Sam reasoned, he had taken his yearnings a bit farther and, having done so, knew there was no going back to admiring a man from a distance.

And, yet, at that time of his life, he could make potent love to Jessie, could give her everything she wanted, he could reach her—he knew that—but she could never reach him. He felt he could live with that, but she obviously couldn't. And who could blame her? Nevertheless, during those six months in London, he had never once cheated on her. He had even given up going to King's after a while just to please her, the only time in his adult life that he ever stopped working out, stopped striving to be in optimum condition. This had left him feeling vulnerable and uncomfortable, and as his body began to shrink, he had felt less attractive.

The simple truth was that a gay man, no matter who he was, no matter how rich or famous, would have a hard time getting a date if he were unattractive. For unlike the world of King's Gym, where the most muscular men accepted the most ungainly, in the mecca of gay life, appearance was everything. And there was always the threat of losing one's beloved to a younger, better-looking version of oneself. Then again, perhaps this trade-up impulse wasn't just typical of gay life but rather of male sexuality in general.

A friend of Sam's who had recently turned fifty often said to him, "You only have ten years left, you better enjoy them. Then you'll be invisible. Nobody will look at you anymore." Though Sam didn't really believe this, the idea of becoming invisible was terrible to consider. In fact, one of the driving forces behind his staying in shape—and therefore staying attractive, if not youthful—was the trading power it guaranteed, power that would otherwise be given away to other men who could take off their shirts and be stunning by anybody's judgment.

Being involved with Jessie had, at least temporarily, delivered Sam from the unforgiving world of gay dating. For one thing, he knew she wasn't keeping an eye out for somebody better-looking or in better condition. He knew he could stop obsessing about being in shape as a way of safeguarding her from being taken away from him. He knew there was no worry about being rejected by her for losing his muscle tone. Women were not nearly so fickle as men, which was why there were so many fat, out-of-shape straight men with beautiful women on their arm—boy, did they have it made! Beyond this, because for Sam sex with a woman was automatically less important to him, whether or not she withheld herself from him was no longer as threatening. Ironic as it might sound, having a girlfriend in many ways had been a relief.

On impulse, Sam went over to the weight rack, grabbed a dumbbell and did a few one-arm curls. Then he decided to leave the gym and hang around the neighborhood to wait. Downstairs, the gym owner promised to keep a watchful eye on his package, and Sam went in search of a cup of strong Caribbean coffee. Strolling along Kingsland Road, past Caribbean groceries reeking of fried plantain and spices, past fabric stores with radiant tropical prints in their window displays, past discount carpet mills, he found himself on streets teeming with West Indians, Indians, and Africans. London, with its many diverse pockets of culture, suddenly seemed like the most vast and complicated city in the Western world—even more diverse than New York. Amid the throng, he noticed all sorts of signaling going on between people standing across the street from one another, between people walking along the sidewalks and passing in cars. On every street corner young and suspicious-looking men were leaning against parked cars, speaking on cellular phones. Sam finally stumbled upon a nearly empty coffee bar with a bamboo counter that served Blue Mountain brew.

When he returned to King's, the Scotsman told him that Bobby LaCour had, indeed, arrived and was on the top floor stretching.

"I didn't mention you were looking for him," he said with a wink.

At the far corner of the weight room, Sam saw, hanging upside down from a chinning bar, a guy whose T-shirt had fallen down to his shoulders. From a distance the torso looked compact with only a scattering of dark chest hair. There was a certain familiarity to the moment, but Sam couldn't place what it was. A harder look, albeit upside down, told him that if indeed this were Bobby La-Cour, the man was younger than he had imagined. Not for the first time it struck Sam as odd that Garland hadn't bothered to show him a picture of LaCour.

Sam walked across the floor mats over to the chinning bar. "Excuse me," he said. "I'm looking for Robert LaCour."

The man let go of the chinning bar with his legs and, surprisingly agile, landed on his hands and pushed himself upright. "For what purpose?" he said with a pure American accent. "What can I do for *you*?"

"I'm sorry, this must seem a little strange."

"Just a little." The man had the faintest hint of a southern lilt. "Why don't you tell me what it's all about?"

He was perhaps six feet tall, with smooth olive skin and dark eyes of an exotic cast, vaguely Asiatic or, perhaps, as the Scotsman said, American Indian. Though his expression was stern, his eyes seemed exceptionally alert and fiery.

Sam backpedaled, explaining that he was there on behalf of Elliot Garland.

The very name seemed to antagonize this attractive "friend." "So, he's had me tracked down. But how did you find me *here?*"

"*I* used to work out here," Sam said but didn't elaborate.

"And how do you know Elliot?"

Sam explained politely, and, as he did so, Bobby LaCour began to look doleful rather than angry. "You're helping him write his memoirs? Garland's writing his *memoirs?*"

Sam hesitated. "Well, to be frank, he's dying."

"That's what I was afraid you were going to say."

As the news took its poisonous effect, Bobby's hands flew to his face. He shuddered and Sam felt an instant compulsion to put his arms around him. Finally, Bobby looked up and exclaimed, "Christ, lately he's crossed my mind a lot more than usual. I've been wondering how he's doing. I guess I was hoping he would just be able to maintain."

"So you knew about his infection?"

Bobby nodded and said he'd known for years.

Sam now explained that Garland had sent him bearing a gift, a piece of artwork that Bobby apparently loved and which was downstairs in care of the Scotsman. Bobby insisted on abandoning his workout, getting dressed, and showing Sam where to catch a bus that would stop within walking distance of Jessie's street in Hampstead. Once he emerged from the dressing room, Sam handed him the wrapped package. "Have you seen it yet?" Bobby asked.

Sam shook his head.

They left the gym and strolled along Kingsland Road, Bobby now carrying his gift. As they walked, he told Sam how he'd first arrived in Manhattan from Louisiana in 1985 and that Elliot Garland had been the first New Yorker he had ever met. Then he stopped in his tracks and looked completely overwhelmed. "I can't believe this is happening. That's he's finally gotten sick. How does he look?"

Sam told him that Garland had already become quite ill by the time they'd met.

"Well, is he . . . I don't know, has he lost weight?" Bobby asked with a wince in his voice.

Sam said that Garland was pretty thin. They walked a bit farther in silence. "So," he resumed, "you've been in London for what? Five years?"

Bobby nodded and seemed far away.

"You have no trace of a British accent."

Bobby screwed up his face. "I'm American. Why should I?"

"Well, my friend Jessie is American. To me, she sounds British."

Bobby frowned. "Her accent may be put on."

"She sounded the same when I first met her ten years ago."

"Even more reason to think so," Bobby said.

At this point in their conversation, they were approaching a pie-and-mash shop. Outside on the sidewalk stood several plastic vats holding captive slithering black ribbons.

"Eels," said Bobby, looking at Sam closely. "Would you like to go in?"

"I've never had eels before."

"They're delicious. In fact, this is one of the few eel shops left in London. It's the real thing." With that Bobby waved to someone inside the shop.

Sam looked back at the writhing black forms and shivered.

"Are you hungry?" asked Bobby, smiling.

"I was."

"Come on. Check it out."

The moment they walked through the door, a woman with a bleached-blond beehive called out to Bobby, "Hello, luvie. Where the 'ell have you been?" Her lips were painted cherry red and dangled a cigarette.

"Staying out of trouble." They both laughed.

The shop was filled mostly with middle-aged white people. Evenly spaced on the walls were identical brass symbols made of two eels intertwining. Above these symbols were hung mirrors, strangely placed too high to be functional for any but very tall people. The floor was covered with sawdust.

Sam stood at the counter, looking at the chalkboard menu. "Now, what can I get you two gents?"

"The usual for me," Bobby said, which meant boiled eels, meat pie, and mashed potatoes.

"Can you get them just plain broiled?" Sam wondered.

The waitress turned to Bobby. "Where'd ya get 'im?"

"You can't be choosy here," Bobby said to Sam. "They basically have one thing."

"Then I'll have the same thing as you."

They went and sat on wooden benches that were attached to a crude marble-top slab. Bobby's olive skin was accentuated by the restaurant's gaudy fluorescent lights, and his shock of straight, fine hair, a shade lighter than black, was shot through with silver. Although he was clean-shaven, it was obvious that he had a very heavy beard. Sam found him incredibly attractive.

To Sam's question was he still dealing in nineteenth-century paintings, Bobby shook his head. He said he now made a pretty steady income painting watercolors of local scenes such as the Houses of Parliament and sights along the Embankment that were sold at tourist kiosks along the Thames and at the Tower of London. This allowed him time to do his more important work.

"Your drawings?" Sam asked, thinking of Garland's beautiful *Vanitas.*

"Paintings, really." Bobby suddenly looked curious. "So what did Garland tell you about me?"

Sam had the distinct impression that Bobby's decision to take him to the eel shop had been leading up to this moment. "Just that you had to leave America—for some reason."

Bobby was skeptical. "That's all he said: *for some reason?*"

"Is there more to it?"

Bobby didn't answer the question. "But he asked you to track me down. I find that strange."

"You don't have a telephone."

"I write and receive letters. He has my address. He could've contacted me by mail."

"I guess he was afraid you might have moved. He may have tried writing—"

"Trust me, he didn't."

Then again, Sam could understand Elliot's being reluctant to send a piece of artwork overseas unsure of its reception.

He was saying this when the waitress came over and put down two plates of golden meat pies, huge dollops of mashed potatoes, and what were obviously small pieces of eel—all of it covered with a green parsley sauce. Sam took one bite of his eels and shuddered. It wasn't that they tasted bad, but he disliked the creepy texture: a springy, round black piece of meat filled with cross-sections of little bones. Repulsed, he picked at the mashed potatoes and politely watched Bobby devour his meal.

When Bobby finished eating, he reached over and grabbed the package and hoisted it up into the booth next to him. "I have to say I've been wondering what he sent me. There're quite a few things of his that I wouldn't mind having."

"Garland has many beautiful things," Sam agreed.

"I advised him on lots of important acquisitions," Bobby boasted, but then looked disconcerted, as though suddenly regretting having said this. He managed to smile shyly. "On second thought, I think maybe I'll wait till I get home to open my gift."

"Suit yourself," said Sam, disappointed that after all this he would not get to see whatever Garland had sent.

5   Jessie stood in front of the bedroom mirror in her bra and underwear, trying on one outfit after another. Sam lay on her bed, amusedly watching her attempts to choose the right thing to wear to her thirty-eighth birthday party. Once they'd hammered out their friendship, it seemed silly to be modest with one another. Indeed, whenever he visited now, both he and Jessie would parade around the house in varying stages of undress. "Thirty-eight shouldn't be such an occasion," he mused aloud.

"I wasn't with you on *your* birthday," she said to him. "Was it hard turning the big four-oh?"

Sam shrugged. "Not really. I made sure that everybody I spent it with was older."

"Awfully clever of you. Was that planned?"

"Yeah. In one fell swoop I planned my fortieth birthday and what I'm going to do at the millennium."

"What's that?"

"Well, it all depends on my financial state, but I'd like to hire a party boat from a Pacific island near the international date line. To be aboard when the twenty-first century turns and then have the boat cross back into the twentieth century."

Jessie turned and surveyed herself from the side view. "Sounds wonderful."

"You want to come?"

"I'd love to."

"And Eva will come, too, but that goes without saying. By the way, you look great," Sam said. "You really got your figure back."

As though suspecting that he was deliberately flattering her, Jessie showed him a small spider's web of stretch marks on her hips. "Look at these. I guess I'll have them for the rest of my life."

"You can barely see them. Shut up. You know you have great legs."

"I've gained some weight, Sam. I'm surprised you haven't noticed."

He frowned. "I'm looking at every inch of you. Whatever way you've changed, the change becomes you."

"Well, I don't agree."

"Okay, you look like shit. I'm not giving you any more hot compliments. You've got somebody else for that."

"Rudy doesn't compliment me enough."

"Lack of compliments obviously keeps you interested."

"Don't be sour grapes."

"Too many compliments and you might start looking frumpy."

She ignored his gibe and pawed again through the hangers of clothes. "I suppose I could always fall back on leggings and a tunic."

"So prosaic. Wear a dress, for Christ's sake. Black leggings are a dime a dozen."

"A matter of comfort," Jessie explained. "And also the line if you're tall. It's a wonder that men haven't picked up on that fashion."

"Trust me, they already have." He explained that in New York City certain men with androgynous taste wore tights.

As she reached into the armoire and took out a silk blouse of small violet flowers and green leaves that looked very forties, Sam looked at the blouse with approval. "Now that's beautiful. *That* you should wear."

Jessie put on the silk shirt and Sam watched her button it down. She then retrieved a black skirt, stepped into it, and zipped it up. "Stop ogling me!"

"I like looking at you. What's wrong with that?"

"You're such trash. It's no wonder Rudy gets jealous of you."

"I don't ogle you when he's around."

She took a pair of black pantyhose out of her drawer, gathered them in her hands, and finally stuck a pointed toe into the gossamer fabric. "So you found him right off, huh? What's the guy like, anyway?"

"Hard to know. Seems aloof. Inscrutable."

"Your type, sounds like."

"Yeah, right. He's also lived for two years without a telephone."

"I take it back," Jessie cried. "You couldn't last twenty-four hours without a phone."

"Neither could you."

"No doubt this Bobby LaCour is gay, right?"

Sam felt wary. "Why would that make a difference?"

"Just curious," Jessie said and began fixing her hair, gathering it on top of her head and then letting it fall. Sam suspected that she wasn't quite telling the truth, that even after all this time, she still felt a twinge of regret whenever he professed to be interested in another man—which was why he'd refrained from telling her that Bobby LaCour was sexy.

And, yet, only a few years after they'd broken up, she'd become Sam's confessor, the person to whom he confided his conquests. There had been more than just a few. He'd explained to her that immediate consent between two men was more usual because sex itself was more recreational. Unlike women, neither party worried that consent had been given too easily, that dignity had been undermined. He'd admitted to her how much he liked the hunt, liked sighting a beautiful stranger and luring him into a one-night stand.

Jessie said, "My hunch is that he was, at some point, involved with Garland."

This had been Sam's assumption, too, but he played innocent just to hear what else she might say. "What makes you say that?"

"Just the feeling I get. Mostly because Garland made such an elaborate gesture by having you deliver the artwork. . . . By the way, did you get to see it?"

"He decided not to open it while I was there."

"Hmmm," Jessie said as she checked out her final appearance in the mirrored panel of her armoire. Then she gave her full attention to Sam. "There *is* something that puzzles me. . . . Correct me if I'm wrong, but you mentioned that he fled the U.S."

"Apparently."

"Why?"

Sam was well aware Bobby had avoided elaborating on this. "I couldn't ask."

At that moment the phone rang and Jessie grumbled that it was probably somebody calling at the last minute to say they would be unable to come to her party.

"Hello . . . yes." The patient tone of her voice gave way to slight exasperation. "Do you need something? Because I'm just getting dressed." Jessie's face was suddenly written with concern. "Luvie, tomorrow is Saturday. You know we planned the whole day together. Remember, we're going to the Serpentine." There was a long pause. "Because there will be lots of people who will be making noise and the house will be smoky, too." At this point

Jessie cradled the phone to her neck and whispered to Sam, "She wants to come home *now*." Then she spoke back into the receiver. "Okay, then why don't you let me speak to Alex's mum?"

A moment later her friend Claire was on the phone. "I guess I should've foreseen that. She was being so reasonable, wasn't she?" Jessie laughed. "Tell me something, which Barney videos do you have? Do you have the one with the ship that sails on land? That's her favorite." Jessie's eyes alighted on Sam. "Not to worry, I'll send it round with my friend Sam, who's staying with me."

"What am I, chopped liver?" Sam murmured, smiling.

When Jessie put down the phone, she said, "Darling, I'd go myself, but she's going to want to come back if she sees me. Just take it over for me, will you? Claire will meet you at the door."

Holding the video against his hip like a schoolbook, Sam walked along the row of identical eighteenth-century houses, catching glimpses of Londoners watering their gardens and doing touch-up maintenance on their ancient houses. Nobody made eye contact with him. Even though it was early evening, he knew the light would linger for a long time and this gave him a cozy feeling. Still woozy from his transatlantic crossing, he was thinking of how much he loved the easy banter with Jessie, a snappy back and forth that he had with no other person. Their rapport was rare, especially because she came from such a different background. Her father had been one of those fire-and-brimstone Baptist preachers who brought up his children with so many rules and restrictions that, as Jessie once put it, "he was begging us all to revolt." Indeed, one by one, Jessie and her two brothers and sister defied their unyielding tyrant of a father and struck out on their own. Unfortunately, each child was so determined to put distance between themselves and the family that they all ended up in far-flung corners of the world—permanently out of touch with their parents and one another. Jessie's mother had died when Jessie was twenty-one, and she hadn't spoken to her father in nearly twenty years. This familial dislocation was why, Sam knew,

Jessie's closest friends were so important to her. And, yet, she always said that one important lesson she'd learned from her blustering, raging father was self-reliance, how not to depend on anyone for anything. All her life she'd worked hard to support herself, and had achieved a strong sense of personal dignity, which Sam thought gave her the strength to be a single parent. Perhaps this was why she never spoke of her father bitterly.

When Sam arrived at the address Jessie had given him, he could hear a child crying inside the house. Hesitating, he finally knocked. The door was answered abruptly by a stocky woman with overly permed hair who introduced herself as Claire. "That's Eva," she explained. "She's throwing a fit to go home." Taking the video out of Sam's hands before he could even offer it, Claire whispered, "I didn't tell her you were coming because I knew she'd insist on accompanying you home."

Not wanting to complicate matters any further, Sam gave Claire a hand salute and quickly retreated.

When he arrived back at Jessie's, she answered her door, frantic. Rudy had shown up unexpectedly and was upstairs in her bedroom, drunk and sobbing like a fool, claiming his wife had thrown him out and told him not to come back until he'd broken off his love affair. Rudy was apparently so drunk that he'd stumbled and knocked over a Victorian lamp and smashed its globe." This is the second thing he's broken today." She winced. "I've told him to leave, but he's refused. What can I do?"

"Do you want me to . . . escort him out?"

"No, Sam, I do not!" Jessie warned. "I'd like you to avoid him, if at all possible."

"But this is totally insane. You're about to have a party!"

"I realize that, but if he's stinko, he's better off left alone."

"You should let me go deal with him."

"I told you—stay out of it!" Jessie was emphatic. Then, under her breath she said, "I'm secretly hoping he'll just pass out."

At precisely that moment Rudy's head appeared over the railing from upstairs, wavering. "Jessie," Rudy sneered down at them.

"I think you should come up here and talk to me and let the *mincer* answer the door."

The rest happened fast. Sam rushed upstairs despite her entreaties, shouting, "What did you call me? You got something to say?"

Rudy's eyes looked zombielike and bloodshot, his normally pasty complexion as red as if he'd run all the way to her house from where he lived in Crouch End. With surprising softness he said, "Yeah, you're the fucking mincer. Let the guests in."

Sam punched him square in the face, shocked to hear the grunting sound and the clock of bone.

"Goddamn the two of you!" he heard Jessie shriek behind him.

Grappling with one another, they shoved each other into Jessie's bedroom, and bounced around, colliding with the walls and furniture. Sam heard something cracking every time Rudy got a good one in, but curiously he felt no pain. "Both of you! Get out of my house!" Jessie's screams were like distant tolling bells, futile warnings for some kind of maritime disaster. But Sam was caught up in the maelstrom of his own fury, amazed at how much he wanted to hurt this man. "Get out of here. Get out!" vaguely came to his ears again, shortly followed by the stinging jabs of hardcover books pelting his arms and shoulders. Then he felt somebody grabbing him, wrenching him away from Rudy, the interloper a fellow he didn't recognize. "Oh, God, please stop them!" Jessie was imploring. "Make them stop!" Rudy, he noticed, was being restrained by another stranger—the first of Jessie's guests to arrive. And then Sam heard the seesawing sound of a siren growing louder until it alone finally broke the spell of hatred. From where he stood, he could peer into the street, could see the white car with blue flashing lights pulling up to the curb in front of the house. Stunned, he stopped struggling to free himself from whoever held him. "Oh, for fuck sake, who called *them!*" He could hear Jessie cry—now from downstairs. "Sam, the police are here! You've got to leave. You're a foreigner. Right now! Go out the back door."

6   Sam bolted down the stairs and into Jessie's kitchen, past counters laden with platters of canapés and fruit and wedges of Stilton cheese. He grabbed a cluster of dark grapes and hurried outside, dodging the white tablecloths that held constellations of glittering wineglasses and cutlery and platters of hors d'oeuvres shimmering under cellophane. He sprinted to the far end of the garden, the dark recesses where Jessie had planted clematis and dug graves for her cats and placed stone markers. He leaped over the back stone wall and hurried through the neighbor's garden. A family dining outside turned in astonishment to watch him and only thought to protest his trespass when he'd run well past them and was entering the road beyond their lawn.

Once he reached the road, he slowed to a walk, thinking how ridiculous it was to be fleeing the house of his closest friend in the world. Who could have called the police? One of the caterers? A neighbor? He supposed the commotion could have been overheard in other houses along the row. His triceps smarted from being punched and his neck was stiff from the sudden exertion of the encounter. Knowing he'd have to wait some time before returning to Jessie's, he followed the road until he spotted a pub with an ornate blue-tiled entrance and two cornets above the door.

The place was brimming with locals gathering in the warm night, holding half-filled pint glasses with great heads of froth. Sam went inside, ordered a Bass ale, then, clutching his mug, emerged. When a rash of black cabs whizzed by, he couldn't help wondering if they were carrying guests to Jessie's birthday party.

After a beer and a half hour's hindsight, Sam felt he had been wrong to interfere in the lovers' argument—never mind what Rudy had called him. After all, Jessie *had* told him to stay out of it. With anyone else he would have heeded the warning and deliberately kept his distance. A fistfight! God—it'd been years since he had been in a fistfight. But he clearly remembered the last one, which had occurred for a similar reason.

He'd gone to McSorley's Ale House in Greenwich Village with an old college buddy who was straight but well acquainted with Sam's personal life. After they'd had a few drafts, Sam happened to overhear a truly vicious remark made about homosexuals. He turned to the guy who'd made it and said to him, "You got a problem with fags? It probably means you're one yourself."

"Oh, shit, *Sam,*" he remembered his friend saying. Luckily, the other guy swung first, because in New York City the one who swings first gets arrested. Although the fight was a blur, he remembered saying to his opponent after getting a particularly good blow in, "Give the fag a kiss, you fuck face!"

Shortly after one of McSorley's owners had manhandled Sam out of the bar, his friend emerged, shaken and despondent; he'd never imagined Sam capable of such violence. But Sam had always been infuriated by the assumption that being attracted to another man automatically meant an abdication of one's own masculinity, or a lack of combative aggression. And he had wanted to show the guy in the bar that he could be fearless and that all homosexuals weren't necessarily effeminate and retiring.

Rudy's remark had raked up remnants of that anger; but what made it all worse was that Rudy was far too sophisticated ever to fall back on casting direct aspersions. His insinuating nastiness was, of course, infuriating. But Sam could see how Jessie would feel that it was he, not Rudy, who had been wrong. And *had* Sam overreacted? By now, various other parts of his body had begun aching. When he finally left the pub, he strolled up a winding hill until he reached Hampstead Village, draped in the long blue haze of summer twilight. Now, as opposed to when he was strolling with Eva's video, he felt emotionally marooned. It almost reminded him of the time he'd been lost as a child—a time in particular when he'd gotten separated from his parents for two hours at a beach in Maine.

He walked along until he reached the end of a row of shops and paused. It was still too soon to return to Jessie's house. He finally headed to the Tube station and caught the Northern Line to Leicester Square, and then in Soho he strolled up and down Old Compton Street, watching the activity in the outdoor cafés. He wandered along St. Martin's Lane until he got to a bar called Brief Encounter. The place was packed, patrons spilling outside pub-style, leaning on makeshift tables, eyeing one another as well as the passersby. Still nervous about the police, Sam hurried inside and quickly put away a straight vodka, then continued downstairs to the discotheque. Within minutes he was bored with the crowd and stupefied by the flashing fluorescent lights. He left.

Crossing St. Martin's Lane to a phone booth, he called Jessie. Her phone rang and rang until somebody finally picked up—a voice Sam was certain he didn't recognize. The background noise was at high volume: music and raucous voices, the party going on despite the turn of events. How stupid of Sam to assume that his fight would have had any lasting effect on the evening, much less on Rudy. By now Rudy was probably playing host! The thought was so depressing Sam hung up without speaking.

At just that moment a vacant black cab came barreling down St. Martin's Lane, and Sam impulsively hailed it. He found himself giving Bobby LaCour's address on Ridley Road, excited by the idea of begging sanctuary from Garland's old friend. On the way Sam and the elderly cabbie ended up chatting about London and New York, and Sam flattered the man with tales of how bad New York taxi drivers were and what a pleasure it was to take a cab in London, a far more complicated city. By the time they reached Kingsland Road, the driver seemed to have taken a liking to Sam and cautioned him to be careful in the streets, explaining it would be harder to get a black cab after eleven. "It's easy to get stranded in London without transport," the driver said solemnly. Admonished to make it his business to get the number of a minicab company in the area, Sam found his loneliness had disappeared.

As the cab drove off, the empty outdoor market, with most of its carts boarded up, didn't seem as desolate as it might have. True, the pavements were littered with fruit pulps, with oily leaves of newspapers that probably had once wrapped fish and chips, and the stalls themselves were filmed in shadows. And even though Sam thought he heard the scuffling sounds of rats, as he hurried along he now felt hopeful. When he got to the address, he looked up and saw light flooding a huge warehouse window. He surprised himself that he wasn't nervous about showing up here uninvited. Then again, perhaps after everything that had occurred, he was numbed.

Feeling for the intercom button in the darkness, Sam closed his eyes and said a little prayer before he pressed. It took a while for Bobby to respond. "Hi, it's Sam Solomon." There was a significant pause.

"What do you want, Sam?" Bobby finally responded, clearly agitated.

Sam explained that he'd wound up in a bit of a jam, that he'd gotten into a fistfight with the boyfriend of the woman with whom he was staying, that the police had arrived. Sam tried humor. "I figured you'd sympathize," he said through the intercom.

"Sympathize? I don't get into fistfights," said Bobby as he finally answered the door. He was holding a very fine brush covered with fresh yellow paint and wearing the same navy-blue sweatpants he had had on earlier. The T-shirt said "Loyola."

Sam stared at the paintbrush. "Did you bring that down here for effect?"

"Don't be a smart-ass."

Sam noticed an accidental streak of white in Bobby's hair. "Are you painting the apartment?"

Bobby grimaced. "No. What time is it, anyway?"

Sam glanced at his watch. It was just after nine o'clock.

"I guess I lost track of the time," Bobby said, beckoning Sam to follow him and climbing a steep flight of linoleum-covered stairs.

Nice ass, Sam remarked to himself. "Is that the Loyola in New Orleans?"

"Yeah, but I didn't go there. This shirt belonged to my sister."

"Did she?"

Bobby chuckled. "No."

"Garland said you were from New Orleans."

"Not originally New Orleans. . . ." He pronounced it *Orlins*, with a very soft lilt. "I moved there when I was eight. From a small town called Thibodaux. Cajun country."

The space they entered, the living room, wasn't quite as vast a loft space as Sam had expected; indeed, it was the normal size of an apartment living room, except for the ceilings, which were fifteen feet high. Every inch of two walls was plastered with tat-tered theater posters. There was a framed printed program of a play performed in the eighteenth century. The floor was covered in mustard-brown carpeting of a thin pile that had been worn threadbare, and there was a fireplace with plastic flames that housed the rings of an electric heater, a common contraption in England, but novel to Sam. Two matching sofas upholstered in a sun-faded floral print abutted a small round marble table with a reading lamp. Next to the lamp was a high-backed armchair. Over-all, the place was rather grim and depressing.

Sam asked if Bobby were a theater buff and Bobby explained that the posters belonged to the guy who had lived in the apart-ment before him and who still had a legal right to it—although this fellow had been living in Amsterdam for several years. An-other wall was covered with yellowed snapshots collaged together. Sam approached the display, and as his eyes traveled over the busy images, he kept finding Bobby in all parts of the world, alone or with groups, and rarely smiling.

In the careful layering, the photos seemed to cover many dif-ferent geographies and dates: what looked like powdery beaches in the Mediterranean with azure water at the fringe, barren land-scapes with denuded trees in what could have been Wales or Scot-land. Among the largely unfamiliar faces, he spotted Bobby sitting on a split rail fence in a countryside with mountains in the dis-tance; posing for a group portrait with some friends somewhere along what looked to be the Embankment; standing in the Piazza Navona; on a boat in what seemed to be an Alaskan or Scandi-navian setting. In another, an attractive, light-complected black man was sitting alone at a café table, leering at the camera.

Sam turned from the photographs to find himself locked in Bobby's gaze much in the way he felt locked in the gaze of the black stranger in the snapshot. "You look so grim in many of these," he remarked. "Weren't you enjoying yourself?"

"Does there have to be a smile on my face to prove happiness?"

"I'm surprised there isn't a picture of you and Garland." Sam watched Bobby's expression.

Bobby seemed to sense the significance of the question. "There must be one of us somewhere," he said matter-of-factly.

"Well, if you ever find it, I'd love to see it. For continuity's sake."

Just beyond the photographic collage hung a cluster of several unframed watercolors of recognizable London landmarks. Those had to be the paintings Bobby had mentioned as "paying the rent." Beyond these formulaic watercolors were a few others that were far more interesting. They were painted on thicker, richer paper that was ivory-colored and ragged-edged and bubbled attractively in the aftermath of having dried. There was a very detailed painting he'd made of a Mediterranean building with palm trees, a flagstone courtyard, umbrellaed tables of a café, people in the sun wearing beach jerseys and hats. The other was of a rocky coastline in the shape of a whip that suggested, at the very corner of the page, a far-off assembly of white buildings. The dreamy effect came from its strong suggestion of distance.

"I like these," Sam murmured, nodding at the two.

"I did them in Corsica. They're just sketches."

"They have something in them, though."

"Well, I was inspired," Bobby said, for a moment scrutinizing his own work. He frowned. "I love it there. I often think of just living there and trying to paint my own stuff and sending my touristy watercolors back to the galleries I deal with."

"You wouldn't feel isolated living in Corsica?"

"I never feel isolated. I like solitude," Bobby said.

Sam noticed a hanging watercolor replica of the photo of the black man sitting at that café table. The likeness to the original snapshot was extraordinary, the cast of the sun and the drape of shadows across his features, the delicate and sensual lips, the sexual leer—all of it perfectly captured.

"I guess you must've been there with him," Sam said.

"Yeah," Bobby said vehemently. "It was great. It was the first time he'd ever left England. He took a child's delight in everything we saw. He was really a great guy."

"*Was?*" Sam asked.

Bobby looked away. "Yeah, he's gone now. Another one. Another casualty."

"I'm sorry."

"Strange that he's gone. Because he wasn't afraid of anyone or anything. We used to walk around London, at all hours of the day and night. Through some pretty rough neighborhoods. If people would ever try to hassle us, no matter how many of them there were, he'd face off with them."

Bobby went on to say, however, that the man's light skin created problems for him. There were times when they'd be out walking even in the West End and pass other black guys who would call him *white nigger*.

"Did he try to fight them?"

Bobby shook his head. "No, he did nothing. Said nothing. He was too hurt by the remark. He always felt the lightness of his skin was his Achilles' heel."

"When did he die?" Sam was, once again, looking at the watercolor.

"Two years ago."

After a moment Bobby said, "I'm going to make some tea. Want some?" and without waiting for an answer, he led the way into the kitchen, where the walls were covered with more theater posters. He filled the electric kettle and switched it on. Almost immediately the sound of water stirring filled the lull in conversation. "So, you have nowhere to stay tonight?"

Sam could tell Bobby was nervous about being asked to give shelter. As they each took a mug and walked back into the living room area, Sam reassured him. "If worse comes to worst, I'll try to get my interviews done tomorrow, spend the night in a hotel, and then go back to New York."

Holding his mug with both hands and blowing on his hot tea, Bobby smiled for what seemed to be the first time. He sat down on one of his threadbare sofas and motioned Sam to take an armchair. "You hardly strike me as the kind of guy who'd be writing the memoirs of somebody involved in the decorative arts. How did Elliot find you in the first place? Do you write for *Architectural Digest,* or *House and Garden*—one of those decorator magazines?"

"No."

"Do you know much about the art world, or about antiques?"

"Very little."

Bobby slid a few inches down the sofa and looked appraisingly at Sam. "So, then, why *are* you writing this book?"

Sam felt uncomfortable. "I need the money, okay?"

Bobby shook his head. "No, something about this, about you, doesn't make sense."

"I could say the same thing about you," Sam said.

"Why about me?"

"For one thing, neither you nor Elliot has been very forthcoming about why *you* had to come over to England."

"Why should we be forthcoming? What does it have to do with Garland or with his book, for that matter?"

"I don't know if it does or it doesn't. But why so cagey? What's the big secret?"

"There's a reason," Bobby said ever so gently. "And that's all."

"That's the kind of answer that only makes me wonder and then assume things."

"Assume what you want. I've told you nothing. And I don't know what Garland has told you," Bobby added.

"If he told me anything, why would I be asking you now?"

Bobby stared at him. "I don't know you. And I don't trust you. But perhaps you're asking me questions to corroborate what he said."

Sam shrugged. The moment had grown quite awkward. Then something caught his eye in a room off the living area—a very large canvas draped with a sheet. He indicated the direction with his head and said, "What's that in there?"

Bobby swiveled around to look at the far room and then faced Sam again. "Something I've been working on. That's my studio."

"May I see what you're working on?"

"I don't let people see my stuff until it's finished."

There was yet another uncomfortable silence. "You're really jumpy," Sam remarked. "I can tell you don't want me here. Maybe I should get a minicab."

Bobby ignored the remark. There was a significant lag before he said, "Maybe I'm disturbed."

Sam took this as a signal to continue the discussion. "By the news of Garland's illness?"

Once again, Bobby was looking agitated. "Did he show you what he was sending me?"

"I told you he didn't. That it was something in the gallery. Why?"

Bobby shook his head. "Go and look in the studio."

Sam practically leaped from the couch. It was a small room that reeked of turpentine. Pushed up against a wall was a white vinyl drafting table covered with squeezed and smudged tubes of paint, coffee cans jammed with drying natural brushes, and oil-encrusted rags. A single wooden easel supported a sheeted canvas, and a small yellow plastic boom box was stationed on the floor next to the easel. Leaning against a wall across from the easel was the *Vanitas* drawing that Sam had fallen in love with.

Reeling, he hurried back into the living room. "*That's* what I brought you?"

Bobby was looking at him suspiciously. "You really didn't know."

"He lied to me!" Sam yelped. "He . . . I can't believe it."

"Where did you see this before?" Bobby demanded.

"I saw it . . . hanging in the bathroom . . . near his kitchen. I knew you were the artist. He told me that. And I made the mistake of asking him to sell it to me."

"Sell it to you? You must be joking," Bobby scoffed. "Garland never sells any of his acquisitions. Asking him to sell something would be like asking you to sell your mother."

"But why would he have *me* carry it to *you* but make me think I was carrying something else?"

Bobby now got up and began walking toward his studio. "Why?" he said, laughing. "Why not? Because that's vintage Garland, sending *me* a message by using something he knows *you* want. It's the sort of double whammy for which he's famous."

Bobby went and stood before his *Vanitas*. Sam followed and marveled once again at the sensual shading of the naked form, the bare outline of the face, the erotic languor of the limbs, the sunken hollows of the skull. "It's so well done," he murmured. "So incredibly sexy. You must be very proud of it."

"Not really," Bobby said. "It was a commissioned work. I actually find it depressing."

"Well, I find it beautiful."

Moments passed. When Sam finally turned around Bobby asked, "Do you thrash around in your sleep?"

"No one has ever complained."

"I only have one bed and one toothbrush."

"My finger does for a toothbrush in a pinch. But I don't sleep well on sofas."

"It figures," Bobby said.

His bedroom was small and it smelled of sandalwood incense and had a barbell with plastic-covered weights suspended over a vinyl bench. Two redwood wardrobes stood side by side along one wall; along another was a battered chest of drawers with stubby candles on it and brass incense pots and joss sticks. There was a considerable mound—six feet high and the entire length of the room—of paperback books. Bobby explained that the books, like the theater posters, belonged to the man who owned the flat, as did the furniture, as did the weights. "Nothing you see except the artwork is mine." His tone suggested he liked it this way.

They stood there facing one another. Sam felt tense with desire but was uncertain of the next move. Bobby finally yawned. "Let's just go to sleep," he said. "I'm pretty tired, anyway."

With that, Bobby removed his shirt and his sweatpants. Underneath he was wearing boxer shorts. In the bedroom light Sam noticed that he had a faint but attractive line of hair that began at his chest and stopped just below his navel. Bobby climbed into bed. Sam took off his clothes and got in next to him. Bobby hunkered down under the duvet but turned to kiss Sam sweetly on the cheek before falling almost instantly asleep.

Sam lay awake for a long time, thinking about the *Vanitas*, wondering why Garland had deliberately made him believe he was sending something else to Bobby. Was it because Garland distrusted Sam and perhaps feared that he'd somehow try and make off with the drawing? No, that couldn't be it. But was Garland really as manipulative as Bobby made him out to be? Although these two men had not had any recent contact, Sam sensed some kind of lingering collusion going on between them.

How odd it seemed to be sharing the bed of a man he'd just met but hadn't touched. Sam was used to such sleeping arrangements being prefaced by sex. And Bobby certainly was sexy, in a slow-boil kind of way. Yet, counteracting his heat was a circumspect nature. Which had made his unexpected, gentle kiss so touching. Lying there, Sam wondered about him with the greatest tenderness, about what mysterious history had brought this man this far. He couldn't help wondering if Bobby might be ill himself and if illness had led to his exile.

The sound of horses' hooves just outside the window woke Sam. He jumped out of bed and parted the curtains to survey the street below. A parade of mounted police were riding by in the early morning light. They were all wearing helmets and yellow rain slickers, their dangling billy clubs bouncing against the saddles. He was amazed.

"What is it?" Bobby's voice was groggy.

"I had a dream and then I heard these horses."

"They come by . . . sometimes early."

"Why?"

"Don't know. Go back to sleep."

Sam turned back from the window and in the muted light caught Bobby staring at him. There was a moment of eerie, tense calm after he climbed back into bed and then, as though responding to a mutual call, they turned to one another at the same moment.

7 Jessie was still in her dressing gown when she answered Sam's knock at one o'clock the following afternoon. "So, you finally decided to put in an appearance," she commented, so frostily that he hesitated before coming inside. "Was I just supposed to assume you were okay, that no harm had come to you?"

"Come on, Jessie, did you really expect me to come bounding straight back after all that? Besides, I tried you last night. But I got a guest and background noise. It sounded as if your party was a success."

"Was I supposed to call it off because two gorillas had it out in my bedroom?" Jessie stood aside to let Sam pass into the house.

He was surprised to see that the place looked exactly as he'd left it, as though last night had never happened, despite the slight residue of cigarette smoke in the air. Clearly, the party ladies had already been there to clean up.

"I don't suppose you ever got rid of Rudy?"

"Well, it was hard to—and I have to give him credit for dealing so brilliantly with the police."

"They couldn't see that he'd been drinking?"

"He sounded quite sober, actually."

"What did he end up telling them?"

Jessie laughed. "That the commotion was a row that I had with my rowdy American brother, whom I threw out of the house."

"Oh, my God. Let me go take a piss," Sam said.

Leaving Jessie standing in the front foyer, he hurried down the hall and went into the bathroom. His resentment for Rudy momentarily faded as he remembered Bobby and himself having sex. He sniffed at his forearms, smelling the sweet residue of dried kisses that remained there despite his having taken a shower. He fell into a racing reverie of a-new-man-under-my-skin. As he peed, he studied himself wearily in a wooden mirror. He noticed a small purple welt on his neck that might have alarmed him had he not known it had been made by Bobby's mouth. Indeed, shortly after they began their lovemaking, Bobby had stopped to declare himself virus-free and then asked Sam about his "status." Sam told him the truth: that it had been many years since he'd had "the test," which was done at Jessie's insistence when they first became involved.

"Why not since then?" Bobby had queried.

"Because the waiting was awful. I hated it."

"It gets easier each time."

"I'm sure that's true. I just haven't done it again. And I've felt fine."

Bobby left off the discussion and resumed it later on, after they finished an act during which he so scrupulously adhered to the rules of safe sex that Sam felt the whole experience, though mysterious and intriguing, was a bit of a disappointment.

"Your attitude is a copout. You know that as well as I do," Bobby had remarked when they were lying next to each other. How could Sam argue with the truth?

Now, from within the bathroom, he could hear Eva crying from somewhere far off in the house, crying unabatedly. Jessie called out to her, but Eva continued to wail. Suddenly, the weeping stopped. It occurred to Sam that children cried as often as rain squalled in the tropics. He washed his face and then dried it with a towel that was stiff and fresh from drying outside. The cloth smelled wonderfully of cut grass and dried rose blooms.

In the kitchen Eva was sitting in a cane chair pulled up to the trestle table with what looked like a bowl of muesli in front of her. She was staring out at the garden, waiflike, tears still glistening on her cheeks. Even though her mother was American, to Sam, Eva had the look of an English child, with her enormous dark eyes and fine, slightly unkempt straw-colored hair and lustrous pallor. Jessie was at the stove stirring a pot of porridge. It was rather late in the day for breakfast.

When Sam said hello to Eva, the child turned and looked at him. Her gaze, which had the unsettling quality of a much older person, was at first bewildered, and then, almost at once, became a kind of bemused recognition. She smiled at Sam and slanted her head shyly to the side.

"Say hello to Sam, darling," Jessie said.

"Hullo, Sam." Eva's voice was somewhat high-pitched and crystalline. "Did you come from America?"

"I arrived yesterday. Right before I saw you."

"Oh." Then something seemed to occur to Eva and she turned quickly toward her mother. "Mummy, where is he going to sleep?"

"In the room where your baby cot used to be."

Eva dropped her spoon on the wooden counter. "Then can I sleep with *you*?"

"You can, just for tonight. You were very good at Alex's."

Sam noted a difference between Jessie's accent and Eva's. The child sounded much more authentically British than her mother. Remembering Bobby's suggestion that Jessie might be putting on her accent, he said, "How come she sounds so plummy and you sound more transatlantic?"

Still stirring her pot Jessie explained, "She's much more influenced by the way her friends speak. That's quite usual."

Sam sat down next to Eva and was almost hurt to see how she automatically recoiled. Yet, she did so with a primness, a certain willed reluctance. Some children, he realized, seemed more like little adults, or rather the adult in them was already anxious to emerge. Eva struck him to be such a child. Her face, particularly her large, unsettling eyes, looked nothing like her mother's—in fact, Jessie said, Eva was the spitting image of her vanished "literary editor" father—but her delicate features, her elegant gestures, were Jessie all over.

"So, the party went well?" Sam asked. "In spite of the bumpy start."

Glancing at Eva, Jessie said, "Mummy's making porridge. Would you like some?"

Eva shook her head.

"I guess that means we'll talk about it later," Sam murmured.

Jessie served up steaming bowls of oat porridge and passed Sam a cut-glass flask of Vermont maple syrup that he'd sent her last Christmas. Even though Bobby had made a huge omelet for their breakfast, Sam was still hungry after having eaten it—ravenous, actually—which he put down to his having just had an encounter. The porridge was delicious and comforting and Sam ate a lot of it while Eva ate some seven-grain toast that Jessie had grilled for her on the gas stove.

Sam watched Jessie moving about the kitchen—there was party stuff for her to put away—and he mused how relaxed he felt with her, even though he could see, in the way she refused to glance toward him, that she was annoyed. Strung out as he was, with the unshared, the forever private images of a night with another man flashing through his brain, he felt immensely close to her. He'd felt close to her from the first time he sat on her bed and listened to her describe growing up Baptist in the Midwest.

"Try as I might I can never get my oatmeal as good as this," Sam remarked.

"Cold water and oats together from the start, that's the key." Jessie sat down next to him.

"I do that and it still never tastes as good."

She smiled. "Some things, I guess, just don't translate."

Yet, as soon as Eva climbed down from her chair and drifted out of the kitchen, Jessie turned and said with feeling, "The party was *not* the success it would have been had I known you were okay."

Sam felt a bit ashamed that he hadn't bothered to call her. He ate in silence, and after an interval commented, "Eva's well behaved, isn't she?"

"That's her way of flirting with you."

"Come on, she hardly said anything to me."

"Trust me, her whole mood changed the moment you came downstairs. She was very cross up until then. She's still peeved that I didn't let her come home last night." An awkward silence fell and Jessie began to rub the counter with a cloth. "I really worried about you. I couldn't even enjoy my own party."

Sam said nothing. It was always best to let Jessie talk when she was upset.

"I mean you could've told him to go fuck himself instead of coming out swinging, right?"

"It doesn't work that way, unfortunately," Sam said. "I got mad." He didn't feel the least bit sorry about the fight and wondered if she wanted him to say he did.

Jessie looked at him more severely. "Oh, really? Well, there is a notion of carrying a quarrel outside. You two thugs broke one of my favorite vases, not to mention cracking the headboard on my bed."

Sam felt awful and apologized at once. When he suggested reparations, Jessie refused to speak of payment for the damages.

"Should I find somewhere else to stay?" he asked sheepishly.

She made casting-off gestures with her hands. "Absolutely not. You're my guest."

"But at the very least, don't you think it's going to be uncomfortable—Rudy and me, both here at the same time?"

"I told you he's not often here . . . especially when Eva is around. Anyway, he's coming over tonight to apologize."

"To me or to you?"

"He's already made his peace with me. His drinking can make him crazy."

"Oh, so I'm just another step on his sobriety program?" Sam shook his head and shoved his empty bowl forward. "Jessie, I don't want his apology."

"Please, please!" Jessie rinsed the oatmeal pot in the sink. "Don't get on your high horse. You're only going to make things worse."

"You know, I can get my business done today and fly back tomorrow. It's not going to kill me to spend one night in a hotel."

Jessie looked confused. "One night? Where were you *last* night?"

Sam said nothing.

Jessie looked wounded. "Look Sam . . . I don't want you to leave. I want you to stay here as planned. I mean, that's my choice. If Rudy doesn't like your being here, sod him."

Sam was thrilled to hear her say this. "All right."

"He's going to be on best behavior now."

"Well, you can never trust anyone who gets like that when he drinks."

"He's promised never to come to my house drunk again."

"Famous last words."

"Yes, all inebriates are quick to lie and deny, aren't they?" She gathered the remaining dirty dishes, ferried them to the sink and began running the water. Grabbing her bottle of liquid soap, she said, "So you're not telling me where you spent the night?"

Sam hesitated.

"It's an easy guess," she said. "At the artist's flat."

Despite himself, Sam blushed. "I guess you know me."

She turned around, smiling, "You little tart! What did you do, call him up and beg a place to stay?"

"No, I showed up at his house. And begged." They laughed.

"Then why couldn't you have rung me from there and said you were staying out?"

"He doesn't have a phone, remember?"

"No, I don't remember. Or at least I didn't last night."

At precisely the same moment they both realized Eva had returned to the kitchen. Her voice said, "You little tart," and she imitated her mother further by wagging her finger.

Sam started to laugh. Jessie turned off the water and said firmly, "Now, Eva, unfortunately that's a very rude word. Not something a girl should say to anybody."

"But you just said it, Mummy."

"I'm not a girl. Sam is a very old friend of mine. And he knew I was joking."

"He's my friend, too, and he knows when *I'm* joking!" Eva said.

Sam was always impressed when Eva sparred with her mother. Jessie often lamented aloud that the child was as willful as she was.

"Eva," Jessie said, pointing to the T-shirt and shorts that her daughter had changed into. "Is this what you're wearing to the Serpentine?"

The child looked down at her clothes.

"I thought we picked your sundress?"

They agreed Eva would return to her room and change. Then she turned toward Sam and held him steady with her soulful eyes. "Mummy, I want Sam to pick my accessories."

"Accessories?" Sam repeated, incredulous.

Jessie gave Sam a "You see what I mean" glance. Eva crossed the kitchen, took his hand and began to lead him. Jessie only shook her head as Sam and her daughter headed out of the room.

As Eva led the way upstairs to her bedroom, Sam reflected that this would be one of those sacred moments of sharing he'd once imagined when he dreamed about being a father. But the child was Jessie's and *not* his and this was always difficult. He'd always thought that a child born of him and Jessie would be such an interesting paradoxical blend of different backgrounds—Jessie, the Baptist, and Sam the lackadaisical, secularized Jew.

Indeed, when they first met, Sam was fascinated by Jessie's tales of growing up in a God-fearing household, the mandatory churchgoings (at least twice a week), her father's long-winded sermons at the dinner table, his repudiation of "liberals," and, particularly, his condemnation of homosexuals. In fact, when Sam first got involved with Jessie, he would fantasize about her bringing him home to Ohio, where he would "out" himself during one of her father's dinner table diatribes. Sam's parents were, by contrast, so lax in his upbringing that sometimes he wanted to beg them to create more household rules, even to give him a curfew. They were almost too accepting of his misbehavior. Once, for example, his mother found a marijuana plant growing on the roof outside his bedroom She very reasonably asked him to transplant it to a place where, if the police were to find it, they wouldn't arrest her or his father. His mother's mild reaction had been infuriating. Sam had half-hoped that she'd at least lose her temper. Jessie had howled with laughter when Sam first told her this story; she'd been impressed by his mother's handling of the situation. But what Jessie didn't realize was that such an unorthodox upbringing, one in which his parents never challenged him, allowed Sam to grow up aimless, without any real overpowering ambition. Had their acceptance of him been less equivocal, perhaps he would've developed a more aggressive approach to getting what he wanted out of life, even if only as a knee-jerk response to their disapproval. He was certain, for example, that Jessie's driving ambition to succeed in a career, to be a single mother, was a positive reaction, a means of escaping the stifling nature of her childhood and the tyranny of her father.

Eva's small bedroom was located off a landing between the upstairs and the living room floor of the house. Oddly, it was a windowless space, but Jessie said that Eva preferred it over the upstairs guest room that Sam was now sleeping in. Two of the walls were lined with shelves that were wide enough to hold both toys and books. Sam was always surprised to see how few toys they contained; in fact, there were many more books. The child had even had books galore as an infant.

Sam was sitting on her small bed. "Where are all your toys?"

Eva frowned. "They're here." Diffidently, she pointed out a stuffed animal giraffe, a box containing a jigsaw puzzle, a single Barbie doll with a pillbox hat. "Here are the necklaces," she said, showing Sam a series of small boxes made out of marbled Florentine paper. Opening each of them, she displayed an assortment of costume beads and clip-on earrings and bracelets. She decorously pulled out a strand of beautiful round amber nuggets and draped them around her neck. "Do you like this?"

Sam said, "What about the beads you've got on already?"

Eva frowned again. "They're too long. And too dressy. Here." She selected one of the boxes and handed it to him. "Open that and you'll see the others."

Inside were various choker-sized necklaces, one of fake turquoise, and one of coral, and a strand of pearls he couldn't tell were real or not.

"Who gave these to you? They're all very beautiful." He wished he'd given her jewelry, not the clothes that might not have fit. He rarely brought presents for children and always felt awkward when he did.

"Mummy," Eva said proudly. "She brings them back when she goes on trips. And some were hers, too."

Hearing this made Sam more aware of the bond between mother and daughter. "Well, how about this one?" He selected a very small but beautiful apricot-colored coral strand.

"That's not a necklace, silly, I can't wear it around my neck. It's a bracelet. Don't you see?"

"I'm sorry, I don't."

Eva appropriated the piece of coral. "You wind it twice round your wrist. That's how it's worn. . . ." Admiring the bracelet, Eva said coquettishly, "Are you married?"

Sam hesitated and said that he wasn't. "Why are you asking?"

"Mummy's not married." Eva said this with a shrug.

"I know she's not married."

"Do you love anybody?" Eva asked.

"Of course."

"Who?" She looked at him with delight. "I know, you love Mummy."

"You're good at guessing."

The child looked happy as she opened a box of little rings.

I could be this child's father, he reasoned to himself, and felt almost resentful. Helping Eva choose what to wear could have been a daily ritual rather than a novel event in his life. Sam often wondered if Jessie had been afraid he'd catch the disease that was killing the young men of his generation, that he'd get sick and die. Or, worse, that he'd pass the disease to her. They had, once upon a time, spoken of this obsessively, and Sam had meant it when he claimed he would be faithful. As a father, he hoped he could be. Fatherhood, he felt, could have made him very strong, very different. But now that he was past forty the most he could hope for was being one of those older single parents who stand outside their child's school, bald, aging, and for that reason conspicuous.

Jessie now poked her head in the room. "Sam, telephone . . . Oh and by the way, Matthew called last night while you were out."

Expecting this to be Bobby LaCour, Sam trotted up the stairs to Jessie's bedroom, where there was a phone extension that would allow him to speak in private. To his surprise, it was Rudy.

"Look, Sam, I want . . . to 'pologize for insulting you." The voice was heavily accented and quavering. "I should not have done that. I was drinking. And there is no excuse."

"I'm over it," Sam said, hesitating. "And look, I'm sorry I popped you one."

"You were provoked."

"Still not the way to handle things. Especially when you're in somebody else's house."

"I understand we broke things."

"We should probably do something about that."

"I'll take care of it, don't worry. You don't have much time while you're here."

There was an awkward silence, and Sam wrestled with the urge to ask Rudy if Jessie had put him up to apologizing but then thought better of it. What was the point?

"Is she standing right there?" Rudy asked.

"No, she went back downstairs."

Clearing his throat, Rudy said, apropos of nothing, "I want you to know that I really love her."

"Oh?" was all Sam could respond.

"Yes, I'm married," Rudy said. "So that is a bit of a problem."

A bit of a problem—I'll say it's a bit of a problem, thought Sam. Provocative though it was, he couldn't help but ask, "Does that mean you're planning to leave your wife for her?"

"It would be hard to do that right now."

Right now? The guy was so full of it.

Saying no more than a polite goodbye, Sam hung up the telephone and wandered back down the stairs to Eva's bedroom. He found her standing before her mirror, patiently trying on a blue necklace. Its beads were made to look like cornflowers. She smiled the moment she saw him.

8   At first Bobby worried that Sam was not quite as guile-less as he appeared, that Garland had coerced him into something he wasn't admitting to. After all, it made no sense that a man who knew so little about art was writing the autobiography of an art dealer. But the wall of Bobby's suspicions was rapidly demol-ished; in the wash of mutual attraction, he knew instinctively that any kind of willful attempt to deceive him would already have be-come detectable. He ended up concluding that Sam was a com-plete innocent.

Sam had said he wanted to look at the paintings in the Na-tional Gallery, and so Bobby met him in the late morning the day before Sam was to go back to America. Sam seemed particularly captivated by Bronzino's *Allegory of Time*, the sexual imagery of Cupid kissing Venus, his tongue touching hers while his fingers tweaked her left breast, the lurid smile of the infant getting ready to throw the garland of roses—amazed that such sexual subject matter was dealt with so explicitly in the sixteenth century. Bobby explained that, indeed, some of the more suggestive parts of the painting had been zealously covered over by conservators in later centuries and that the original work had only been restored about fifty years ago. He pointed out Bronzino's intention to portray time in ephemeral images such as roses, the reminder that everything in life, even the most powerful attractions, cannot last. In this vein the painter introduced figures of an old man and an ailing woman in the background, presumably to stand for the aged alter egos of Venus and Cupid, as well as to remind the viewer of the inevitable transformation of the physical body.

As they continued walking through the halls of the National Gallery, Bobby said, "For me, Bronzino is one of the great portrait painters." He told Sam how when he first came to England, he spent two months making a copy of *The Allegory of Time*. Later on, he traveled to Florence to copy some of the portraits in the Uffizi, trying to recapture the soft, luminous realism that made Bronzino's paintings appear more lifelike than life itself.

Sam asked why Bobby didn't do more portraiture. There wasn't much call in his day-to-day work, said Bobby.

"I mean, in your own artwork."

"Sam, the world isn't waiting for me, I'm afraid." Bobby had long since come to the conclusion that his talent as a painter was limited and that at least he was good enough to realize his own shortcomings.

"Well, Garland's *Vanitas* is beautiful."

Bobby explained there was a particular reason. "I established a real connection with the model." A man had come to him, knowing that he was going to die, wanting to preserve his beauty so that when he no longer had it, he could still look at himself and believe that he had been handsome. "And I understood that. Being an artist myself, I could certainly appreciate the idea of saving beauty. After a short time, even though I didn't know him, I got a feeling for his life, for all its pain and pleasure. I somehow picked up on what he'd been through."

"So he died of—"

"Yeah," Bobby interrupted. He didn't want Sam to mention the illness. "Now, Bronzino could do this every time out, look deeply into his subjects, even those with whom he had little personal connection. He painted them all with unruffled expressions, but if you look closely enough, you can see their entire lives in their faces.

"Uh-oh," said Bobby, interrupting himself. He nodded to someone standing near the end of the corridor, a large-boned Spanish-looking man with jet hair and a ruddy complexion.

The fellow hurried over and demanded, "What are you doing here?"

Bobby was worried what Sam would think and said the only thing that came into his head. "Last time I checked, the National Gallery was open to everybody." The man's face twitched with fury. "I don't think you should make a scene in your own museum, do you?" Bobby said composedly. The man began sputtering unintelligibly in Spanish and scurried away.

"What was that all about?" Sam asked and Bobby explained reluctantly that he'd met the guy, a curator, at the Tower of London, one of the places that sold his commercial work. They'd gone out to dinner a few times and had slept together once, which turned out to be a big mistake. "That was it for me. But he wanted more. And in the end, he got pretty insistent about it."

Bobby noticed that Sam had fallen conspicuously silent, as though finding this admission worrying. "But not in your case," he joked. "So, let's skip lunch and go back to my place . . . you're leaving tomorrow. I can't believe it."

On the Tube riding toward the Angel station, Bobby let his head drop against Sam's shoulder. Sam, he thought, had a beautiful profile, a high forehead, a small, straight nose, lips that looked slightly swollen and were a pleasure to kiss. On him, thinning hair was an asset: it graced a well-shaped head; it gave his face and forehead more prominence.

Bobby rarely made public displays of affection, and he could tell that his gesture was making Sam nervous. However, he found the hard shoulder comforting; actually closed his eyes and drifted off for a few minutes.

Back at his place, with the market cries coming up through the windows, the summer sunlight rinsing through the living room, they began on the uncomfortable love seat, Bobby resting his forehead against Sam's knees. He untied Sam's shoes, tore off his socks, and mouthed his toes until Sam started laughing. He took off Sam's shirt and marveled that the hair on his chest was a lot darker than the hair on his head. He found this incredibly sexy. Finally, Bobby stood up and unbuttoned his own shirt, yanking the shirttails out of his trousers. Eyes riveted on Sam's, he took his hand and led him into the bedroom, where he drew the shades and lit several candles. Bonnie Raitt began to play.

They had not yet made love enough times to establish a rhythm. They were still exploring: a dusting of hair just above Bobby's knees, permanent welts in Sam's back engraved by an onslaught of hornets in a Florida swamp, a faint scar running down the middle of Bobby's chest from a stomach operation that corrected a childhood ulcer, a scar on his leg from his having accidentally shot himself when his father had once taken him out for target practice. Sam's scalp had the wonderful toasty scent of suntanned skin.

Bobby noticed how Sam seemed a bit miffed at how scrupulously self-protective he was—how, for example, he avoided oral sex because it was considered a "gray area" of safety. He listened as Sam tried to tell him that in America even the most cautious people presumed that oral sex without orgasm was "relatively safe." Bobby said "relatively safe" was not safe enough for him and that being "completely safe" was the only way he could enjoy himself. Especially now that Garland was ill, Bobby was determined to avoid dying as the result of a reckless act of love. He looked at Sam's eager face—still trying to convince him to do more than he was willing. Sam Solomon seemed very reckless to him, and this gave Bobby pause.

And yet, making love to Sam was beginning to get to him, touching pockets of sorrow, the confusion of the ending of his last significant relationship—with Gary, the man he took to Corsica. Then came the news of Gary's death: they hadn't been in touch for more than a year when the phone call came. He hadn't even known Gary was infected, much less ill, and the person who called explained that it was one of those mysterious, precipitous declines: hale and hearty one day, dying the next. Death came wildly fast, the mutual friend had said. Still, Bobby sensed that Gary probably preferred his ex-lover not to see him, even in the throes of dying, denying Bobby a chance to say goodbye. It was a cruelty that, at the time, seemed vindictively orchestrated to bring him the greatest measure of pain. Only later did Bobby understand that Gary had cordoned himself off, partly out of vanity, loath to have someone he'd once been in love with see him wasted.

Bobby remembered all those nights after Gary died when he could barely sleep, all the physical sensations of grief revived: the clammy weight of bereavement pressing down against him like an incubus, every single waking moment singed with horror and regret. Remembering it so clearly now must have to do with the fact that the molecules of his body were now in transition. They were reprogramming themselves; he could feel the subtle shifting inside, like the glass shards in a kaleidoscope that form a new beautiful image, while the former configuration was being lost forever. All this as Sam was planting a row of kisses down his spine, and looking up for his reaction. "You look so grim," Sam finally said.

"Thinking . . . about something in the past," Bobby had to admit.

"Want to tell me?"

"Trust me, it would spoil the mood."

"Okay."

By the time they finished making love, the Bonnie Raitt album had already repeated itself, her songs flavoring their sex.

"Better?" Sam asked, stroking the side of Bobby's cheek.

Bobby was touched by the tenderness. "Yeah."

He was feeling especially trusting and soon found himself telling Sam about his family life, about his parents' loveless marriage. About how his father, a river pilot on the Mississippi, constantly belittled his mother, his younger sister, and him. His father was a highly intelligent, complicated man who worked for the Port of New Orleans as a harbor pilot. Captains of oceangoing ships would stop and line up their vessels at a designated spot in the river just outside the port, and the pilots would arrive by launch and perform the tricky job of guiding the ship into the port. The reason for this, he said, was that the Mississippi narrowed, and its currents, notoriously treacherous, could send a ship barreling into the shore. Nearer the port, the currents eddied and vortexed and could suck down even the most powerful swimmers.

One day, as his father was climbing out of the launch and up a ladder to a tanker, he suffered a stroke and fell into the water. Witnesses said his head broke the surface of the chop and one of his hands feebly flagged for help. But then the launch lurched against the tanker and crushed him between the two vessels. He disappeared into the depths of the river and his body didn't wash up until the next day, when it was several miles away. The incident was reported on the front page of the *Times Picayune*. His father didn't leave proper insurance, and his mother, who worked long days as a medical secretary, was now faced with supporting the family, which consisted of Bobby and his sister, Aurora.

Nineteen at the time, Bobby had just won a scholarship to the Georgia branch of the School of Visual Arts but turned it down to help his mother make ends meet. He worked as a hotel clerk, a bartender, and a swamp tour guide, until he met somebody who restored paintings and became his apprentice. When Bobby showed a great deal of natural promise, he was given more and more responsibility. "I'd probably still be struggling in Louisiana if Elliot Garland hadn't come down on a buying trip," he said.

Not knowing how much or what Garland had told Sam about him, Bobby was deliberately brief in his description of how he'd gotten to New York. Garland had arrived at the gallery to make inquiries about having an early-nineteenth-century French painting restored. The head of the studio, an old friend of Garland's, had already told him about his talented apprentice. After Garland looked at Bobby's work, he commissioned him to do the restoration. When he saw the completed painting, he was so pleased that he convinced Bobby to move to New York, promising to find him a job.

Sam asked, "So you lived there for how many years?"

"Five years."

Lying there, Bobby watched as Sam shifted his head and looked at him fixedly. "Can you explain now why you had to leave America?"

Bobby considered the request for several moments. "Tell me again, what exactly did Garland say?"

"That you did something naughty."

A guttural exchange in an unidentifiable language filtered through the window. Bobby had worried all week about what might be going into Garland's memoir. The fact that Sam knew so little about him seemed to suggest, at least so far, that Garland had avoided talking about him. However, the interviewing process was far from complete. Clearly, Garland wanted him to know this, to know that he still had the power to put certain things into print. Bobby would have to watch his step. And, yet, weighing against caution was his disquieting attraction to the man lying next to him.

"Well, let's put it this way," he began. "'Something naughty' translates to being accused of falsely authenticating a painting. A painting by Géricault. Do you know who that is?"

Sam nodded his head vaguely. "Art History 101 . . . it's coming back to me . . . didn't he do that painting of the raft with all the dying people?"

"*Raft of the Medusa*," Bobby said. "Have you ever seen it?"

"I have. It was very dark, as I remember. So, anyway, you sold a painting that wasn't authenticated?"

"No, it *was* authenticated, but wrongly so. But because I was an art restorer, I was accused of making it seem so—deliberately. After all, an authentic Géricault brings a hell of a lot more money than one of his imitators."

Bobby explained to Sam that around renowned artists of any given period, there were clusters of students or followers or even other painters of the day who were heavily influenced by the master's style. These adjuncts would produce works of art similar in subject matter and atmosphere and tone to the master's; however, each painter's technique remained as unique as his own fingerprints. One hundred years or more later, and sometimes not even that long, when paintings—particularly those that were unsigned—by such artists (usually labeled as "school of" the renowned artist) came under professional scrutiny, there could be a question as to their autograph. It might simply be a case of someone rubbing out the name of the follower and replacing it with that of the recognized master. Or it might be, more compellingly, a case in which someone, most likely a restorer, had brushstroked the painting in the direction, technically speaking, of the master. "I'll show you what I mean," Bobby said, jumping out of bed and grabbing his blue sweatpants. He stood there, staring down at Sam, who, sleepy-looking and tousled, just gaped at him. "Do you want to see or not?"

Sam got up hurriedly, put on his underwear and followed Bobby into his studio. Leaning against the easel was a large canvas that looked as though it had been painted over in black. Sam noticed that the *Vanitas* was nowhere to be seen.

"I've just taken this out," Bobby said, pointing to the canvas, "though I've had it for over a year."

He watched Sam examine the black, uneven surface, which had only hints of other pigmentation, looking at it as though peering into the fathomless depths of an ocean. Bobby could tell Sam was afraid he was looking at some contemporary masterwork that was too subtle for his poorly cultivated appreciation. Amused, Bobby reassured him the canvas had been deliberately painted over and he'd acquired it from a London junk dealer who didn't realize what it was.

"By the looks of the frame, it's probably nineteenth-century French, which is my specialty. Somebody decided they hated it and covered it in black paint."

In the restoration game, one frequently encountered this sort of situation. Something in this particular painting had offended someone, who took the trouble to obscure its aesthetic message, but for some reason never destroyed it. Now the trick was to remove the outer paint without stripping away the original surface, as well as to restore those sections of the original that had suffered damage. In some cases this meant using a very weak solvent; in other cases it involved a laborious, time-consuming scraping away of the painted outer shell. A restorer's work, for the most part, was undoing what someone else in an earlier time had done.

"But see this," Bobby said, pointing to the top-right-hand corner of the canvas, where there were blooms of grayish-blue color, the only place where the paint had been conspicuously removed. "I began here. Looks like it's going to be a beautiful sky. Come closer. See how toneless the colors are. Now watch this." He moved back to the drafting table, grabbed a large blond brush and dipped it into a small metal trough. He approached the painting and with a few deft strokes rubbed the brush into it. "Now, look," he said.

The colors had puffed out to reveal the careful shading of clouds. There was also an artery of red running through the darker pigments. "I just put very thin varnish on it. What's called 'working varnish.' It enhances the painting so I can see what I have." He put the brush down and turned to Sam. "The point I'm trying to make is that with a few powerful tools of the trade, a painting can be subtly pulled in another direction. Now that I can see the sky, I can add to it or take it back. More importantly, I can change the pattern of the brushstrokes. Sometimes such subtle changes are all it takes to make a picture, one without an autograph, seem to be by a different painter."

"And so a painting that might, say, be worth ten thousand dollars will suddenly be worth one hundred thousand dollars," Sam suggested.

"Precisely."

Bobby told him that sometimes even the artist himself was unable to recognize a painting falsely attributed to him. Picasso, for example, in the 1930s, actually certified a painting that bore his signature, one that he supposedly completed around 1900. The painting ended up in a Texas museum, which later discovered it was actually by a friend of Picasso's, Joachin Sunyer y Miró. Sunyer, when he was down on his luck in the 1930s, refurbished one of his old paintings in the manner of his more famous colleague, rubbed his own name out and signed Picasso's in its place.

"Picasso didn't recognize that it wasn't his own painting?"

"He'd obviously done a lot of paintings since 1900."

Sam was looking around the studio. "Where is it?" he finally asked.

Of course Bobby knew what he was looking for. "I keep it out of sight. In the closet."

They both laughed at the notion of closeting.

"Why don't you hang it up?"

"You know why. I told you why."

Sam squinted at him, as though disbelieving, and asked if he could see it again. Bobby instinctively knew that unless Sam were given some kind of explanation, he would never stop asking questions about the drawing. Perhaps a measure of honesty might allow him to put the drawing behind them—at least for the time being. With that, Bobby left the room to go to his storage closet. He returned carrying the *Vanitas*, which he placed on the easel, on top of the blackened canvas.

They both stared at it and Sam murmured once again how erotic he thought it was. Up close the drawing appeared slightly more blurred, reminding him of a grainy, black-and-white photograph that managed to suggest depth and shadow, the muscled ridges, the private places of the male body. Arched just above the crown of the skull was the armpit whose tufts of hair were divided by a faint line of skin and gave the figure a youthful touch. Looking at it now, Bobby was particularly proud of the way he'd managed to suggest the fabric swaddling the skull, the luxuries of life rubbing the bone of death. Yes, he thought there *was* something at once intangible and yet immediate about the reclining, languid figure that almost compelled the viewer to imagine himself in bed with the shadowy man, mesmerized by the soft touch of his lovely limbs. Somehow it seemed quite fitting to see how the gold leaf on the simple frame was already flaking away.

"So he just came to you and said he was going to die?" asked Sam.

Bobby nodded. "And begged me to draw him while he was still lovely."

Sensing the man had very little money, Bobby deliberately undercharged for the commission. He had a little studio adjacent to his East Village gallery space, and the man came there every day for two weeks during the deepest part of the winter. He lived in a railroad flat on East Fourteenth Street and would walk along the Bowery to reach Bobby's studio. The weather was particularly severe that year, the mantle of snow that usually arrived and then swiftly disappeared with a kind of whimsy clung to the street gutters for weeks while the sidewalks were often iced over with a treacherous glaze. But, no matter, the man came each day, his face and neck wound with scarves, his body encased in many layers, which he would decorously shed one by one in front of Bobby until he was nude. In the midst of the work, he made many advances toward Bobby, who managed to maintain his distance. The work proceeded splendidly until the man's weight began to rapidly decline, and his body, which had seemed blessed with a kind of immortal beauty, began to waste. By the time the sessions were over, Bobby's charcoal pencil had been forced to lie.

"What about the skull?" Sam asked.

"That was his idea. Not mine. I had mentioned seventeenth-century Dutch painting and the *Vanitas* tradition. I told him about Cézanne. He said that a *Vanitas* was exactly what he wanted."

"And did he die right after that?"

Bobby shook his head. "Ironically, no." The amazing thing was that after they'd finished the drawing, for a while the young man actually got better. "Like I'd given him a transfusion," Bobby said.

Bobby would always remember how Sam visibly shuddered, as though something had triggered an uncomfortable association. Moments passed and then he asked impulsively, "Will you sell this to me?"

Bobby stared at him, thinking, But if I sell it to him, I'll have to see it. This drawing will follow me; I will never be able to disown it. It will trail after me like a bunch of tin cans tied to the tail of a car. I'd rather sell it to a stranger. "No."

"Why not?"

"Because it's bad luck."

"I'm not superstitious. I'll take my chances."

Bobby shook his head, hating the fact that they were both standing there, half-clad, wishing he weren't so attracted to Sam, wishing he could dispel the breaker of dread that rolled over him every time he looked at his own creation. "I will never sell it to you," he told Sam emphatically. "Please don't ask me again."

"Now *you* sound just like Garland," Sam told him.

9   Flying into daylight always made the return to America seem endless. Sam, who had lain awake most of the previous night talking to Bobby, decided to medicate himself to ensure that he slept during the flight. Valium filed down the edge of having to sit still for so many hours; it coaxed the droning of the plane into a lullaby, eased the sense of hurtling forward. Napping intermittently, Sam dreamed of entering an abandoned subway station and seeing the man in the *Vanitas*; but it wasn't *him*, it was "the angel"—once again. This time Sam was not so surprised. Wearing a trench coat, the angel appeared to be waiting for a train. Next to him on the platform was a sleeping bed made of an ultraviolet coil that spiraled off the concrete up into several tiers of tubing that ended at a pillow. This time Sam spoke to the angel first and the face that turned to him had not eyes but spectral hollows.

A squalling infant roused him from sleep, and when he turned to the window, he saw not a reflection of his own face, not the angel, but rather the skull in Bobby's drawing—but only for a split second. He blinked at the osseous mask that stared back at him and cried out, frightening some of the other passengers and embarrassing himself. Two flight attendants, buzzing down the aisle like a pair of wasps, descended on him, demanding what was wrong. By the time they reached him, the skull had disappeared and Sam found himself telling them he thought he'd seen something falling past the airplane.

New York became a long line at customs, a repellent blast of heat and humidity, a long wait for a taxi without air conditioning, traffic on the Van Wyck knifing through visible streamers of heat waves radiating above the concrete. To avoid congestion, taxi drivers were now taking a new route that looped in and out of the Long Island Expressway and the Cross Island, which ended up costing three or four dollars more on the meter at the other end. When the driver announced this change, Sam grilled him as to why exactly this longer route would be better. Even though he had grown up in Vermont, Sam was well aware that life in New York City was stabilized and sustained by a certain level of suspicion.

Sweltering in the back of the taxi, he kept scrutinizing the driver, a man of indeterminate race, wanting to give him the benefit of the doubt for making the proper decision in the face of an onslaught of traffic, but unable to relinquish knee-jerk skepticism. "Has the BQE really been that backed up?"

"Oh, yes, terrible these days." The heavy accent could've been from anywhere.

"When I left two weeks ago it was fine."

"Oh, no, construction since then."

Palming the plastic, heart-shaped radio dispatcher, the man began burbling in an unidentifiable foreign tongue, blathering on for a few minutes while Sam eyed the meter. A friend had told him that speaking on the car radio enabled the cabdrivers to somehow accelerate the fare. The meter numbers *did* seem to be going faster suddenly—he was determined to end the man's conversation with his contact.

Sam interrupted. "What language are you speaking?"

The man glanced at him in the rearview mirror. "My language. My country," he said defensively and then began addressing the plastic heart again.

"I need to speak to you, sir," Sam said. "Could you please?"

The man finally put down his radio. "What is it?"

"I want to go a different way. I know a shortcut through Queens. Get off at the next exit."

"But I go a different way," the man protested.

"Look, I'm paying for this ride and I want you to take the next exit."

The alternate route ended up presenting a very clear passage along wide boulevards of decrepit shopping malls and chain stores, as familiar, yet as foreign, to him as those outlying suburbs of London. Other lives, other cultures he'd never know because Manhattan would always loom for him as it had for everyone else who flocked there from small-town life. The driver followed his directions dutifully until they hit a traffic snag. "You see, you see," the man complained.

Back at his apartment on East Twenty-fourth Street, the pileup of bills immediately set Sam to worrying about his dwindling finances. The first installment of the book advance had gone to pay outstanding debts, and he hadn't even been able to cough up enough to pay his phone bill the previous month. The depressingly fat blue NYNEX envelope wedged into his mail stack would, he knew, reflect the latest charges added to those still owed. Two credit card statements screamed hefty balances that he was nurturing every month. Before leaving, he'd delivered the second one hundred pages of the memoir and was due an additional installment from the publisher. But they were allowed to request rewrites and thereby hold up the next payment until these were completed.

Sixteen flashed the answering machine. Sixteen messages. Sam switched on the air conditioning, tore off his clothes, and flipped through the rest of his mail, probing for magazine article payments—of which there was only one. He put the rest of the bills to one side. He would open them when he felt more in the mood to cope with the idea of financial peril. Then he listened to his messages: a few friends, a few second-tier magazine editors, nobody he needed to contact immediately. Two were from his ex, Matthew; and then his mood skyrocketed to hear the last one from Bobby saying that he missed him already. Bobby's outward reserve made him seem a lot cooler than he actually was, and Sam was pleasantly surprised by the sudden gush of affection. Then his mood plummeted. What the hell was he going to do about money?

He showered and looked at himself in the three panels of his bathroom mirror. Although he usually gained weight in London, this time he seemed to have lost some. Once the drug of Bobby LaCour had taken effect, Sam's appetite for food had been cut in half. To prove the weight loss to himself, Sam put on a pair of cutoff jeans that had been a little tight when he'd left. They fit perfectly, even somewhat loosely.

Sam reached Matthew's answering machine and left a message and was just going out to the grocery store when the phone rang. He half-hoped it was Bobby.

"When did you get home?" It was Matthew.

"I just called you."

"I know. I heard you. I was . . . in the bathroom."

"So, how are you?"

"Not great . . ." There was a strange pause. "Sam, why didn't you call me back?"

"Things got really crazy over there. I'm sorry. Why, what's going on?"

"I'm not sure."

"You're not sure? That doesn't sound like you." While they'd been together Matthew had been almost too vocal about the way he felt and about what Sam was doing—right or wrong.

"I actually called in sick the last two days."

Sam fell silent. What the fuck was wrong? Of course, he feared the worst: that Matthew was sick. "I was about to go grocery shopping. But I can do that later and come over now."

Matthew lived in the East Village in a sprawling two-bedroom tenement, which he was subletting from an acquaintance who'd had the lease since the 1960s, and paid a ridiculously low rent. Located only a block away from noisy, carnival-like Saint Mark's Place, the painted brick building was peeling, in a state of disrepair; it came equipped with metal fire escapes but no elevator. In the year since they'd split up, Matthew had furnished his new place rather scantily, particularly so for someone who was a well-paid law associate. For some time Sam had been harboring a suspicion that Matthew had acquired a recreational drug habit. After they broke up, Matthew starting clubbing and hanging out with a body-beautiful crowd that dropped a lot of Ecstasy.

Sam had his own set of keys for emergencies and let himself into the building. He passed what looked like a bag lady whose hair was tied back with a dirty kerchief and who was leaving the building accompanied by a mother/son pair of German shepherds. He climbed three flights of stairs and knocked on Matthew's door. When nobody answered, he tried the knob and was surprised to find it open.

The moment he walked in, he was hit with a strong smell of sweat and dirty laundry and, oddly, something starchy. The apartment, which had a coveted southern exposure, brimmed with light. "Where are you?"

Matthew's voice summoned him from the bedroom.

To get there, Sam had to pass the kitchen. An electric grain cooker stood on the counter, opened and half-filled with dry, spoiled-looking rice. Two cockroaches were feasting on some stray grains that were lying next to it on the counter. As he passed, they flew across the Formica and disappeared behind the stove.

Matthew's bedroom was darkened by pulled-down shades, his mattress-on-the-floor covered by a blue down comforter. He was completely submerged in his bedding, covered except for his elbows and head. He lay there, peering groggily at Sam. The stagnant atmosphere in the room reminded Sam of rooms he had visited in the past, rooms of men who had since died. Upon closer scrutiny, he could see that Matthew had the beginnings of a beard, which still could not conceal a gaunt look about him. Sam was so shocked by his appearance that he couldn't help but blurt out, "What are you doing in bed?"

The familiar syrupy-brown eyes fixed themselves ruefully on Sam. "I told you I'm in a funk."

"I want to know the truth right now."

"Stupid. I told you I had another test two months ago and that I was okay. You just don't remember."

The giddy sense of relief made Sam feel guilty. It would have been too ironic if Matthew got sick, too, for it would mean that, besides James, another one of Sam's lovers would have died. Then again, perhaps not ironic so much as grim, the grim reality of the law of averages. He knew many men who had lost more than one lover. In some cases, it was true, nursing the dying had oddly become a kind of career, as it had during wartime. But often people met and fell in love before they found out that all too soon one of them would sicken and die.

Suddenly, buried memories surfaced with long-forgotten but familiar faces. They tormented him now, captivating men he'd rejected because they'd bravely confessed to having been infected. He'd explained to them that he just couldn't go through again what he'd been through with James. Sam had no idea if they were dead or alive now, but he knew they might certainly have loved him had he allowed them to. It was such a scary thing to love; it took so long to let one's defenses down. How could he possibly have given himself to someone he knew was standing on the brink of leaving him forever?

He sat down on Matthew's bed. "Jessie is always chilly to me whenever I call there," Matthew complained.

"So why do you care?"

"I don't care, really. I know she never liked me. But it takes no effort to be cordial."

"If it bothers you so much, I'll say something."

Matthew waved him away. "Don't. I just don't get why you're still so close to her."

"Would you say that if she wasn't a woman?"

Matthew glared at him. "That's insulting. I have female friends, too."

"So then what's the problem?"

"It's just the way the two of you carry on. It's like . . . I don't know . . . you're still together." Matthew had always been jealous of Sam's post-breakup closeness with Jessie. "Case in point. When I called and she said you weren't there and she didn't know where you were, I could tell she was worried. . . . I thought you might be with somebody else."

"Well, there were extenuating circumstances." Sam explained about the fistfight and having to run out of the house to avoid the police.

"That's the other thing. Every time you go to England, it seems like somebody is getting drunk and losing it."

"The flip side of having to maintain a stiff upper lip."

The joke fell flat. Matthew was looking preoccupied. After a few moments of ruminative silence, he looked away and said, "So where were you the night that I called?"

Sam wanted to avoid the truth. "After the fight I didn't want to go back. I went out to a few bars."

"How were they?"

"Boring."

"Hummm," Matthew said. "So how's the daughter?"

"You giving me lip service now?"

"No, I'm curious."

"She's wonderful."

It suddenly occurred to Sam that Matthew was probably waiting for him to ask why he'd been hanging around in bed. And so he did.

Matthew shrugged. "I went out last weekend, stayed up all night, and I think I'm paying for it now."

"You've got to stop taking that Ecstasy."

"*That* Ecstasy." Matthew's eyes mocked him.

"Well, that's probably what's doing it to you. Normal life no doubt seems boring after you've been on that stuff."

"How do you know? You ever tried it?"

"I know that too much of a good thing is always bad for the status quo."

"Listen to you," Matthew said, propping himself up on the mattress. His chest was now visible, pinkish-tan, with small freckles on the upper planes of his pectorals. He was proud of his chest and Sam knew that he was trying to be seductive. The gesture, however, left Sam cold.

He glanced around the room. "Your place is still a shit hole, Matthew. I don't get it. You used to be so anal. Christ, I can't believe you still haven't bought a bed."

"Haven't gotten around to it."

"You used to be so organized."

"People go through phases."

Could Matthew's black mood possibly be due to the fact that the Brazilian man he had been seeing had thrown him over? Matthew shook his head.

"Na, he calls me every day. Apologizing and begging me to go away with him."

"Must be nice."

Matthew was peering at Sam with bewildered astonishment. "Does it even occur to you that it might have something to do with *you?*"

Sam blinked, incredulous. "Me? What to do with me?"

"Maybe it's . . . I don't know, maybe I'm still screwed up over our breakup."

Sam sat there for a moment, slack-jawed. "Come on, that doesn't make any sense. We've been functioning as friends for like eight months now."

"Well, maybe there hasn't been enough of a transition," Matthew pointed out. "A readjustment period, a time when we weren't in contact."

"Is that what you're angling for, that we *not* be in contact for a while?"

Matthew looked exasperated.

"Well, come on! This is coming out of left field. If this has been the case, then why did you invite me to have dinner with you and your Brazilian boyfriend—what's his name?"

"Jorge."

In fact, Sam had found Matthew's inamorato superficial and overly talkative—in short, hardly threatening. Beyond this, Matthew didn't seem to be all that interested in the guy.

"Maybe that was a mistake," Matthew pointed out now. "Maybe we shouldn't overlap like this. Straight people don't do it. Former wives and former husbands never break bread with their ex's current lovers."

Sam still found it hard to believe that Matthew could have relapsed into such distress over breaking up with him. After all, they'd already been through the hard parts, the months of self-doubt and bewilderment. They'd always been able to talk about what went wrong.

"Maybe it's different for you now," Matthew said suddenly. "Maybe you've got somebody else in your life."

Sam wondered if Jessie had somehow tipped Matthew off. He'd have to ask her. "What makes you say that?"

"It's coming out of every pore," Matthew observed. "You've lost weight. You look splendid."

Sam hit the inevitable wall of jet-lagged exhaustion at around seven-thirty that evening and crashed. He slept through until 4:00 A.M., then lay in bed fretting over his finances until around six-thirty and was just drifting off to sleep again when the phone rang. He picked it up to hear the overseas sound of white noise and blips and thought maybe Bobby was calling, but there was nobody at the other end of the line. Five minutes later it rang again. It was Jessie.

"Did you just try and call me?"

"Yeah, I couldn't hear anything."

Sam couldn't help but be disappointed.

"So how was the flight?"

"Fine except for around thirty minutes." Oddly, she didn't ask him to elaborate. She called him rarely to chitchat. He sensed something must be wrong. "You sound distracted," Sam said.

"I'm stewing."

"So tell me, already."

She hesitated and then said, "Oh, it's just Rudy. I think he's in the process of buggering off."

The day Sam left, Rudy had arrived at Jessie's to break the news. His wife, Carolyn, having tried for years, had finally gotten pregnant. Carolyn was now insisting that Rudy end his extramarital liaison, and he was wavering but seriously considering it.

Sam exclaimed, "Is this a total shock? Did you have any idea this might happen?"

"I don't know. I don't know what I wanted," said Jessie morosely. "I don't know what I *expected*, either. Perhaps that he and

I would keep on sleeping together and talking politics—even if he had six kids."

Sam was taken aback but forced himself to say nothing more than "Six?" Once he'd said it, he realized it sounded as if he'd said *Sex?*

Jessie went on describing her horror at the news. "I guess I felt my parenthood gave me 'one up' on Rudy. Or at least some equality. He had Carolyn to care for, I had Eva. We met in a space between, to indulge ourselves."

"Indulge?"

"Well, that's what an affair is about, isn't it? Fun. Relaxation. Stimulation. New perspectives."

Sam shuddered at the thought of Rudy. "I suppose so."

"And then you get to cut out when the going gets rough." Jessie sighed audibly. "Rudy's going to throw me over. He doesn't exactly want to, but he's fairly aglow at the idea of his baby. And you know what?"

"What?"

"I am *not* aglow. I'm . . . envious. Very envious. That's been a real shock to me. Perhaps the worst shock of all."

"But you've always said—"

"Oh, I know, I know. Eva's quite enough, no more babies. God, it was really hard."

Sam wondered if, all along, Jessie had envied the solid triad of Mother, Father, and baby. "Single motherhood—," he began.

"I know, it's what I chose. And I've done a darn good job, if I do say so."

"Of course."

Jessie said wearily, "I always thought Carolyn would just let the affair burn itself out."

She explained that Rudy had confessed to having had other affairs during his marriage. According to him, none had been as serious as his and Jessie's. "But I never wanted it 'serious,' of course. He kept thinking I was hoping he'd leave Carolyn. I *wasn't* hoping that at all."

"So what *do* you want, Jessie?"

Sam waited for the response, which was a while in coming. It occurred to him that when they were involved and there were such silences, the burden of them had become unbearable. Finally, she said slowly and emphatically, "I want him to be a good husband and father. Yet I still want to keep seeing him . . . somehow."

10 Looking shockingly more gaunt and wasted than he had just ten days before, Garland kissed Sam on the cheek and asked him to come into his kitchen for a moment. However, as soon as Sam stepped into the apartment, both dogs stampeded from the bedroom. The gray schnauzer rushed over, vaulted up on his leg and managed to nip through his jeans and catch skin. "Jesus!" Sam cried out. "Your dog just took a piece of me."

Garland turned around, looking puzzled. "Gus!" he yelled. He grabbed the unread *New York Times* off a low table in the entryway, halved it, and clouted the dog on its snout. Gus, in response, bared his teeth at his master and then ran off to hide in the living room. "You insolent little shit!" Garland upbraided the animal, then aped his own dog by baring his teeth at Sam. "Are you all right? Do you want some iodine or hydrogen peroxide?"

Sam suddenly felt foolish for complaining in front of a man who was ill.

"Well, I can tell you he's not rabid, and if you get regular tetanus shots, you should be fine."

The distracting little incident gave Sam a chance to recover from his amazement at Garland's precipitous decline. As the art dealer led the way into a fully equipped, Upper East Side kitchen complete with hanging, highly burnished copper pots, a Sub Zero refrigerator, and all sorts of cooking appliances that seemed barely used, Garland explained that he had suffered a seizure and gone into the hospital. "I dropped ten pounds practically overnight. That's why I never got your message that you delivered the package until long after the fact."

"Are you okay now?" Sam asked gently. "I mean, is the condition . . . stabilized?"

"As much as it can be with this disease," Garland said cynically. "They have me on Ritalin, you know, the drug they give to hyperactive children?"

Sam nodded.

"One more irony in my life." Garland went on to explain that when he was a child, his elementary school had urged his mother to put him on Ritalin to combat his hyperactivity. "She downright refused. I couldn't resist calling her to say that I'm on it forty-five years later."

"I'm sure it wasn't easy for her to hear."

Garland was silent for a moment and then turned philosophical. "Yeah, it ain't easy for a parent to lose a child. Then, again, I'd rather be her than me," he said with a devilish grin.

"How can you be so blithe about this?"

"You don't see me when I'm depressed."

Lying on the round kitchen table was a large, salmon-colored ceramic platter wrapped in plastic and bearing a hand-lettered sign: "Don't Touch." Two gleaming copper pots were low-boiling on the stove.

"What's that cooking?" asked Sam.

"It's called Kombucha tea."

Kombucha, Garland explained, was an Asiatic mushroom that was cultivated under plastic wraps in a bowl. He pointed to the platter. "A friend of mine who lives on Central Park West messengered these to me. He says people swear by them. The nutrients are supposed to be a cure."

"I've never heard of it."

"I've been following these elaborate, handwritten instructions for a little over a month now—in between hospital visits, that is."

"Is it working?"

"How do I know? I'm taking it merely to make my friend feel better." Sam was touched that Garland felt obliged to make someone else feel better about his fatal illness. "You want to try it?" Garland asked. "Supposedly cures everything, even what you don't know is ailing you." He dropped a few ice cubes in a tall jelly glass and poured from a dark-green plastic pitcher. "I drink my alternative medicine iced. I pretend it's one of those decaffeinated summer drinks." He handed Sam a glass. "So what else is new? You're looking well. Lost some weight. I think you needed to."

Sam laughed uncomfortably and tried the tea. It had a woody, fermented flavor.

They took their glasses of Kombucha into the Fifth Avenue sitting room. The black Labrador followed them there, but the nasty schnauzer remained in hiding behind one of the sofas. As Sam sank into one of the down-filled armchairs, Garland said, "The other irony in my life is apparently I have this new illness called 'micoavial complex.'" Garland swiveled his eyes to indicate the room. "I might as well have held on to my birds."

The former aviary had once been home to a hundred birds of different varieties and sizes, until a fierce storm blew out one of the windows and at least half the menagerie escaped into Central Park. Garland had recently been urged by his doctor to give away the remaining ones due to all the possible illnesses they were known to carry. After dismantling the aviary, he was in the process of redecorating the room when several friends and business associates threw him an impromptu surprise party and showed up with bird tapestries, bird taxidermy, bird carvings, nests, bird sketches, bird paintings, porcelain bird perches—all of which he'd used to furnish the room

"But maybe it's because—"

"No." Garland interrupted him. "My birds have been gone way too long. I've been tested for this thing before." He looked up at the ceiling. "I must've been shat on somewhere—maybe out in the Hamptons—and just didn't realize it."

It had been several weeks since Sam had sat in this room, and now that he had his affair with Bobby LaCour pressing on his conscience, the fixed gazes of birds, both taxidermic and figurative, were unsettling.

Garland asked how the writing was progressing, how the two interviews had gone. Sam reported that he was forging ahead, but confessed that the two men he had interviewed in London were rather dry and had little to add to what Garland had already told him about handling a certain estate sale of English sporting pictures that included works by Gainsborough, Stubbs, and Wooton. The dealer on New Bond Street had confirmed Garland's recollection of the chain of provenance of a small, D-shaped, formally mounted mahogany console made by Adam Weisweiler, one of the great *ébénistes,* or ebony carvers, of Europe, and which had been delivered to the private study of Marie Antoinette on September 24, 1784.

"I understand Mr. Danforth invited you to attend an auction and that you didn't go," Garland said.

Sam explained that he just didn't think he'd get anything out of it. "For the book, I mean."

Garland peered at him as though he were a curiosity. "Have you ever even been to an art auction before?"

Sam shook his head. "Not really."

"Don't you think seeing one firsthand might help you write my book?"

"I can always go to one here in New York."

Garland's lighthearted mood seemed to shift and he ceased speaking for what ended up to be a troubling amount of time. "You're really not interested in any of this decorator crap, are you?" he said finally.

"That's not true," Sam said unconvincingly, realizing that two weeks ago he would've made a much grander display of hiding his apathy.

"Come on, you're bored silly by all this frill and fop. I can tell." Garland chuckled. "You probably wouldn't know a Fabergé egg if it bit you in the ass."

Sam thought, If Garland senses the truth, why insult him by denying it? "I'll admit to you that sometimes I feel pretty ignorant of it all and pretty dull because it doesn't get me going. Then, again, I've always loved going to museums and looking at paintings. When I was a child, my father used to take me to the Museum of Fine Arts in Boston."

"Well, isn't that nice," Garland said sadly. "As you know, I used to be a fanatical collector. Certain things I would've even traded my own mother for. But not anymore." With a flick of his hand, he indicated the overabundance of objects in the aviary room. "Now, being so fanatical seems absurd. None of this means anything to me." Having said this, he placed his hands on the armrests of his chair and slowly hoisted himself to a wobbly standing position. "Be right back." He headed to the bathroom.

Garland returned five minutes later, shaking his head. "Everything I eat goes right through me. I probably could eat powdered cement and it would come out like a river." Once again he fixed his flinty gaze on Sam. "So, I'm assuming you were able to deliver my gift."

Sam explained that Bobby was still at the same address, albeit with a disconnected telephone, living a modest, extremely reclusive life.

Garland dismissed the description with an imperious wave of his hand. "He's hardly a recluse—that one, it's all a front. He has to be miserable living on a shoestring, doing little curio sketches for tourist museum shops."

"Seemed fairly content to me."

Appearing not to have heard Sam, Garland burbled on. "Let me tell you, he's one grandiose individual. He would never admit it, but he likes the expensive life. As do most people who come from small towns to the big city and reinvent themselves."

"I come from a small town. I don't crave the expensive life."

Garland's smile was crafty. "I'm talking blue-collar, Sam. Bobby is one hundred percent blue-collar. You, my friend, do not fall into that category."

Sam gave Garland a look that meant, how did he know?

"Sam, the world is small—I told you that once. I believe I also told you that New York is a fishbowl."

Sam blinked and waited.

"Let's just say that while you were abroad, I met a friend of yours at a party. And I asked a few polite questions."

"Okay, so what did you find out about me?"

"Nothing dishy, unfortunately. Nothing in the way of *scandale*. For an ex-lover, he was quite complimentary."

Matthew? Why hadn't he said anything?

"So now I know that your father is one of those country doctors turned gentleman farmer."

"An exaggeration, Elliot. He milks a few cows and grows a field of hay and sells it to some of his farmer friends. And he's not a country doctor, he's a shrink."

"What psychological illnesses do they suffer from in the countryside, cabin fever?"

Sam stared at him.

"Nevertheless, you have grown up quite comfortably. I happen to know that in the financial relief map of the United States, Woodstock, Vermont, is a lot higher than Thibodaux, Louisiana. And at least a mile above Bethlehem, Pennsylvania, where I come from. You see, Sam, people like Bobby LaCour, people like Elliot Garland, don't like to remember where we come from. Our childhoods were prisons, not idylls. And so we refine ourselves to the point where nobody would ever suspect our humble beginnings. We refine ourselves until there's a mirrored veneer to reflect what people want to see, sharp edges to turn them away so that they don't guess we have pathetic, sentimental, white-trash hearts. Whereas somebody like you can risk being a little rough around the edges. People with your sort of background can afford to slum it."

Sam ignored the remark. "Bobby LaCour doesn't strike me as being so irreproachably effete."

"You certainly say that with authority," Garland pointed out. "You brought him a gift? How much could you possibly glean from one brief meeting?"

The sharpened, glittering blade was unmistakable. Garland was staring at him keenly, and it struck Sam perhaps for the first time how beautiful the man's eyes were, how when Garland had been well enough to try and make romantic connections with others, that these eyes must've been beacons of attraction. But now he was infirm, horribly aged by his sickness. The disease, almost overnight, could rob even the most beautiful man of his sexual power and of even his youth.

"Let's put it this way. I spent enough time with him to find out what your gift was."

Garland seemed to have anticipated the gibe. "It was mine to do with as I liked."

"You could've sold it to *me*."

"Well, now you can buy it from *him*—if he'll sell it to you."

Sam waited a moment. "Why are you doing this?"

"Don't be coy, Sam, it doesn't become you," Garland said,

barely audible. "You know exactly why. You're oozing it. I knew the moment you walked in the door."

Sam waited a moment before he spoke again. "Come on, Elliot, it had to be part of your plan. Otherwise, why not just ship him the drawing and leave me out of it?"

It was the first time Sam had spoken up in such a way to Garland, who blinked at him, as though trying to calibrate the subtle shift in their relationship.

"Flatter yourself all you want," Garland said in a carefully measured tone, "but I wanted him to come back to see me—that was why I sent the *Vanitas*. I mean, didn't he tell you about our relationship?"

"I didn't ask him and he didn't tell. But of course I knew."

"So he didn't actually explain? Why should I have expected anything different?" Garland said bitterly.

"But you didn't tell me, either. Don't you think *you* should've said something to me before I went to find him?"

"You were taking him a drawing. Not interviewing him."

"I tried to interview him, trust me. And didn't get very far."

"No matter if you did, my personal relationship with Bobby LaCour isn't going into my memoir."

"Of course not. It's probably too interesting."

Garland seemed stunned that Sam would dare to parry in such a way. "I hired you to write this book," he said grandly. "I sent you to England to do interviews. And while you were there, I asked you to deliver a drawing to an old friend of mine."

"If you'd been honest and told me who and what Bobby was to you, I wouldn't have pursued anything more."

Garland was skeptical. "You expect me to believe *that?*"

Sam said sadly, "I do have *some* principles."

Garland dropped his head and shook it weakly back and forth. A sigh turned into a hacking cough. "Okay, so now I'll confess to you. Bobby LaCour was the love of my life."

Clearly agitated, the ailing art dealer pressed on the armrests and staggered to his feet. Sam watched him shamble over to the window, where he placed his hands on the sill and leaned ever so slightly toward Fifth Avenue. In Sam's absence, summer had exploded in Central Park. The trees were lush, their boughs knitting together, and the meandering pathways were burgeoning with annuals. Indeed, watching Garland's display of frailty, Sam wished he could've known the man before all this began, when he was still healthy. Finally, Garland asked, "Well, does he look good, at least?"

"Yeah." Sam's voice was hoarse. Neither said anything for a moment. Sam stared at the back of the dying man. Even though he knew he was looking at a life sped up to the end of its span, somehow he couldn't see the two of them, Bobby and Garland, together. Although Sam was upset, he willed himself to try and deal with the situation professionally. "So neither of you bothered to tell me the truth. Why was that?"

Garland turned back from the window, his brow furrowed. "We were trying to protect you," he quipped and then laughed. He sat down again, and his eyes met Sam's. "I don't know if you should continue working on this project anymore, Sam. It may be that I will ask you to turn over your interview tapes and find somebody else to complete it."

Sam was breathless with sudden anxiety. And yet he knew he couldn't appear to lose composure. "So first you withhold information and then you punish me for acting out of ignorance."

Garland said, "I think it was pretty sleazy of you to bring something to an old friend of mine and then sleep with him."

Part of Sam had to admit this was true. Nevertheless, if he were fired, he thought, he'd probably run out of money before he could get another assignment.

Garland looked at him. "Everything was going so well until now." Then the haughty man burst into a fit of sobbing.

Sam didn't know what to do. When he finally made a move to go and comfort Garland, the man repulsed him with a waving hand. His sobs were so deep and agonized that it was only a matter of moments until Sam, overcome by the man's despair, grew a bit tearful himself. Garland tried to speak as he wept and ended up saying many incomprehensible things.

For Sam, the greatest irony of all was that his subject had been painting a tepid portrait of a life too charmed, too evenly balanced, the manuscript itself rather talky and impersonal. It would be so much more interesting if Sam could only mine the story of this relationship with Bobby LaCour.

"I think you should go now," Garland finally murmured. "I'm obviously not in the frame of mind to do any more today. Why don't you come back tomorrow around noon."

11 After he left Garland's apartment, Sam wandered through Central Park in an attempt to calm down, but only got more depressed and angry as the minutes went by. He couldn't quite face the idea of losing his job, for that would mean financial ruin, having to borrow money to pay his immediate debts, and ultimately financial straits. Beyond this, he now distrusted Garland's motives in hiring him. At first he thought it might be because he lived outside of Garland's social loop and would therefore be unlikely to know about the relationship with Bobby LaCour. But that didn't really make sense. Obviously, Sam would have found out about Bobby sooner or later, and if Garland didn't want him to know about Bobby, then he would never have choreographed Sam's bringing the drawing to London. No, Garland definitely wanted him to know who and what Bobby was in his life, and yet at the same time ban Bobby from being written about in the memoir. Sam had to admit to himself that more and more the memoir seemed to become incidental to something potentially a lot more important. Could it be the scandal with the falsely authenticated painting?

When Sam arrived home an overseas express letter, postmarked London, was waiting for him. He ripped it open, glanced at the signature, and was jolted to see that it was from Bobby LaCour.

Dear Sam:

Even if this is the first you're hearing it, I'm sorry that I didn't tell you before. Although I was never in love with Elliot Garland, we were very much involved. I didn't tell you because I was worried that knowing the truth would make my seeing you too much a conflict of interest. As soon as you left my apartment the last time, I realized I should have said something, that it was wrong not to have. I was attracted to you from the moment I saw you. You're the first man I've been at all interested in in a long time.

You also have to understand that this whole thing came on very suddenly. You appeared in my life not once but twice—in the same day. I made no advances toward you. You know as well as I do that turning up late at night was provocative.

As far as Elliot is concerned, I owe a lot to him. He rescued me from the dead end life I was living in Louisiana and took me to New York, where I was able to pursue a career in painting restoration. I lived with him for two years in that apartment where you go every day to interview him. The place was magical to me. I advised him on many of the acquisitions he made. I spent months painting all the bedroom and closet doors to make them look like exotic wood. When I finally decided to move out, he was furious. He tried to break my self-confidence. He tried to make me feel that I couldn't survive on my own. He kept drumming it into my head that sexual attraction ends up wrecking every relationship between two men. He tried to convince me that even though we stopped having sex that I was better off being with him, because then at least I could rely on some kind of stability. And yet he was always jealous of anybody who ever came into my life, assumed that they were romantic involvements, even if they weren't. I eventually had to move out of his apartment because I knew that if I stayed with him he'd be destroyed by his own jealousy.

But he never forgave me.

Even now that he is dying, it seems that he still won't forgive me.

Yes, I still care deeply for the man.

Over the last two days, I have kept wondering why he sent you to me. He never wanted me to be with anybody else—so there's obviously something he's doing that I don't understand. But Sam, please try and understand why I'm telling you this now instead of before.

Bobby.

Though Bobby's letter augured further complications and even the possibility of heartbreak, Sam couldn't help but be moved by it, to imagine he felt an even stronger bond to the man who wrote it.

Another insomniac night full of speculation. On Sam's professional fate, his solvency now resting in Garland's hands, the die his to cast. At 3:00 A.M., a three-figure bank balance seemed dangerously low, and the knowledge that next month's rent would be delinquent in just another week was paralyzing. Sam prayed that his subject would decide to continue working with him; for, after all, what had happened was something that Garland had had a hand in bringing about.

At around ten the next morning, Sam went out to the corner grocery store for a *New York Times* and a quart of nonfat milk. When he got back upstairs, without even putting the milk in the fridge, he checked his VoiceMail and retrieved a message from Bobby LaCour, calling from his corner public phone box. Goddammit! Important phone calls always arrived the moment you stopped waiting for them. As he was putting the milk in the refrigerator, the phone rang again. Sam jumped on it and heard the whirring of overseas telecommunication, the sound of jets high above the Atlantic.

"Hey, there. Something told me I'd get you if I tried again."

"Well, you figured right," Sam said flatly and told Bobby that his livelihood was now in jeopardy and that Garland might not want to continue working with him.

"That's not fair!" Bobby insisted. "He also had a responsibility to tell you about me. After all, you're writing *his* life story. In fact, when you and I first met, I actually assumed you knew— I figured he would've told you."

"So when were *you* going to tell me?"

"Sam, I thought ours would only be a one-night stand. To be honest, that's what I'm used to." Sam was stung to hear this. "And then every time we got together it became harder and harder to say something—for obvious reasons."

Sam felt frustrated at being so removed. Once again, he was reminded of the old trauma of when he had separated from Jessie, of yearning for someone impossibly far away, the confusion of desire trying to masquerade as something more substantial—didn't matter what, it was there and unavoidable. He now told Bobby how Garland had wept, how he had confessed that Bobby was the love of his life.

"Knowing Elliot, he probably thinks I didn't say anything because I'm ashamed to have been involved with him. Which is hardly true." Bobby explained, however, that though their relationship had been one-sided, he'd always loved Garland, they'd always had a vibrant give-and-take friendship. "I eventually found it impossible to fake the sexual part. I'm sure you can understand that."

"I would never think of trying it."

"Well, excuse me, but I was twenty-five when I met Garland. He lived an exciting life. He invited me to be a part of it. In fact, up until I met him, nobody had ever told me I was wonderful. I thought the attraction would take time, I thought that it would grow. Don't you think it was hard for me to realize that he was becoming less and less attractive to me? You know that would only mean that eventually I'd have to leave him and cause him terrible pain."

Sam was silent, suddenly feeling muddled from lack of sleep. He reminded himself that the few times he and Bobby had slept together, the sex had not been nearly as exciting as he had hoped it might be. Perhaps Bobby was less sexually driven than Sam, enough at least to fool himself that it might be possible to establish a relationship with someone who didn't reach him.

"I just wonder if he's really serious about firing you," Bobby said now. "Or if it might be some kind of game he's playing."

"You know the man better than I do."

Bobby said that he hadn't seen Garland in a long time. He had no idea what Garland's mood might be now, particularly in light of his illness. Anyway, how could Garland simply find somebody new to pick up where Sam left off? Wouldn't such a radical change affect the tone of the overall work?

Sam thought it would.

"Well . . . no matter what happens, even if he ends up firing you, make sure he tells you how he ended up with the *Vanitas*."

"But you'll tell me if he doesn't, right?"

"Look, it's a very personal thing. I suggest you do whatever you can to make him tell you. Because it's really important. If at all possible, I'd rather not get caught in the middle of this."

"But you *are* in the middle."

"No, I think *you're* in the middle," Bobby amended.

They both managed to laugh at this. "But don't worry, if he refuses to tell you, of course I will. Just come back and visit me."

For Sam had mentioned returning to England and continuing to write the memoir there once the interviewing process was completed. Right now, however, it was difficult to even think about London when he might be out of a job. He certainly couldn't return to England without money; at the very least he would have to scare up another magazine assignment to cover his most recent bills. He voiced his worries and Bobby said, "Well, you could come over and write what you wanted to write until you got another long-term assignment. And then you can go back to New York."

"I'm surprised to hear you say that," Sam said. "Because you seem to guard your privacy and your solitude. It wasn't so long ago that the idea of me even spending one night was a big deal."

"I hardly knew you, then," Bobby said. "What can I say . . . besides, I figure you can stay at your friend Jessie's, come and visit me, and that way we won't get tired of one another."

This was not quite what Sam had hoped to hear.

12   Several people manhandled the phone in Jessie's office before she retrieved Sam's call on the speaker extension. "Sounds like you're having a party there," he groused.

"We're on a terrible deadline."

"Do you have a minute to spare?"

"Sure, just hang on for a bit."

Sam listened while Jessie continued to critique an ad layout. He remembered how astute she'd been when they worked together, how her ideas had been responsible for rejuvenating several foundering ad campaigns. To think that in the beginning their association had been all about business, whereas now he rarely thought of her in such a capacity. "I've got to take this now," he heard her say. A click and then her voice was quietly whirring through the receiver. "Darling, let me call you back in two. Stay right there." As she hung up the phone, Sam heard Jessie continuing to insist to someone how important this call was.

When she called him back, the silence in the background was luxurious by comparison.

"So where are you now?" he asked.

"Big boss's office."

"And where is he?"

"*She* is in Corsica."

Corsica? That was Bobby's favorite place. Sam could hear the creaking sound of Jessie leaning back in a chair.

"What are you doing now—lighting up a cigar?"

She said sweetly, "I was just thinking that you know this office."

"I do?"

"Krelis used to be here." Krelis was the firm they had both worked for. "They gave up this space years ago. And Saaks just moved in."

"Oh."

"What I'm saying is that you and I have actually done it in this office."

Sam remembered with a pang of embarrassment but also with pleasure. During their affair he had forced the issue of having sex at work, had insisted until late one night they'd finally made use of an empty office.

"I'm sorry that I have to rush you, but they're all waiting for me. Patiently. I'm sure they think this phone call is about romantic difficulties."

Sam explained what was going on. Jessie mulled it over for a few moments. Finally, she said, "I think each of these men has something to hide. Garland probably had something to do with the reason why Bobby had to leave America, the false authentication of the painting, the scandal, whatever it was—he could have been involved in it also."

"I was already thinking that. But what do you think Bobby is trying to hide?"

"For starters, that he was in deep with somebody he wasn't really in love with. I mean, Garland's got plenty of money, right?"

"Seems to." Then again, Sam pointed out, in their brief acquaintance, Bobby never struck Sam as being particularly venal or materialistic. In fact, quite the opposite.

"Come on, don't be naïve. Everybody is venal to some degree. And you don't really know this guy."

"That's true."

"Even though they're not in contact, they're still collaborating. And since neither knows what the other is telling you, each of them is telling you as little as possible."

Sam took this in and then said, "From what I know, I can't see Bobby and Elliot as a couple."

Jessie giggled. "That's because you're infatuated with one of them. Besides, each relationship, and, specifically, what brings two people together, is a mystery. Don't you think?"

Sam said nothing, although he agreed. "Look, I know you have to go. But before you do, tell me how you are?"

At first there was no response. Sam could hear the desk chair creaking. Then Jessie said lightly, "Nothing has changed. He's still in the process of fucking off."

"You sound very flip when you say it."

"That's something I've learned from them," she said, meaning the English. "When you're feeling like shit, be as ironic as possible. It really does make you feel better."

"But has he ended it officially?"

European men weren't like American men, she explained. They didn't have the decency or the balls to spell things out. They just vanished slowly back into the woodwork.

"So have you seen him or not?"

Jessie hesitated before saying that she had. "After telling me that his wife has insisted that he end it, he called me up the other day and said he just had to see me." They'd ended up sleeping together. She admitted that was a wrong move on her part, giving into Rudy. She should make the break clean, it was the best way.

"I probably would have done the same thing."

"Probably?" Jessie laughed. Then her voice got serious. "Sam, he said the weirdest thing to me, after the fact, of course. He was being oh so meticulous with a condom, mind you. Doesn't want to trust *my* precautions any more. Doesn't want 'even more complications,' as he put it, in his life. But what stunned me was his suggesting that I should have a child with you."

Sam held his breath.

Jessie laughed nervously. "Did you discuss this with him?"

Sam explained how Rudy had told him in the same breath that he really loved Jessie yet couldn't leave his wife. "Our conversation ended before he could go much farther."

Jessie now confessed she'd worried that Sam had told Rudy how distraught he'd been when she broke the news that she was going to have Eva with another man, or how Sam had once accused her of being ashamed of his sexuality, of how having a gay father might affect the life of any child they created together.

"I wouldn't confide any of that," Sam said, shocked. Hearing his concerns, his accusations played back, he wondered if she might have interpreted them as a smoke screen hiding his actual ambivalence about having a child. He hoped not. "You probably shouldn't have put him up to calling me," Sam told her by way of saying something emphatic.

"But what do you make of what he said to me?"

"I think it's all pretty transparent. He's done with you. He's foisting you off on the *mincer.*"

"I just wanted to make sure you saw it the same way that I did." She sounded hurt.

There was a long pause. He realized she was waiting for him

to say something to soothe her. Finally, Sam spoke. "Jessie, you know you're going to be okay."

"I know I am. I don't like to admit it, but I'm going to miss him. Twisted though it may sound to you."

"No, it doesn't sound twisted. It's like you said before, what brings two people together is always a mystery."

A few hours later Sam arrived back at Garland's apartment. This time the dogs answered his knock by yipping and scratching on the other side of the door, but nobody shooed them away and no one came to the door. Wave after wave of cold paranoia broke over him. Was Garland petulantly refusing to answer? Was he somehow incapacitated and unable to get up? Was he perhaps at the hospital again? Sam was just about to go back downstairs and ask the doorman if he knew anything when he heard the locks on the other side unbolt and the door swung open.

Garland, looking tousled and groggy, was peering at him over his reading glasses, which were noticeably askew. "I think I must've fallen asleep," he said with a yawn. "What time is it?" Sam said that it was going on twelve-thirty. They had an appointment for noon, right? Garland said he had just started on a new medication, which was making him sleepy. He told Sam to follow him into the bedroom.

Like the rest of the apartment, Garland's bedroom was chock-full of art and furniture. There were two satin-covered armchairs, and hanging on the wall opposite the bed was an old Flemish tapestry with scenes of feudal life centering around a castle. The weaving was worn in places, but the colors were rich and earthy and vibrant. Next to the tapestry was a drawing that Garland had told him was by Beardsley: a willowy, androgynous figure with a corona of flames around the head. It was a rather whimsical choice to place the two very different pieces next to one another, and yet it was a good example of Garland's iconoclastic sense of decor.

As soon as Sam entered the room, the two dogs rushed past him from the hallway. The gray schnauzer leaped on Garland's bed, brandishing its teeth, and began a frenzied barking. "Gosh, he's really taken a dislike to you, hasn't he?" Garland muttered as he grabbed a nearby magazine and swatted the dog, who whimpered and finally lay down, trembling. Sam took his usual armchair while Garland climbed back under the covers. Occupying the other side of the bed, where Sam imagined a lover might sleep, was a white tray with slatted side compartments that held a cordless telephone, the remote controls for Garland's television, as well as a gathering of pill bottles. Garland pulled the tray in front of him as though it were some kind of armor.

Fixing his gaze on Sam, Garland said, "I've decided what I want to do. The only way I can continue collaborating with you is if we work very closely together and I see your progress every few days."

Puzzled, Sam waited for Garland to clarify what he meant. "What I'm trying to say is that, at least while we're finishing this book, I'd rather you not go back to England to see *him*."

Sam was disappointed. He figured Garland would do what he could to prevent him from seeing Bobby, he just never expected it to be the sole condition of their continuing the collaboration. Sam shut his eyes for a moment, trying to focus on what was important. He wanted to lash out at Garland, to leave in a huff, but knew he had no choice—and Garland knew it, too. That's why Garland didn't really seem to be waiting for his response.

"That's too bad," Sam whispered.

"What's too bad?" Garland asked, crossing his arms and staring coolly at him. He might be enfeebled by illness, but his will was still incredibly strong.

"Oh, just that you feel you have to make that condition."

Garland made a gesture of deference and then said, "If you were really hurt by somebody, would you so easily grant them happiness in the arms of someone else?"

Sam remembered how he'd felt when Jessie told him she wanted to call it quits. The anguish, the implacability of the vast physical distance between them—which made it both easier and harder. While being so far apart argued against continuing the relationship, it also distracted from the possibility that they might not be right for one another, or (even more delicate) that Jessie didn't trust Sam's love enough to continue seeing him only part-time until one of them decided to move clear across the Atlantic. Still, it had been brutal to have it end over the phone, without an actual meeting. He'd always felt robbed of seeing the impact of the situation on her face, in her body language. No, he'd just heard her halting words strung out over an unfathomable distance, beamed from a satellite, or relayed digitally through fiber optics under the bed of the ocean. A fatal conversation and then he'd had to put down the phone and go on living his life, lonely in the city, nurturing the hope that she might change her mind.

"When it happened to me," he now told Garland, "it wasn't easy, but I did it. I had to, knowing it was the other person's choice."

"You're still pretty young," Garland reasoned. "And healthy. Your life hasn't broken you yet."

There was brittle silence between them and then Sam spoke again.

"I just don't understand why, from your standpoint, from where you are . . . in your life now, wouldn't you want the people who have meant something to you, to find—I don't know—a safe haven with another person if they *could* find it?"

"As far as I'm concerned, Bobby had his opportunity to be greatly loved. He turned it down. Most people only get but one chance. I never got another one. And now I never will. So why should he?"

"But nobody can take away from you that you loved him," Sam offered tentatively.

Garland snorted "If you were me, Sam, wouldn't you be furious to have your life cut short? Are you actually naïve enough to think that people become more noble and magnanimous when they realize they're finally on the way out?"

"Some people do."

"Who? Christ? Gandhi? Perhaps. Most of us aren't so saintly." Garland sighed. "Believe it or not, one of the things that gets me through the day is telling myself that nobody else is immortal. That at some point, every one on the planet will face what I'm facing now. Fifty years from now, *you*, Sam, will most likely be dead."

Despite himself, Sam shuddered at the thought.

"No, Sam, facing death, most people just hold on even tighter. You wake in the morning, you see the light out the window, you look down at the street and see people walking to work or taking a stroll, the proof that the rest of the world is going to go on as usual. And even though you feel like crap, you're afraid to let go. Dying is like skydiving. You know the parachute is going to open and that you're going to glide. But the idea of being out there thousands of feet up and free-falling is completely terrifying. You don't want to do it. Somebody is going to have to push you out of the plane."

At that moment the Labrador lying at Garland's feet stiffened and stood at attention on the bed. A muffled yip escaped him. The schnauzer also went on alert. Then both dogs began baying. "Tell them to be quiet, please!" Garland huffed with hardly enough breath to speak aloud.

The force of Sam's yell instantly squelched the dogs. And then he asked Garland, "So you're saying basically that you still can't forgive Bobby?"

Garland didn't precisely answer. "I *do* want to see him again. That's why I sent him the drawing."

"The *Vanitas*—"

"So that he would know that I . . . well, that I was next."

The rest of their meeting was business as usual. Sam had made a list of questions regarding Garland's acquisition and sale of several seventeenth-century Dutch paintings, one of which turned out to be a forgery. Garland found himself explaining how a forger must bake a painting at a relatively low temperature in order to dry the pigment enough for it to seem as though it might be a few centuries old. He also illustrated how forgers deliberately created cracks in canvases as a way of imitating the natural aging of paintings—what historians called *craquelure*. All throughout the description, Sam kept thinking about the falsely attributed Géricault. He was determined to ask Garland what he knew about it and why he hadn't mentioned it but decided to wait a few more days until things had settled before bringing it up.

When they were through interviewing, Garland took a small can of chocolate-flavored nutrient off his tray table. He popped the metal cap, swallowed some, and then said, "Sam, I know you're unhappy about my caveat. But maybe one day you'll even thank me for it."

"I don't think so."

Garland refused to leave the subject alone. He felt it necessary to point out that Bobby LaCour was a deeply troubled man whose relationships had never been very successful, that he had already proved himself incapable of romantic love.

Sam could finally contain himself no longer. "Elliot," he agonized. "Why did you send me there? Why did you send me to London with that drawing?"

"I told you why—"

"I think there was another reason. A more compelling reason. And I think I deserve to know." For Sam was only just beginning to realize how difficult it would be to be barricaded from seeing Bobby.

Smiling, Garland admitted, "I guess I really need to have my head examined. I jeopardized everything by bringing the two of you together. I know what I did was mean."

"That's why I told you yesterday pulling the plug on me would be unfair."

"Well, I got very upset yesterday."

Sitting upright in his bed, Garland suddenly seemed to lose his balance and steadied himself with both hands on the mattress. Then he grasped the white plastic tray table as he would the steadying arm of a partner.

"Are you all right?" Sam asked nervously.

"Yeah, just got a little dizzy. The blood rushing to my stomach."

Sam waited for Garland to speak, and finally the older man threw up his hands. "I don't know. I guess I thought that having the drawing delivered by a young, healthy man like yourself whom Bobby would find attractive would make it all the more poignant."

"So then you *were* encouraging something to happen."

Garland reflected for a moment and then admitted that he did relish the idea of dangling somebody in front of Bobby, somebody associated with him. "It would be like I conjured you up, somehow. Someone rugged, someone brusque—someone so completely his type. The moment I set eyes on you, I knew that Bobby would want you."

"So that was why you hired me."

"It was the main reason, yes," Garland admitted.

Something occurred to Sam, but he mulled it over for a moment before deciding to come out with it. "I don't know if you remember this, but you once told me you wanted to work with me because you thought my name was . . . 'euphonious' was what you said."

"I remember."

"Well, the name Solomon also invokes a biblical character who was a truth seeker."

Garland stared at him, waiting.

"So the most important thing in your whole life, the most important relationship you've ever had, is not only being left out of your memoir, you're acting—on paper, at least—like it never happened."

"Maybe I'm ashamed of myself and how I behaved." Garland was candid.

"Mistakes are human, romantic ones, especially. People, readers, understand that."

Garland now folded his hands on his lap and stared at Sam with a peaceful glimmer in his eyes. "Just think of what you could do with this book if I gave you free rein."

Disgusted, Sam made a deliberate display of reaching for his pocket-sized tape recorder, pulling its plug out of the wall, gathering the cord and winding it. He picked up his notebook and his pen and slipped them into the small backpack he'd brought with him. Then he held up both hands in a gesture of surrender. He now realized that Garland's vanity had been flattered when the publisher had offered him handsome money to write a memoir, but that he was far too proud to be candid about himself on paper or otherwise. The book had been faked.

Now knowing he had nothing to lose, Sam scrutinized the withering, elegant man. "Bobby said that I should ask you about the *Vanitas*."

Garland nodded. "Yes, I imagined he would."

"He avoided saying much of anything about it to me. I suppose you could call that a kind of lingering loyalty."

"That's one way of looking at it."

The white cordless phone on the white tray table rang and Garland frowned at it, waved his hand as though he was not going to answer, and then finally decided to pick it up. "Hello," he said. "Oh, hello, Pablo." Garland suddenly seemed agitated. "I see. No, I can't, obviously. Because Sam is here, that's why. Just come by around five." He put down the phone without saying goodbye and then suddenly looked at Sam, despondent. "I want you to know there is a part of me that wants Bobby to be happy. Especially because his happiness, even with somebody else, really doesn't make a difference anymore. . . . So." He clapped his hands together with false enthusiasm. "What were we talking about?"

"The *Vanitas?*"

"Oh, yes, the *Vanitas.* The *Vanitas.* Where did it all begin. How did it all begin?" Now Garland's tone was sardonic. "I'll tell you about the *Vanitas,* Sam, so long as what I tell you is strictly off the record."

So Garland still was insisting on keeping up the charade. Fine. "What isn't off the record, Elliot?" Sam said wearily.

Garland laughed. "I'm glad you have a sense of irony. You'll need it for this story. Because, you see, Sam, that drawing was basically my undoing."

Long before Bobby had moved out of Garland's apartment, they had stopped sleeping together. One night in bed, Bobby had simply turned away from him and said, "I'm sorry, Elliot, I can't do this anymore. I'm faking it. And it's making me angry." Garland was devastated. And once Bobby rejected him, Garland suspected he was sleeping with anybody attractive who came into their lives. He became plagued with fantasies that Bobby was having secret trysts whenever he was late coming home. Then a wealthy man Bobby had met through his restoration work offered to back him in opening up a small gallery. With that guarantee behind him, Bobby finally moved out of Garland's Fifth Avenue apartment and migrated downtown to the East Village, a section of Manhattan that Garland never visited.

Up until that time, Garland felt he'd made many personal sacrifices to keep Bobby living with him: avoided friends Bobby didn't like; cut down on his grand scale of entertaining because Bobby abhorred big parties; was very selective about accepting weekend invitations with socially prominent people because Bobby felt such people discounted him as "Garland's boy." Garland had even sold a small house he owned in Amagansett, because Bobby hated spending weekends around rich people.

"Even after he moved, we never lost touch with each other,"

Garland said. He was now leaning against the television tray, as though needing to prop himself upright. "It was rare that even a day went by when we didn't speak at least once. I was surprised, actually, at how desperate he seemed to stay in touch. It was only then, only after he left me, that I realized how afraid he was of losing me. And yet, whenever we tried to get together, with the best intentions, something would always go wrong. One of us would say something to set the other one off and we'd end up arguing. We clearly couldn't get along, and yet we couldn't leave one another alone.

"It took me a year before I could even visit him at his new place. And when I finally did, I saw these photographs of a beautiful young man, a Godlike man, spread out all over the worktable in his studio. I asked Bobby who they were of and he said, a model, somebody he was drawing. But that was all he would say. So of course I was suspicious, anyone would be, of somebody that rapturous, that beautiful. He *was* one of those golden boys, Sam, he was one of those all-American types, from Idaho. He was fresh-faced, with regular but not too delicate features and an incredible smile. Beautiful teeth. Of course, he wasn't smiling in the pictures, but I saw that smile later on when I went to an art opening. The moment I saw him there, I knew who he was. Then again, his face was already branded in my memory."

The boy had certainly heard of Garland, and was impressed to be the focus of the renowned art dealer's attention, which Garland used as a seducer's tool. Their affair was brief and lasted but a few months.

Sam interjected, "But didn't you know about—"

"He told me eventually, but not immediately. Which, if you'll remember, is what many people were doing then. And still do. Because otherwise they assumed they'd be treated like lepers. It was an unspoken rule that precautions would be taken. And we took them. Truth is, by the time he told me he was infected, I was too hooked on him—sexually, that is—for it to really matter."

"But didn't Bobby know? Didn't he tell you—"

"That's just it. I never told Bobby. I kept it a secret."

"You were getting back at him."

"Perhaps I was," said Garland. "And I'll tell you this, though you may find it hard to believe me. The boy, that beautiful boy in the *Vanitas*, was very attracted to me."

"Why wouldn't I believe it?" Sam said.

Garland went on to explain how his so-called revenge backfired one night while he'd been having sex with the boy and there was a mishap.

"A mishap?" Sam asked.

Garland nodded and his attention seemed to drift for a moment so that there was something trancelike in his face and manner. "The condom broke," he said finally. "And I knew that was the moment. Not a month before I'd had the test and my doctor had given me a clean bill of health."

Sam thought to himself, Like some women know when they conceive a life, Garland knew the moment he conceived his death.

According to Garland, that night was also the night the boy admitted that there had never been anything between him and Bobby LaCour. Garland now shrugged. "Another great irony in my life. Like you, Sam, the boy was out of the loop. He never even knew that I knew Bobby. Until I brought it up. As he did with you, Bobby never told the man anything about his life with me.

"And so the affair ended. As affairs are wont to end. And six months later I got a phone call from this boy, who pleaded with me to buy the drawing. He said the money would provide medicine that wasn't covered by Medicaid. And so I bought it to help him. By that time Bobby and I were getting along a little better. And one night he dropped by the apartment and saw his drawing hanging on the wall.

"I didn't want to hide anything," Garland now explained sheepishly. "Not that I could have, anyway."

This had happened five years ago, only a few months before Bobby had fled to England.

Sam just sat there, taking it all, the almost macabre humor of Bobby's arriving at Garland's apartment and seeing the *Vanitas* hanging on the wall, and then learning the awful truth of how it got there. Garland, in his jealousy, had pursued an infected man merely because he imagined this man had once been a lover of Bobby's. It could almost be said that jealousy was killing Garland. Or that Garland had infected himself.

There was an audible commotion in the outer hallway, and the dogs once again erupted into barking. But Garland made no attempt to quiet them, just let them carry on until they finally simmered down. "Keep writing," he said when Sam finally got up to leave. "Let's finish this book."

It was at that moment Sam realized Garland didn't mean to finish it.

13 Sam had been surprised by Garland's candor, by his willingness to finally divulge intimate details about his relationship with Bobby, to clarify how he'd gotten infected—after having resisted doing so for so long. The confession was almost too easy, and Sam, though moved by it, couldn't help being a little suspicious.

Still, as Garland related the story of how he'd become infected, Sam had become overwhelmed by a feeling of hopelessness. He could well imagine the pain of being involved with someone like Bobby, and having the younger man decide that they would no longer make love. If that conversation, that rebuff, was the beginning of Garland's end-of-life dirge, then it was the most mournful movement of all.

Garland had asked Sam to avoid using the term *AIDS* in the memoir, simply because the acronym implied that the illness itself was too terrible to name. The request reminded him of what a doctor, whom he had once interviewed for a magazine article, had told him with great sadness—that the disease's taboo status conferred its own measure of pain, as cancer had for generations before any of the modern cures were developed.

After leaving Garland's apartment Sam headed east and wandered along Lexington Avenue. The weather was blistering and when he ventured down into a subway station, he felt as though he were entering a furnace. Standing on the dirty, crowded platform, he knew that when a train arrived and he got on, if he searched the faces of the passengers, he'd be able to spot a face afflicted by wasting, and that if he eavesdropped carefully, he'd glean the mutterings of people discussing the malady. Every time he recognized someone who seemed to be infected, he would feel a terrible despair. The mantle of a dreaded sorrow was cloaking the city like a thin layer of ash. And it had been gathering there long enough so that it was becoming as much a part of the landscape as the other urban eyesores: refuse in the gutters, nomadic homelessness, toxic air. Sam couldn't help wondering if he'd go on to live his whole life threatened by an affliction that was such a mouthful it probably deserved an acronym. And what a strange name to give it, as though the horrifying disease could *aid* anyone.

That night, Sam met Matthew at one of Manhattan's innumerable moderately priced pasta restaurants that was long on atmosphere and short on flavor. Before them rested a shallow plate filled with pale-green virgin olive oil and chopped garlic into which both of them were dipping their bread. Matthew had rolled up his shirtsleeves and loosened his tie. They made easy banter and Sam was relieved that Matthew seemed like his old self again.

"You're out of your funk," he remarked, "and although you probably don't want to admit it, I think you were depressed over breaking up with Jorge."

Matthew shrugged. "Well, I don't miss Jorge."

"Why did he break it off with you again?"

"I refused to go to Brazil with him."

"That's as good a reason as any, I suppose."

"His other reason, which I never mentioned, was that he was tired of hearing about you."

"You're joking."

"He felt I referred to you too much. And why did we break up? I told him you were still my closest friend, and that it was tough shit if he didn't like hearing about you."

"Speaking of me . . . I keep meaning to ask . . . Did you happen to meet Garland, the guy I'm working with, at a party?"

Matthew picked up his fork and waved it, looking vaguely embarrassed. "Yeah, I'm glad you brought that up."

"Oh, really, and when were you going to tell me?" Sam asked irritably.

"Hold your horses, there. I did try and tell you. That was one of the reasons why I called London. Then I filed it away. It was hardly a monumental conversation."

"Maybe not to you. But, according to him, you told him all about my father."

"I told him you come from Vermont. That your father gave up psychiatry to become a farmer. A decision which, I must say, I appreciate more and more as time goes on. Whatever conclusions Garland drew from that are his own."

"Well, I have a professional relationship with the guy, Matthew. I don't want him to know about my family, particularly about my father's financial status."

"Why, you afraid he's not going to pay you? You have a contract with him, don't you?"

"Yes, but—"

"I was minding my own business, and he sought *me* out. He came over to *me*. Batted his eyes like the queen that he is and started pumping me for information. The point here is that he knew exactly who I was. In fact, I think that's why he showed up at the party."

"What do you mean? Where was the party?"

"At the office . . ." Matthew, for once, looked unsure of himself. "Didn't I tell you that? That Garland is a client of the firm?"

"No! What an amazing coincidence."

"Not really." Matthew explained that major players in the art world tended to patronize the same handful of law firms. "What strikes me as odd, however, is that he attended an office party. Clients don't go to those. He was at the firm for an appointment—or so he said. And just kind of mingled in the festivities. Thinking about it, it all seems very orchestrated. Like he was expecting or hoping to run into me."

"But how would he know who you were?"

"He called dial-a-fag—how do I know? *You* know how incestuous we all are," said Matthew. "I'm sure somebody he knows knew either you or me. Every city shrinks as you get to know more people. The connections between everybody become exponential."

Wait a minute, Sam thought. What if Garland's law firm had some documentation about the falsely attributed Géricault? He described what he knew of the story to Matthew, who listened thoughtfully and said, "I've told you, I'm more involved in contracts. Whereas this has to do with possible fraud."

"Could you find out if there's anything on this at the law firm?"

"Sam, you're asking me to do something that's unethical."

"I know."

Matthew grimaced. "Is this why you were sounding so wigged out over the phone?"

Sam shook his head. "No."

"So what is it, the *new* romance?" Matthew sounded sarcastic.

Sam hesitated.

"Come on, just tell me already. I can handle it."

And so Sam elaborated about bringing the *Vanitas* to England, about getting involved with Bobby, and the conflict that involvement had invariably caused.

Midway through his story, Matthew started shaking his head. "I can't believe it. You're doing it again. You got yourself into the thing that you always said was anathema to you, the love triangle."

Matthew was specifically referring to the ending of their relationship, when Sam had spent a summer in Vermont, working as a staff writer for an on-line magazine. It was Matthew's first summer as an associate, during which he had been required to work most weekends. In short, he couldn't leave New York City and didn't want Sam to go, even pleaded with him not to, and when Sam insisted on doing so, Matthew retaliated by having an affair. An affair that he had announced and then refused to end. For Sam, it had been a terrible period of panic attacks, of lying awake at night and listening to moths hurl themselves against the screens of the cabin he had rented. A time when he painfully discovered how the habits of a relationship perpetuated themselves in the midst of estrangement. In a way, suddenly not having Matthew declaring his love every morning and evening—in twice-a-day phone calls—began to ache more than the idea of Matthew giving his body to somebody else. Infidelity, no matter how painful, remained somehow in the abstract, whereas it seemed that the human spirit came to form a chemical dependence on certain morning and evening emotional fixes. No matter what catastrophe was happening between them, the nerves of their relationship were still very much alive through the trauma.

Sam now observed, "This may be a triangle but it's hardly a *love* triangle."

Matthew was quick to illustrate. Garland desired Bobby. Bobby desired Sam, while feeling beholden to Garland in some way. And Sam was in the middle. What was it if not a love triangle?

Sam had never looked at it this way, and yet he felt it was unfair of Matthew to say he'd courted the situation. After all, both parties had initially lied to him.

"Come on, you had to sense it on some level," Matthew insisted. "Okay, first Garland sends you over to London with a gift for Bobby, and you arrive there not knowing but suspecting that Bobby is Garland's former lover. The gift turns out to be a drawing by Bobby that Garland knows *you* covet and which is an image of the man Garland thinks he got the disease from, a person he never would've gone after if he hadn't thought this man had been involved with Bobby. You get involved with Bobby, Garland finds out, he freaks out and then finds a legitimate way to prevent you from going back to London to see Bobby. What does that sound like to you, Sam?"

"Well, put like that—"

"Pardon me," Matthew interrupted with a bemused look on his face. "But you have gotten yourself involved in a textbook homo soap opera of the first order."

Sam hoped he had seen at least one flaw in Matthew's facile scenario. "But they haven't been involved for over five years."

"Look," Matthew said. "I have a friend who went through a relationship very similar to Bobby and Garland. And my friend told me that he remained completely caught up in the older man even though it had stopped being a sexual relationship."

"And did he say why that was?" Sam asked.

"It took him a while to realize it, but he said that the real glue, what was holding them together, was the father/son thing."

Sam looked at Matthew in amazement. It was a different twist all right, something neither Sam nor Jessie had quite put their finger on. Nevertheless, it rang true.

Over the next two days, Sam was unable to meet with Garland, who, according to Pablo, was suffering from some sort of internal bleeding and remained too weak to be interviewed. Early in the morning on the third day, he received a call from Jonathan Wade, the book's editor, the man who had once asked Sam to pick up Garland's lunch on the way to his interview with the art dealer.

"I have bad news," said Wade, with no preface at all.

He's firing me after all, Sam thought. I can't believe it. After all this, Garland is fucking firing me.

"Garland died last night."

"What?" Sam cried out. He'd heard the words, but his realization was slower-moving. "But I just saw him," was all he could think to say.

Wade laughed, as though Sam were being naïve. "This has been the danger all along," he said.

Sam managed to ask if there was going to be a funeral and the editor said he hadn't gotten that far. Surely, there would be something, a memorial service, which might not be immediate. He figured that Garland was being cremated.

"Now, listen"—Wade continued in a manner that, considering the situation, was, Sam felt, a bit too businesslike—"because of what's happened, the publisher and I would like to meet with you at your earliest possible convenience."

Sam remained silent.

"Are you there?"

"Yeah, I'm here."

"We need to discuss with you how far along you are and exactly how you intend to proceed. So how soon can you meet with us?"

"Look, I'm a little shell-shocked. I've been spending a lot of time with Elliot and I need to sort out my thoughts—about the manuscript, I mean."

"How's lunch the day after tomorrow, then?"

Sam felt too confounded to resist. "Sure. Fine. I guess . . . that sounds doable."

"Meet me at my office and then we'll go out from there." The editor said this in a cajoling tone, as though trying, for once, to be soothing.

Sam put down the phone, feeling as if someone completely well had just been decimated by a heart attack. Even though he had met Garland in decline, had always known that it was only a matter of time, he nevertheless expected some kind of warning—a final festering illness, some pathological manifestation. After having finally established some kind of real connection to the man, Sam was undone by the news of Garland's death.

Then he remembered that there had been a new medication. Could Garland have reacted badly to it? Nevertheless, the timing certainly was eerie. Sam thought about Garland's confession about Bobby, about his infection, about the *Vanitas*, and wondered if, perhaps, it might have been motivated by some inkling of the actual proximity of his own death.

Sam automatically dialed Garland's gallery and was informed that Pablo would be unavailable for the next few days.

"Do you know what they're doing about funeral services?"

"I don't think they've quite decided yet." The woman sounded completely unfazed and yet in possession of the facts, which was unnerving.

"Well, obviously since Elliot and I were working together, there are things that I have to be concerned about. . . ." Sam wanted to be delicate. "Things I'll have to get from his apartment at some point. Certain papers and letters that we were going over together."

"I'll have Pablo call you."

The phone rang five minutes later. "Sam, it's Pablo. I understand you need something."

"I just got the news. This is all very sudden. Even though—"

"Look, there's a lot on my plate right now. How can I help you?"

"Well . . . I just want to make sure that the papers we were working on don't get filed away anywhere. Because he wanted me—"

"You won't be getting anything more for the time being. And I mean, this *is* kind of premature, don't you think? Mr. Garland has just died."

"I'm doing this for *him*, there were things he wanted me—"

"Sam, he was very upset. I'm sure you know that."

"No, we straightened everything out."

"Well, I got a slightly different impression. Anyway, I can't talk right now. Hold off and do no more work for the time being."

Pablo hung up the phone without even saying goodbye.

Sam sat down on his bed. Paralyzed. In one fell swoop everything seemed to have hit rock bottom. He had no idea what he should do next, whom he should call, where he should go. Garland was dead and right now there seemed to be no promise of anything.

Whether it was perversion or momentary insanity, Sam found himself reaching for the phone and dialing Garland's number, as if he didn't quite believe the man was gone, or that everyone he'd spoken to was lying collaboratively to dislodge him from writing the memoir. The number kept ringing and ringing and he imagined the two dogs picking up their heads to hear the chorus of telephones tolling throughout the house. Suddenly, he heard a voice: "Hello, this is Elliot. I'm unable to take your call right now. Please leave me a message."

Two

14 Bobby LaCour flew in to New Orleans over the Gulf of Mexico, which lay below him like a great bruise that lightened along the continental shelf until it reached the landfall of the Mississippi Delta. During the plane's final approach, he pressed his forehead against the window and peered downward. Shadows of thunderheads were stippling the green templates of the marshland and the mangrove shrubs, and farther on, the spiky fronds of the *cheniers*. The plane rose, banked again, and then swooped into a low glide over Lake Pontchartrain and its endless causeway, until in the distance he could finally make out the evil, snaking Mississippi. It was the river that carried the detritus of chemical by-products, the heat of electrical plants, the river that had taken his father's life.

It was also the river that had once brought his ancestors down from the far north: wandering Acadians who originally fled Brittany and journeyed across the Atlantic to Nova Scotia and New Brunswick in search of a secular paradise. The Acadia they searched for then was called "Akade" by the Micmac Indians who intermarried with them and so, too, became his ancestors before the English overran Nova Scotia and burned the beautiful city of Grand Pré.

As the wheels of the plane touched down on the runway, Bobby realized he had to figure out how to get from the airport to his mother's apartment at the River Bend. Five years ago there'd been a bus that went directly to the Loyola campus; he wondered if it still ran. His mother had no idea that he was arriving today; she'd been expecting him several days from now, as he'd originally planned to stay with Garland for at least a week. Indeed, Bobby had crossed the Atlantic with every hope of a final rapprochement, of being a comfort to his dying friend. But Garland, true to his nature, had managed to say things that made Bobby want to flee from him.

"Don't be surprised," Garland had tried to warn him, when Bobby had first called from London and Garland insisted on paying his plane fare to America, "if you find me as rail-thin as those rich ladies who used to invite us for the weekends we never went on because you couldn't bear them—"

"Come on, I already feel badly enough. Don't make me feel worse."

"Bobby, I'll tell you this now before you see me. Unless you have a sense of humor, you won't be able to get through this."

Flying across the Atlantic, Bobby had tried to form a mental picture that mirrored ones he'd seen of other men who had perished prematurely, but the only image he could conjure was that of an exuberant Garland with a rosy complexion, a man passionate for so many things—most of all, beautiful objects—a man who could never be idle and had to stay busy. In New York Bobby had arrived at the Fifth Avenue apartment to find Garland lying in bed, listless, subdued, looking ghastly and emaciated in a pair of cotton pajamas flocked with a print of the Egyptian pyramids. How eerie it was to see the fast-forwarding of a life. Almost like previewing his own mortality.

Their embrace felt as though he were hugging a loosely gathered bundle of bamboo. The man's skin sagged from malnutrition, he smelled of antiseptic unguents, which could not mask the unmistakable odor of bodily decay. Somehow, despite the horror, Bobby ground out a smile.

Garland was the one who'd made it easier—at least at first. "Come sit by me. Sit close," he had said, taking Bobby's hand. "You're still so beautiful. I love the gray in your hair. Distinguishes you, gray at the temple. Who would've ever thought this boy would get gray at the temples."

"I started going gray when I left New York."

"It's been so long," Garland muttered. "Shame on you. Shame on both of us." Shifting uncomfortably in bed, Garland had slowly turned his head to scan his night table, covered with amber pill bottles of varying heights and widths, the miniature edifices of failing medical intervention. In the midst of the medications was a tall plastic liter of water. "That's distilled," he explained to Bobby. "Germ-free, it's all I drink. The New York City water would kill somebody in my condition. Could you pour me a glass?"

Bobby complied and Garland drank a few ounces in loud slurps. And then handed Bobby the empty glass.

"So now, what's with the phone? Why did you disconnect your phone? Just like that?"

"Because I hated being disturbed. Especially when I was working."

"What do your museum shops do when they need a word with you?"

Bobby explained that in England people were much more willing to resort to letter writing if necessary.

"Don't they use answering machines over there?"

"Of course they do. But I don't want to be burdened by having to return phone calls either."

"As misanthropic as ever," Garland remarked. "And just as contrary. And just as disagreeable."

"Believe me, I don't want to be. Especially because I haven't seen you."

They stared at one another, each imagining what the other was thinking.

"Come on, Elliot."

"What?"

"Why did you have to cause so much trouble? Sam's an innocent, for God's sake."

Without missing a beat, Garland said, "Because you love trouble, Bobby—I know that now. And I realize I didn't give you nearly enough of it. I probably should have."

"You're making up for lost time?"

"No, but you should realize that having a relationship with Sam Solomon would be a total pain in the ass for all the wrong reasons."

"Relationship? Let's not jump ahead of ourselves. Affair is more like it."

Garland went on. "Besides, he's not established enough to get work over *there*. You'd have to come *here*. And you've refused to do that." He smiled.

Bobby waited a moment and then remarked, "I was sure you were finally getting it."

"Getting what?"

The fact that he could have involvements and still maintain his loyalty to Garland. "That's why I thought you sent Sam to me; you'd finally accepted that I'm going to have sexual relationships with other people. If only you could have accepted this earlier, we might have stayed together."

"No, Bobby," Garland said. "I sent Sam with the *Vanitas*. Your own drawing. To tell you that my life finally caught up with me. You should have paid attention to that."

"I did."

"Sending the drawing with Sam was a measure of how I really *don't* care anymore. I don't care about my art acquisitions, I *don't* care about this apartment." Garland now looked away. "I *don't* really care about you. That's the grief and power of dying."

Bobby, instinctively, disbelieved this. "Okay," he said. "So you're too sick to care any longer. But why involve a third party who has had nothing to do with *us?* Why set him up and then disappoint him? Don't you think that's perverse?"

"It must be my delirium," Garland said cynically, tilting his head back and looking up with an air of drama. "I mean, here I am dying because I once tried to be vindictive and it backfired on me."

"You could've just written me a note and asked me to come and see you. Instead of orchestrating all this nonsense."

"I didn't think you *would* have come," Garland said. "I figured I had to send you a message with a spin."

"You just never believed in my devotion."

"You haven't been back once in five years."

"You could have come there just as easily."

Garland spread his arms wide, to indicate his present state of illness. "How?"

"Before this happened."

"You know I deplore England."

"I guess that was why you suggested that I live there."

"You wanted to live there. You wanted to get away from me."

"Hardly," said Bobby. "I think you've conveniently forgotten how insistent you once were that I remain thousands of miles away."

Silence followed his remark, a mutually miserable silence. "You still had your own reasons for staying there," Garland said finally. "Please don't blame me."

"I wonder if you even know what they were."

"You want to get laid without my breathing down your neck. Or calling to find out if you're home or not."

"That's the least of it, Elliot."

"What, that you could make money doing those kitschy paintings?"

"At least it was a living."

"So is restoration."

"Restoration always made me feel unworthy of myself. I'm glad I burned my bridges."

Garland fanned a withering hand before his face. "Bobby, you were a big boy. You made your choice. Nobody was holding a gun to your head."

The sniping had gone too far and Bobby was desperate to stop it. "Please, let's just call a truce, okay?" he begged.

"Fine. We'll cease." And there was edgy silence between them for several minutes. Finally, Garland said, "So, have you called Sam yet?"

"I just got here. How could I?"

"From the airport, I don't know." Garland waited a moment and then asked, "Are you going to?"

"At some point," Bobby said vaguely as he noticed a tear in the hanging Flemish tapestry and got up off the bed to more closely examine it, to gently trace his finger along the damage. "How did *this* happen?" Somehow he felt personally responsible for all the objects of art in Garland's apartment.

"The bitch jumped up and did it," Garland said. "Got a little overexcited."

"Which one?" Bobby said, regarding both dogs.

"The bitch with a cock, for Christ's sake. The black one."

Bobby laughed and then turned back to Garland. "You know, Elliot," he said. "I haven't had a successful relationship in five years. Don't you think that tells you something about me?"

Garland shrugged.

"Look, Sam is sexy, I'll admit that. But seeing him is not at the top of my list."

Garland seemed relieved to hear this. When next he spoke, his tone was more moderate. "I must say, Sam turned out to be a lot more shrewd than I gave him credit for."

"You told him I couldn't come back, that I had to remain over there."

Garland looked worried. "Did you contradict that?"

"No, though I wish I had. This all would've been so much easier if you'd sent me a set of instructions on what I could and could not say."

"Well, as you know, I hate writing letters. But, now, please don't give Sam an interview about our relationship. I don't want it in the book."

To think Bobby had worried that Garland had intended to tell all when in reality Garland had intended to tell nothing. Now, Bobby couldn't help asking Garland if his intention to keep their relationship out of the memoir was the embarrassment of being publicly known as a homosexual.

"Me?" Garland had laughed derisively. "You must be joking. Hardly. I'm just mortified about the way I behaved toward the end, about what I did to try and keep you."

"In other words you're afraid of being perceived as a desperate man."

"If you will . . . and as far as the Géricault is concerned—"

"Again, you didn't help matters any by mentioning it to Sam."

"One oblique reference?"

"You said I did something naughty. That certainly piqued his interest." Garland looked stricken. "Don't worry, Elliot, I didn't go into graphic detail, I didn't say that *you* were involved in all of it."

"He's only supposed to write what I want him to write."

"And what happens when you can't control that?"

Garland smiled. "Who says I can't control it . . . even *after* I'm dead?"

Something restrained Bobby from asking Garland what exactly he meant. He felt it was best—at least for now—to squelch the conversation. No matter what, he couldn't allow their first face-to-face encounter after five years to end on a bitter note. After a while, he said, "You have such beautiful eyes, Elliot. That was the thing that struck me when I first met you."

"But tell me honestly, I look like shit, don't I?"

"You're not well, what do you expect?"

"You didn't answer my question. You'd probably pass me on the street without recognizing me."

"No, I would see those eyes and know you instantly."

Moments passed and when Garland spoke again, it was with tenderness. "Well, I feel awful, Bobby. I'm glad you haven't been here to watch it all."

"I wish you hadn't waited so long to tell me."

Garland shrugged and made no response and seemed momentarily uncomfortable. Finally, he said, "You should probably call your mother and tell her you arrived here safely."

Bobby left the room and walked down the hallway to where he knew there was a phone. He reached his mother's answering machine and left word that he was in New York. After being away from America so long, it certainly felt odd to be bypassing New Orleans. But afraid that Garland might be on his last legs, Bobby had rushed directly to New York. This, clearly, was not quite the case. Although noticeably ill, the man was full of love and fury, spilling over with all his usual contradictions.

When Bobby came back into Garland's bedroom, he said, "How would you feel if I went to see my mother sooner than I'd planned and then came back and spent more time with you afterwards?"

Garland looked distressed. "When would you go?"

"I don't know. A day or two."

"Is that really necessary? I mean, you just arrived."

"She knows I'm in the country now. I feel terrible that I haven't seen her in so long." After all, Bobby had had to give up seeing his mother when he gave up living in America. "And she's never complained about it, not once."

Garland took this in for a moment and then said, "Unlike me."

Bobby laughed. "Well, you are two very different people."

"What can I say."

"You've paid for the ticket."

Garland dismissed such an idea. "I don't own your time because I bought your ticket."

At that point they were interrupted by a knock on the door. A woman in a white nurse's uniform came in bearing a jade-colored teapot and a single black teacup. "Just put it right over here," Garland said, pointing to his small white tray table that was resting on the bed adjacent to him. "I'll get around to drinking it sometime before the end of the century. . . . So boring," he said to Bobby when the nurse left. "Being ill. The regime of pills every few hours, and if that isn't enough, all the alternative *shit*. Remember how I used to sneer at all the New Age people and their remedies? Well, guess what this is?" he said, pointing to the pot of tea.

"Tell me."

Garland lifted the lid and took a whiff. "Christ . . . I grow these Japanese mushrooms in my fancy kitchen and brew tea like a fucking witch."

Bobby chuckled and asked if the tea was helping.

Garland shook his head and said morosely, "No, Bobby, nothing helps when you're on the way out. The tea, the pills, everything is a sham."

"You still seem to have a lot of life left in you," Bobby had assured him.

Bobby ended up taking a taxi from the New Orleans airport to the River Bend. The taxi had no air-conditioning and they drove with the windows down. New Orleans, as usual, was sizzling hot, its greenery wilting, the swamp water in the low-lying areas seething and scummy. Living in England, he'd grown unaccustomed to heat. Living in England, he'd forgotten how much light there was in America, long stretches of violent sun that jabbed shadows out of palm fronds, burned lakes against the stucco buildings, relentlessly reflected the chrome of automobiles. Bobby drank the heat into his bones. How depressed he had been those first few years in Britain, where there would be weeks, sometimes whole months, of gray. Lack of light made him sink into depression, quickly brought him to understand the appeal of a cocktail in the darkening afternoons. And those were the years that he hated Garland for creating his state of exile.

"Wing . . . wake up, Wing . . . honey, wake up." He opened his eyes to the sound of his childhood nickname.

His mother, Christine, was sitting beside him on the bed where he'd fallen asleep, wrapping her arms around him until he could smell her Chantilly. "I'm sorry I couldn't come get you at the airport," she murmured. "I tried to get off work, but they wouldn't let me. Why didn't you let me know earlier? Lucky my neighbor had a set of keys."

"I decided on the spur of the moment to go to the airport. I had an open ticket. Sorry it was so sudden."

"I'm sure I'll get over it."

She released him from her embrace and held his head in her delicate, overworked hands and peered at him. "And look at you, gray at the temples. You probably wouldn't remember, but your daddy's hair had the same pattern."

"I do. I remember."

"I can't believe you're finally back! God, I've been missing you. I've been missing you so much, I'm still missing you right now."

"Missed you, too," he said, slightly uncomfortable with her scrutiny.

Due to their limited finances, he'd seen his mother once during the five years he'd been away. He'd saved up his money for six months and sent her the plane fare. His sister, Aurora, who lived ninety miles away in Baton Rouge and earned a pretty good salary at a beauty salon, had paid her own way and accompanied their mother on the overseas excursion.

His mother was olive-skinned and dark-haired, as he was; although even at sixty-three, her hair had yet to begin turning gray and fell in a long, bouncy wave around a face that had few lines. Her nose and mouth were small and sharp, her figure had always been thin, sometimes verging on emaciation: whenever she got what she called "a case of nerves," her appetite would die.

"So, how was the flight?" she asked in a slightly higher pitch. The awkwardness of the reunion was making her jittery.

"Went by pretty quickly," he said. "Nothing in comparison to flying from England."

"Good weather for flying, though."

"It was okay. We came in over the Gulf, which was unusual. I guess there must've been heavy air traffic from the north. I keep forgetting how beautiful the Gulf of Mexico is."

With that, Christine went and made a batch of stiff rum and tonics and they began sipping their way through the rest of the afternoon.

"Wing, does it look any different to you?" his mother asked when she was pleasantly fogged. "The city, I mean?"

He shrugged. "How much can a city change in five years. Particularly New Orleans . . . You know, I miss being called 'Wing.'"

"You used to hate the name . . . when you were young."

He hated the name because of the way he acquired it: like Garland, Bobby had always loved exotic birds. When his father created the nickname, Bobby secretly feared his father thought that this appreciation of birds was some kind of effeminate predilection. He topped off his glass with a thread of dark rum.

"Well, come back to New Orleans and Wing will be every other word out of my mouth," his mother said.

This was uncharacteristic in a woman who normally did her pining in silence, a woman who was so self-contained that it gave her a kind of dignity. She had accepted his far-flung absence without complaint, which was not easy because she knew it had been caused by his rift from a man as old as his father. Now, as though to avoid broaching the paradox of his absence any further, Christine brought him up to date on all the personal disasters that had occurred in their neighborhood, as if to say, "Now this is real heartbreak." She told him about the people down the street who had lost three of their family to freak accidents. She told him about the suspiciously high incidence of stomach cancer and leukemia in their old neighborhood, the Ninth Ward, fatal illnesses that made people fret about the airborne poisons released by all the industries that had sprung up along the Mississippi, and particularly across the river in Chalmette, which cloaked itself in sulfurous-looking clouds. She told him how one of his classmates, a dentist with a wife and three children, recently shot himself to death in the bathroom of his office, in despair because of drug habit he was unable to break.

Finally, she brought out a photo album containing the pictures of his sister Aurora's wedding, a small affair that had taken place the year before in Baton Rouge and which Bobby had been unable to attend. Aurora had always been overweight, but managed to slim down for the event, and in every photograph taken of her, she faced the camera defiantly with dark, hooded eyes full of a rancor that Bobby imagined was aimed at him.

"So, is she going to come and see me?" Bobby asked. Aurora still lived in Baton Rouge, which was an hour and a half away by car.

Christine looked away and fidgeted with her bony hands. "She probably will at some point but she hasn't said anything definite."

His sister was still angry at him for missing the wedding. "Mother, what was I to do? I had no money. We couldn't even afford to pay for the wedding ourselves. How do you think that made me feel?"

"I know. I've told her all that."

"I mean, how do you think I got here this time?"

"Did Mr. Garland pay your ticket?" Christine asked, looking at him expectantly.

"That's the only way I could've made it. It's expensive to fly all over the continent like I'm doing."

"Well, it was nice that he paid your ticket down here to see your mother."

"It was the right thing to do. How could I come back to America and not see you?"

His mother paused. She gathered up her slim legs, which were visibly afflicted with varicose veins, cocked her head to the side, looked at him studiously, and then asked quietly how it had been seeing Garland after all this time. Clearly, it was not the easiest thing for her to do.

It was difficult, he tried to explain, for different reasons than he'd imagined. He thought it would be really hard to see Garland so ill, and it was, but only for a moment. He'd quickly gotten used to his friend's altered appearance, only to realize that even though Garland looked completely different, he was exactly the same man with the same agenda. "I came to see him with the greatest affection. And then right before my eyes both of us went back to the same old behavior. It was like I'd never gone away. Five years ended up being like nothing."

"But you *were* shocked to see him so ill?" she asked, not quite registering what he'd said.

"There was no way I could prepare myself for how he looked."

"All I can say is thank God *you're* okay."

"I am. I get tested every six months like clockwork. I'm fine."

"That's one blessing at least that I can count on," she murmured.

His mother was still unable to assimilate the true complexity of Bobby's relationship with Garland. Bobby knew that she thought of Garland as his father's surrogate and that was as far as she could go.

When Christine got up and left the room to start dinner, Bobby noticed his favorite photograph of his father propped against the wooden collar of a tall lamp. Taken when his father was only twenty-five, still slim, before his great dissatisfaction with his lot in life set in. He was dressed in a tuxedo, holding a clarinet—he used to play in a local jazz band—and grinning seductively, showing two slightly crooked front teeth, as he raised the instrument to his lips.

After his father's body had washed up, Bobby and his mother were summoned down to the levee. It was just before Christmas. As they drove, they passed several wooden pyres being built on the top of the levee by their fellow Cajuns for the holiday bonfire. They had driven until they spotted the revolving lights of the emergency vehicles, lights that reminded him of lights on buoys, weak against the night of a storm, lights of warning. When the pool of policemen and paramedics parted for them, there was his father, lying on a stretcher completely stilled, so inconceivably dead, a six-foot-four tower of a man with a raspy, booming voice, who, only a few days before, had called Bobby "a pansy" for choosing to attend art school. Crushed between a launch boat and a massive freighter, his familiar clothing shredded into tatters, his flesh was so white it looked blue in the sultry light of the afternoon. As Bobby stood there, staring at his father's remains, he could feel a great pit widening and twisting inside, and all he could think was that the drowning was a mistake. It would take him many more months to admit how much he had loved his father, despite his abuses. Each word of discouragement, each comment on his physical frailty, each gibe at his artwork curiously bonded them while it damaged his future capacity to reach out to others for love.

It was night by the time Bobby and his mother had driven home and all the pyres along the levee were burning high and bright, burning like their ancestral Acadian city, Grand Pré.

His reverie was disturbed by the telephone. "Wing, would you get that?" his mother called from the kitchen.

Bobby answered, still half-dreaming of his father, but was quickly wrenched back to the present by the foreign-sounding voice on the other end of the phone.

"Is that Bobby?"

"Yeah."

"It's Pablo Fortes."

There was a pause during which he could hear the man's tremulous breathing. And then he knew. "Is everything okay?" he asked, still hoping he was wrong.

"Bobby . . . I'm sorry to have to call you like this. But Elliot has died."

He froze and could not move or say anything.

"The night nurse said he died in his sleep. She said there was no sound, so we're supposing, we're hoping it was a peaceful death. It's really a mercy if you think about it."

The flight to New Orleans had been an early one and Bobby had left the apartment at seven, passing Garland's closed bedroom. Slipping out into the corridor, he had actually heard the two dogs rustling around, probably trying to rouse their keeper.

"He didn't want me to come down here now," Bobby muttered. "He wanted me to wait. But then he said there would be some warning, that I could always be called."

"Please don't blame yourself," Pablo said. "At least you got a chance to spend time with him. Maybe that's what he was waiting for, waiting for you to come back."

"Well, I'll come back to New York tomorrow," Bobby said. "What about the funeral?"

"It'll be in two days' time," Pablo told him.

His mother had overheard the plaintive tones of the conversation and now stood at the threshold of the kitchen with a vacant look on her face. She had hung some wind chimes near an air-conditioning duct and in the dreadful silence the chimes orchestrated the news, crystallizing his disbelief. An utterly foreign yet somehow familiar feeling—for it was the second time they'd been together for such bad news. But now she was unscathed by it. And she probably realized that the aftermath for him would be a lot worse now than it had been when his father had been killed.

"Did you hear?" he asked and she nodded. "I've got to go back tomorrow, I'm sorry." She looked crestfallen. "But just as soon as I can deal with everything, I'll come back for a while. Don't worry. I promise to come back."

"Just as long as you do."

"Don't be silly."

He opened his arms toward her and she came forward and they both held one another. He was too stunned to do much else. Finally, his mother ended the embrace and looked at Bobby in bewilderment. "Wing," she said. "Why did he wait so long to contact you?"

"Who knows? Fear. Shame. Most likely ambivalence."

"None of us liked that you didn't have a telephone, but I always wrote you when I needed to tell you something. Garland could have done the same. But instead he waited. Almost like he was trying to get you to come back, but was afraid of seeing you."

"Or was afraid for me to watch him die," said Bobby.

15   Sam ended up meeting Garland's editorial director, as well as his editor, at a trendy restaurant on the West Side of Manhattan. A typical, minimally decorated place-to-be-seen in the magazine and publishing world, Trentanove was staffed by earnest-looking actor types with angular faces and fashionable haircuts. He had shown up wearing a battered-looking tweed jacket, an Oxford shirt, and a paisley tie and felt immediately out of sync with the dark Armani and Prada suits of the other patrons. He'd ended up being squeezed into a bar booth by Jonathan Wade, a strapping, impeccably dressed man in his early forties, and the editorial director of the publishing house, Anna Pontic, a patrician, fiftyish woman with seashell ears studded in diamond earrings.

"Isn't this cozy," said Anna of their seating arrangement. "They gave us a very good table," she informed Sam. "It'll be so much easier to talk over here."

It was so cramped, Sam didn't see how this was possible.

"I hope you've been okay," Jonathan Wade said, and then elaborated, "with everything that's happened."

"I've actually been feeling out of the loop," Sam told them. "Nobody from Garland's gallery has told me how I can continue getting work done."

Jonathan and Anna exchanged a glance. "Well, you know, they've been topsy-turvy with him dying," Anna said. "It's just what happens," she said, her voice warbling like a flute. At this peculiar juncture the waiter arrived for the drink order and to ask if they wanted menus. Without skipping a beat, Anna Pontic requested a Campari and soda and her usual Cobb salad, no bacon, no blue cheese, and then glanced inquiringly at Jonathan, who said, "I'd also like a Campari and soda. And for my main, spaghetti with basil and tomato."

"Now would you like a menu or can I suggest something for you?" Anna said with motherly sweetness, turning to Sam. "Order something nice and enjoy it. I insist."

Sam supposed it was more chic to order without a menu. "Don't they have a famous steak burger here?"

Anna nodded to the waiter. "Medium-rare good for you?" she asked him.

"Sure."

A brief silence ensued and Sam took the opportunity to ask the editors what they thought of the book so far.

"It's good," Anna said as the waiter arrived with the drinks. The moment her Campari was put down, she grabbed the glass and took a quick sip. "Oh, lovely," she said. "Wonderful to have this in the summertime. Now . . . the book. Well, the book seems to be fine, but I must say, we're a bit concerned—"

"You see," broke in Jonathan Wade, "we were hoping that his life might be more juicy than it's turning out to be."

Sam now tried to explain that there wasn't much that could be construed as "juicy" in Garland's life except for the art auctions he was involved in and anecdotes of celebrities who came to his gallery and of his buying expeditions all over the world. Garland had been a much more amusing character *in ex tempore* than he was on paper.

"Well, you can understand how that might be worrisome to us," Jonathan said. His voice, somewhat nasal and nerdy, seemed at odds with his impressive stature.

Anna Pontic continued, "There's nothing at all in the manuscript about his personal life, his 'great loves,' as he described it in the book proposal."

Sam went cold. "His great loves? He actually promised to write about his great loves?"

Jonathan looked bewildered. "Didn't you read the proposal?"

Sam explained that he'd asked Garland the very first day they began working together. "He wouldn't show it to me. Said it was sketchy, basically a formality because you'd already decided to buy the book."

Both editors stared at Sam. "That is completely untrue!" exclaimed Jonathan. "He was very precise. He said it was going to be a *tell-all* memoir."

"Hang on, hang on a second," Anna told her colleague. "Let's just keep moving along here." Her eyes now riveted on Sam. "Let me ask you this," she said delicately. "How well do you know Pablo Fortes, Garland's assistant?"

"Not very."

"Apparently, the night of his death, Garland's assistant called up to ask if any of the delivered manuscript pages contained material about his relationship with a man named Bobby LaCour."

Sam swallowed and said he didn't find that surprising.

"Well, we told him there wasn't," Jonathan said. "But why *is* there no mention of Bobby LaCour in the pages you've handed in so far?"

"Because I didn't know he existed until recently."

"So then tell us who this Bobby LaCour is," Anna pressed confidentially.

Sam hesitated.

"It's all right," Jonathan said with a languid wave of his hand. "We already know about your affair with him."

"Pablo was kind enough to tell us," said Anna.

Sam could feel the pinpricks of a flush in his face.

Anna put her hand firmly on Sam's arm. "Just start from the beginning. We're all ears."

Sam felt he had no choice but to explain everything he knew, that Bobby was the love of Garland's life, how the *Vanitas* came to be executed as a commission and the tragic way it ended up belonging to Garland. How Garland had sent the drawing under his aegis to Bobby LaCour, and that neither Garland nor LaCour had been willing to divulge the story behind the falsely attributed Géricault. Anna said, "But if we could back up just a wee bit. Once you knew they were lovers, you *did* ask Garland to tell the story of his relationship with Bobby and he refused."

Sam nodded.

"But then I don't understand something," Jonathan said. "If, from the beginning, he had hidden from you the fact that he was involved with this man, then why did he send you to see him in England?"

"It's probably not going to make sense to you, but I was meant to be some kind of lure."

"Lure?" Jonathan said.

"Garland thought we'd be attracted to one another."

Anna looked perplexed. "But why would *Garland* of all people want you to be attracted to Bobby?" She glanced at Jonathan. "Am I missing something here? Is this a gay thing?"

Jonathan flashed a conspiratorial smile at Sam, who thought to himself: I never would have known this guy was "queer." Then, again, it makes sense somehow.

Sam reminded them that Garland and Bobby had been out of contact. "Garland was using me to get Bobby's attention."

"Which he couldn't have done otherwise?" Jonathan asked.

"Clearly, he didn't seem to think so."

"Does that make any sense to you?" Anna asked.

"No," said Sam, "but I do think that's what was going on."

She continued, "But now do *you* believe that Garland might have been implicated in the sale of that falsely attributed Géricault?"

"Yes."

"Did you ever interview him about it?" Jonathan asked.

"Never got the chance."

"I see," Anna said just as the food arrived. She waited until the waiter finished flourishing around the table, then leaned toward Sam and said breathlessly, "I've got to be honest with you. We're in a lot of trouble here."

Sam just blinked at her. He feared what was coming.

They had a manuscript clearly in need of a transfusion of vital material, which didn't seem likely to be forthcoming. They could easily reject it and leave it at that. The problem was that when the book deal had been set up, Garland's agent had been very cagey and insisted that his largest payment would be due him once the publisher was notified that the interviewing process was complete and it was understood that "the writer" would be able to finish the manuscript—whether or not Garland survived the process of writing.

Sam said nothing for the moment, wanting to see where the conversation would float them.

Anna continued, "We received a letter from his agent two days before his death, informing us that before you left for England, you'd completed the interviewing process."

This was a flagrant misrepresentation. "As you can see, that's not true at all," said Sam. "In fact, we were far from being finished."

Anna said, "But this is puzzling. Would he propose a book he had no intention of writing?"

"He got cold feet," Sam said.

"Yes, of course he did," said Jonathan. "But why try to tell us that the interviewing was done, and force the payment of an entire advance for something that he knew wasn't going to be publishable?"

"I mean, it's not as if he needed the money," Anna pointed out.

No one was eating. Sam glanced down at his burger, which looked as if it would bite him back if he bit into it. Anna speared her Cobb salad and then, on second thought, let her fork drop. It seemed as if the whole restaurant had hushed to hear the outcome of the conversation.

Sam said, "I think that by telling you we were done, by trying to force you to pay him the rest of the money, he was really asking you to put the kiss of death on the project. He knew if he did this, you'd pull out."

Yes, Garland had originally agreed to do the book. He'd momentarily let vanity override his sense of shame and desperation-in-love. But Sam believed that Garland had also wanted to make Bobby worry that their very troubled relationship as well as their illegal business venture would be written about and therefore publicized, something Garland would, in fact, never dream of doing.

"But why manipulate someone like this?" Anna asked. "It was clearly to his own detriment."

The answer was simple: Garland couldn't help himself. Manipulation was his nature.

Anna gazed at Sam fondly for a moment and then clapped her hands in applause. "Sam, we are soooo grateful to you," she said. "You've really helped us."

"Yes, it's beginning to make sense now," Jonathan said. "Now, if you wouldn't mind, we'd like to have you sign a statement to the effect of what you just told us."

Sam hesitated. "That's all well and good for you, but your canceling the book is going to break me. It's going to put me in major financial trouble."

Anna thought about this for a long moment. "Well, you *have* been very helpful. You're saving us quite a bit of money in the end. How about if we pay you seven thousand of the fifteen thousand dollars that we owe you for the second installment and call it a day?"

The settlement would at least pay some outstanding bills and buy him a few more months. Sam had no choice but to agree, knowing that Garland died with the wish that his book die with him.

He left the restaurant feeling a curious amalgam of many different emotions. Despite all the impediments that Garland had deliberately thrown in his path, despite the dearth of good material, Sam still felt sad about abandoning the writing project. He never liked to give up on anything. He also found it curious that a man, facing his impending death, would deliberately leave his world in a state of chaos, rather than try and put things in order. There were so many loose ends in Garland's life, unresolved relationships, unresolved personal history. Garland had never even said goodbye to Bobby.

Bobby LaCour, the great love of Garland's life, probably didn't even know the man was dead. Bobby was unreachable by phone, and who would bother to try and write to him? Sam imagined the artist painting in his London loft—his curio sketches, the works-in-progress kept from public view—completely oblivious to what had happened. Bobby had to be told—and Sam decided that he would be the one to tell him.

Back at his apartment he called around to all the airlines until he could find the cheapest spur-of-the-moment fare to London. He booked himself on an evening flight. And it was only after he'd paid for his plane ticket with the only credit card that hadn't been charged to its limit, and was in a taxi en route to Kennedy, that Sam dared to ask himself why, outside of breaking the news about Garland, was he flying back to England on a whim. Why was he so determined to see Bobby LaCour?

The answer was simple: In just a short time, Bobby had left

his mark, had stirred up something wild and profound in him. Not since Jessie had this happened. Matthew had caused him great pain, but the pain derived from Sam's wounded ego, from having been momentarily eclipsed in Matthew's affections by somebody he knew would turn out to be insignificant. Whereas Bobby, who could claim but a fledgling presence in Sam's life, had awakened a terrible yearning that made absolutely no sense. For Bobby at times had seemed remote and ambivalent, and Sam often wondered just how attracted to him Bobby actually was. Could this constant speculation, this insecurity, have something to do with why Sam was so drawn to him?

But then, high above the Atlantic, Sam was dozing when he thought he saw "the angel" at his window, this time with a look of such sorrow in his vitreous eyes, mouthing words: "Forgive me, but don't ever forget me," he seemed to be saying. Can I forget? Sam groaned to himself. The longing he once felt for the angel flooded back and became a part of the longing he felt for Bobby LaCour. Sam shut his eyes and pressed back against his seat, wondering what it was about flying that brought on such memories. When he opened them again, the angel's face faintly lingered at the oval of the window glass.

Completely unnerved, he broke down and dug into his carry bag for his emergency bottle of Valium. He took two five-milligram pills, and told himself he'd somehow have to weather the next half hour until the drug kicked in. It was an interminable interval, but finally a haze began arriving like a downy blanket; it was daylight forcing the angel to reluctantly relinquish his place at the window, leaving a milky mist and the first traces of the Outer Hebrides. Soon the islands appeared in high relief, reminding Sam of the way Bobby had varnished the sky in the blackened painting to revive the shapes of the clouds.

16   Even after having lived so many years abroad, Bobby felt no thrill in seeing the magisterial graph of the Manhattan skyline, milky blue against the late summer fumes. London did not have a skyline, it was a great sprawling metropolis that couldn't be properly viewed from any one angle. Something about the New York skyline seemed two-dimensional to him, like a cardboard cutout, or a stage set.

Back at Garland's building, he didn't recognize the corpulent, middle-aged doorman on duty and was momentarily afraid that he wouldn't be able to get back into the apartment. Why didn't I consider this possibility before I left? he chastised himself. The answer, of course, was that he never allowed himself to consider that Garland might die while he was in New Orleans. With trepidation, Bobby approached the doorman and introduced himself. To his great relief, the man retreated into a little office and returned with a white letter-sized envelope with Bobby's name written in Garland's scrawl.

The strange, left-slanting handwriting on the notes sent early in their relationship, the handwriting of the long, rambling letters full of recrimination and pain after Bobby had left. Now, it spelled out his name and was, he supposed, a kind of relic. The man was dead. And although the building lobby was quite warm, Bobby shivered. Inside the envelope was a note: "Bobby, here are the keys. I hope your mother is well."

Garland's last ironic words—it was still inconceivable to Bobby that the man was dead and gone from the apartment. The only real certainty in his life had been Garland's great love for him—even when Bobby was living so far away—and his great love for Garland. So why, in that last conversation, couldn't they have expressed more affection, why had they torn one another down? Bobby wished he could have at least told Garland he had been by far the most important person in his life.

The doorman broke his reverie.

"Mr. Garland was a kind man. He took good care of us all." The man was Irish.

"How long have you worked here?" Bobby asked.

"Going on eight years."

"I figured you had to be here less than ten. Because I used to live here. Before that."

"No foolin'," said the doorman.

Bobby delicately asked if there was anyone upstairs and the doorman said, "Just the dogs." That Garland's assistant from the gallery had been coming over to walk them.

"What are their names again?" Bobby asked. "I forget."

"The schnauzer, the mealymouth one, is Gus. I wouldn't try and pet him if I was you."

Bobby found himself delaying by the elevator, not pushing the button while the doorman kept eyeing him. Suddenly afraid to go upstairs.

"It's working, isn't it?" the doorman finally asked.

"Yeah, I just haven't pressed it. I—" Bobby broke off, wondering why he had to explain himself to this man.

"Take your time, collect yourself. Don't worry about it," the doorman said.

Standing outside Garland's apartment, staring at the *faux bois* that he had painted himself, Bobby smelled the vetiver scent. He thought back to his very first night in New York all those years ago, standing there with all his nylon duffel bags and the Samsonite carrier he'd borrowed from a Cajun uncle and smelling a scent he found exotic. But after living several months in New York, the fragrance grew cloying and he convinced Garland to stop wearing it, complaining that its scent was too effeminate. Of course, when they split three years later, Garland defiantly began wearing his signature cologne again.

Fingering the key, he began unlocking the door and could hear the scrambling toenails of the dogs responding to the sound.

Both animals began barking at him, the schnauzer actually baring its teeth. His leaning over to pet Diane, the black Lab, infuriated Gus, who barked even more frantically and then began inching toward Bobby, still snarling. Without even thinking about what he was doing, Bobby lunged at the dog and yelled, "Get out of here!" Startled, the dog froze, pressed itself against the floor and then skittered away, darting into Garland's room.

Bobby looked around. Now that the dogs had stopped yipping, the apartment seemed especially quiet. Conspicuously clean and, as always, overstuffed with all the objects that Garland had obsessively collected over the years. Bobby strolled through the living area and into the aviary room that faced Central Park.

The first time Bobby had ever seen the extent of the menagerie he was delighted. Garland loved having the birds, thrived and doted on them, and though Bobby shared his appreciation, he found the whole cacophonous arrangement unsettling, not to mention the fact that so many animals in such close proximity might be unsanitary. Nevertheless, he had happily lent a hand with all the feeding and cleaning. By the time he moved to England, this room had been a mess, like a zoo or a henhouse, its walls slathered with dried feathers and punctuated with beak marks, the parquet floor spattered with bird droppings, echoing with screeches and the wing beating of short desperate flights and endless importuning avian calls. The caged domain had been opened to the wall that faced Fifth Avenue, with the birds given license to chew the moldings on the windows.

Now the birds had been replaced. Paintings of cockatoos, bronze statues of flamingos, various taxidermed horn jays and owls attached to mahogany stands inhabited a room where the moldings had been redone, the walls papered. And even though this transformation had happened only recently as a result of Garland's illness, for Bobby it was the most powerful reminder that ten years had passed.

Before leaving for New Orleans, he'd spent two nights in the apartment, consumed by his visits with Garland. At one point Garland had said, "You haven't even looked around to see what's here and what I've given away."

"I love everything so much, I'm almost afraid to see what's gone."

Garland had smiled and said, "I only gave away what you didn't really care for, particularly some of the contemporary art. I sold the Bleckners and the Motherwells, for example."

"I liked them," Bobby protested.

"But you didn't *really* appreciate them," Garland pointed out dryly. "You never mooned over those paintings the way you did some of the others. But now please go take a look. For *almost* everything you see will be yours."

Only for a moment had Bobby been puzzled by the qualification *almost* and then quickly left off speculating. Because he'd inflicted pain on Garland, he felt guilty about being given anything from the art collection. That day he'd toured the rooms one by one, taking mental inventory of the multitude of paintings and objects, to see what was still there and what was gone. There *were* some new acquisitions: a pair of Victorian parcel-gilt candelabra, a Regency rosewood side cabinet, many more Spode china pieces, of which Garland had once been a fanatic collector.

Of course, it was the nineteenth-century paintings he'd most cared about—Garland was right about that. In the dining room he had found the detail painting of an Egyptian relief at Karnak, depicting the great gilded plume head of Amenhotep III, as well as a watercolor and gouache of Rachel's tomb by Hercules Brabazon, a still life with tulips, morning glories, and a landed tiger swallowtail butterfly. He was happy to see Garland's unsigned oil, probably French, from the 1850s—depicting a monkey with a red cap that they had found at an out-of-the-way antiques shop on Cape Ann in Massachusetts.

However, a drawing by Pietro Benvenuti, an eighteenth-century Italian, of Perseus holding the head of Medusa seemed to be missing and Bobby went from room to room, unsuccessfully hunting for it. A good many other things were gone—Garland *had* given away plenty of things that Bobby loved—but how could he complain if the art did not belong to him? Besides, his absolute favorites *had* remained a part of Garland's collection: a nineteenth-century Italian pastel of a woman in a red silk dress, wearing a broad black hat, a nineteenth-century Russian oil of a boat breasting the ice floes on the Neva River, a nineteenth-century American painting of a horse and a cart making morning deliveries.

Over in England, whenever Bobby would recall his first apartment in Manhattan, he would imagine how these paintings would appear at various hours of the day: early in the morning, when bars of light draped themselves decorously on the canvases and made burning diamonds on the Abyssinian rugs, the lighted air in rooms aswirl with dusty motes; or in the amber tones of evening, the paintings haloed by the dozens of gilded sconces, and beaded, silk-shaded lamps, and Gothic candle trios. He would remember the wind stinging the high windows, the slanted curtains of summer rain pelting Central Park, the eddies of snow spiriting up the air shafts between the oddly protruding wings of the building. He would remember Garland's world, shimmering and gorgeous, and the vision of its beauty made it possible for Bobby to occupy the dingy flats that he lived in during his first two years abroad.

He now stepped into the master bedroom where he'd slept for three years and where he had last sat with Garland only a few days before. The English wing chairs were still there, as was the Empire chest of drawers, and the wonderful Beardsley drawing of two upright conjugal lovers catching fire. There was also a nineteenth-century watercolor by William Ladd Taylor of a young man walking down a hallway, holding a candle, a painting Garland bought because the man reminded him so much of Bobby—who was never able to see any resemblance. The bed was made up with a paisley-damask-covered comforter, and stacks of fashion and art magazines were piled up at the bedside, book-ended by a biography of Lincoln and the autobiography of Pamela Harriman, who had been a good friend of Garland's. The pristine state of the room and the layout of the reading materials almost made it seem as if Garland were on a trip somewhere and was due to return at any moment. At this point the phone rang. Bobby was afraid to answer, afraid of who might be calling, and so just stared at the receiver and waited to see what would happen. Then Garland's voice was there in the room, telling someone he couldn't talk right now, they were busy getting ready for the opera. His explanation cut short by a beep and then a strange sighing silence of an anonymous listener.

A rapping on the door of the apartment threw the dogs into a renewed frenzy. Bobby was surprised to hear a key turning in a lock and the door opening. Then he remembered the doorman saying somebody came to walk the dogs. A short, swarthy man with gel-stylized jet hair entered the apartment with a smile and greeted Bobby. Upon seeing the visitor, the dogs calmed down immediately and allowed themselves to be patted. Bobby said nothing, just stared and waited until finally the man said, "The doorman told me you'd returned. I'm Pablo," and vigorously shook Bobby's hand.

"You know, it's amazing that we haven't met before now," Bobby exclaimed.

Pablo continued to pat the dogs, who were wriggling with pleasure. "Elliot wanted to be alone with you. He didn't want anyone around. Which I can understand." Pablo now stood and stared at Bobby appraisingly. "So, are you going to continue staying here?"

"I'd been planning on it. Garland asked me to. If that presents a problem—"

"No, no, of course it doesn't. I just wanted to make sure. The reason why I'm asking is that we'd like to have a gathering here after the funeral."

"By all means."

Pablo turned away as though to survey the opulent contents of the living room. "It was what Mr. Garland wanted. A party here after his cremation," he explained. "He left explicit instructions for his funeral, explicit instructions for everything. God knows, he liked to be in control."

This made Bobby wonder exactly how Garland had died. "So, did he just pass away in his sleep?" He watched carefully for an involuntary reaction in Pablo.

Still facing away, Pablo murmured, "His heart just stopped beating. They figured it happened around four o'clock in the morning."

Bobby grew momentarily dizzy.

Pablo faced him again and tried to be comforting. "He talked about you a lot, especially the last few months. Now, would you like to speak—at the service, I mean?"

Bobby shrugged, not knowing what he'd say, afraid he'd lose composure. There must be a lot of other people who wanted to say things.

"You knew him better than almost anybody."

Except that the person he knew, nobody else knew. "So, what I might say would probably have no meaning."

Pablo looked skeptical. "I'm sure it would."

"I'm assuming his family will be there."

"Yes. And that reminds me. When you have the time and when you feel like it . . ." Pablo moved to an end table next to Garland's bed where there was a empty white notepad and a pen. He uncapped the pen and wrote something on the top sheet of the pad, which he then tore off. "This is the telephone number of his lawyer. She needs to speak with you."

"Why, what's going on?" Bobby asked suspiciously. Any mention of lawyers instantly revived the sense of anxiety that had once permeated his life when he was accused of falsely authenticating the Géricault.

"Don't worry. It has nothing to do with the lawsuit or anything like that."

Pablo looked around the apartment, as if searching for something. When he spoke again, his voice sounded somewhat raspy. "Now, there's quite a bit of food in the fridge. You'll see a bunch of pitchers full of tea. I wouldn't drink them if I were you. They're some kind of alternative medicine he was taking toward the end. I told the housekeeper to get rid of them, but she hasn't for some reason. Do you have any idea what room you want to stay in?"

Bobby glanced at Garland's perfectly made bed. "What about in here?"

Pablo looked surprised. "It doesn't bother you?"

"Why would it bother me? It's where we used to sleep together."

"But it's also where he died."

"I know. Maybe that's why I want to sleep in here."

"Whatever." Pablo primly dusted his hands together, as though he found Bobby's desire ghoulish. "However, I don't think the sheets have been changed."

"Look," Bobby said. "I just want you to know something. It's not because of me that he died. I did not infect him. I—"

"Bobby, nobody's blamed *you*!" Pablo exclaimed. "I was the man's assistant. Don't you think I might have known what was what . . . in that regard?"

"I guess I don't know how much or how little Elliot told you," Bobby said as he turned away to grab one of his bags.

"Look, there's one more thing. Do you have any objections to Sam being invited to the funeral?"

"Me? Not at all. Why should I?"

"Well, I mean, I know Garland was over . . . well, you know what I'm saying. And I don't know what kind of terms you and Sam are on now."

Pablo's prying was annoying to Bobby, who decided that the best way to deal with the situation was gloss over it. "I'll give Sam a call and tell him about the funeral."

"Would you?" Pablo said. "That would make things a bit easier for me."

He's officious, isn't he? thought Bobby when Garland's assistant finally left, not the sort of man that Garland would normally tolerate. When Bobby first heard of Pablo, he had wondered if Garland and his assistant had been involved. Clearly, this was not the case. The man was a bit too obsequious and deferential. Had Pablo been Garland's lover, Bobby felt he would have been able to detect some resentment toward his being there in the apartment.

A while later, he picked up the phone and dialed Sam, whose answering machine announced that he was out of town for a few weeks. And although it was only considerate to leave word about the funeral, Bobby found himself hesitating before deciding not to record a message.

17 Sam took the Tube from Heathrow to King's Cross, and from there took a black cab directly to Bobby's flat in Dalston. Hoping to at least get inside the building, he was disappointed to find the outside door locked. He rang the bell and waited until a boy in a blue school uniform and a knapsack came bounding down the stairs in response. Scowling at Sam, he demanded insolently, "Who do *you* want?"

"Bobby LaCour."

The kid sneered. "The *poofter* artist you mean."

Sam was taken aback. "How the hell would you know what he is?"

"Fuck off!" said the boy as he pushed past.

Sam's heart was thrumming. He climbed the two flights of stairs. He'd never done this: flown thousands of miles to knock uninvited on somebody's door, and in the expectation of the moment, Sam felt completely alive, like someone who took incredible risks. Naturally, he had visions of an erotic reunion, of Bobby answering the door tousled from sleep, half-naked, and pulling him into bed.

He glanced at his watch—eighty-thirty in the morning—and rapped loudly on the door. The moments passed, finally accumulating as a fatal silence. He knocked again and this time placed his head against the cold wood and listened. His dread of finding a vacant space was becoming a painful reality. Amazing to think that the person who inhabited this warehouse flat in an exotic, unfamiliar part of London had become more and more crucial to Sam's sense of well-being. He knocked, frantically wondering where Bobby could be—possibly with somebody else? His imagination was kindled and burst into several bright and agonizing scenarios, the most prominent of which was Bobby being involved in a long-term relationship in which Sam had just been a momentary wrinkle. He had to admit to himself, he knew very little about this man, whose reticence still made him seem like a stranger. Perhaps Bobby had gone away somewhere—maybe even to Corsica. Then, again, would he have been able to afford a vacation? He seemed to have so little money.

As Sam turned to leave, the door opposite Bobby's opened and there stood a fair-haired woman with pudgy cheeks who looked to be in her mid-thirties.

"Can I help you?" she said. He told her he was trying to find Bobby. "Have we met before?" she asked, peering at him inquisitively over her reading glasses.

"I don't believe we have."

"Oh, sorry. Actually, I think I'm confusing you with somebody else. Bobby's got quite a few friends." Sam cringed at this news.

"But now, I'm afraid you've come at a rather bad time," she said. "He's out of London."

"Do you know for how long?"

"Didn't say. Just asked me to keep an eye on his flat." She looked away when she said this and Sam had a sense that she was deliberately keeping something from him.

"Do you have any idea of where he might be? It's urgent that I speak to him. I have some news."

"I'm sorry, I don't. It's up to you, but you could leave a message with me and I could tell him the moment I hear from him."

"That's all right," Sam said. "I'll write a note and slip it under his door."

At this point he would've expected the neighbor to shut her door and leave him to write his note, but she remained there observing his activity, as though she didn't quite trust that Sam was going to do as he said. A gust of fury overtook him. He disliked being distrusted, and he disliked even more that Bobby wasn't here. Sam's hand shook as he wrote Bobby that he was in London and it was urgent that they speak.

Jessie and Eva were just going out the door as his minicab pulled up in front of the house. He rolled down the window. "Hey, there, you beauties."

Jessie was so stunned to see him that she had to sit down on one of the stone steps in front of her door. Eva ran down the stairs and stood next to Sam as he lifted his bag out of the minicab. "Hello there, my little pea," he said in a bass voice, kissing her.

When Jessie finally stood, Sam saw that she was smartly dressed in a black leather miniskirt and cream-colored sweater. A silk scarf was tied around her shoulders. She was grinning maniacally. "First you disappear without warning, and now you appear without warning." She finally waltzed down the front steps, her thick hair bouncing against her shoulders, the ends of it corkscrewing down her back. Sam could see that the skin on her face stretched tautly over her cheekbones. She'd clearly dropped weight.

She put her arms around Sam, gave him a squeezing hug. "Why didn't you tell me you were coming?"

"I'm sorry, I came over on impulse. I was already on the plane when I realized I forgot to call you."

Jessie was puzzled. "But it's not like you to jump on anything— particularly an airplane. What's going on?"

Sam explained that Garland had died a few days ago.

Jessie looked alarmed. "Oh, I see. Oh, my goodness . . . that's terrible. But I mean, where does that leave you in terms of finishing the book?"

Sam explained, "It's not going to happen. It's been canceled." Before she could say anything, he reassuringly touched her arm. "Everything's okay. I'll tell you all about it after I've gotten some sleep. And just so you know, I *have* been compensated."

"Well, that's a relief. I know you were worried about money. . . . Will you have enough to last you for a while?"

"A few months."

Eva now interrupted them. "Mummy, can I stay home with Sam?"

Jessie looked her daughter in the eye. "They're expecting you at school. And Sam is tired and wants to sleep." She turned to Sam. "God, you're lucky we were still *here*." Jessie fished into her handbag and pulled out a set of keys. "What would you have done if we weren't?"

Sam sheepishly explained that he'd actually been expecting Bobby to be at home.

"Oh, I see." Jessie seemed a bit miffed. "Maybe that's why you didn't call."

Of course, she was right. "Come on, don't make me feel bad."

"Well, for future reference, there's a set at the neighbors' two houses down." Jessie pointed down the road.

"Mummy," Eva piped up again. "I don't want to *go*. I want to stay with *Sam*."

"That's f-i-n-e," Sam spelled, trying to get Jessie to look at him.

She shook her head. "No, but you can look after her later when school is over. She's supposed to go to Claire's in the afternoon. We share a child-minder. But she can come directly home from school if you'd like and if you'll be here."

"I guess I will," he said.

She now looked at him directly. "No guessing," she responded crisply. "*Her* plans become *your* plans, or not. So you'll be here?"

"Yes," he said at once.

"How would that be, darling?" Jessie said, kindly, bending over Eva. "I'll have Claire drop you here."

"No, I want to stay *now*."

"I guess we're going to have a little bit of trauma this morning." Jessie smiled and shook her head. With some cajoling, Eva allowed herself to be placed in the car and Jessie returned to where Sam was standing on the sidewalk. "Strange because she only digs her heels in about going to school when I've had to go out a lot. And I haven't budged from the house in a bloody week!"

"Maybe she needs a dad?" This was outrageous for Sam to say, but he chanced it anyway. To his relief, the remark was taken lightly.

Jessie flicked her fingers at his arm. "Shut up, you." She reached down and picked up a slim leather briefcase that she had laid on the cement. "Now I've got to run because I have a meeting in the City."

Sam said, "So what's the latest?"

"Haven't seen *him* since I talked to you last. But I'm fine, I think." Then she dodged further elaboration by saying, "God, I'm glad I went shopping. There's plenty of food in the fridge. So help yourself to whatever." She kissed him. "Goodbye, love. Get some sleep." Bending down to the car window, she addressed Eva, "Darling, say goodbye to Sam."

"Goodbye, *love!*" Eva effused.

Leaving his bag in the front foyer, Sam walked downstairs to the kitchen. There was a huge basket of fresh fruit on the counter, three covered enamel pots on the stove. The white teapot was standing next to the stove, piping hot and filled. One of his favorite white cups and a saucer were next to it, as if waiting for him. One would almost think that Jessie somehow knew he was arriving. Sam poured himself a cup and held the warm white porcelain and tried to quell the burbling anxiety left over from the nerve-racking flight, and then the disappointment of finding that Bobby was not home. He cut himself a few slices of seven-grain bread and slathered them with blackberry jam. He found a tea tray, piled everything on it and took his breakfast upstairs and lay down on his bed.

He quickly fell asleep and into a dream in which he and Jessie had become assistants of Bobby LaCour and were helping him do preparatory studies for a portrait of an unwell child, searching for a model who would best embody infantile suffering. Scores of children, all tragically afflicted in one way or another, lined up outside Bobby's studio: faces with open lesions, or crusted with purple carcinomas, children with flippers for arms or severely twisted spines or lifeless dangling limbs. Some perched precariously on wheelchairs, which were pathetic accommodations to their skewed body positions. Still others had been wasted by malnutrition to skeletal proportions. A bell would ring, signaling the end of a brief interview and the candidates would, in turn, walk or hobble out, or leave in self-propelled wheelchairs. Bobby would not speak in their presence, but observed them coldly.

Sam was wrenched awake by the telephone.

"Is that Sam? It's Claire. Can I bring Eva by?"

"Sure." He realized that hours must have gone by. It was now midafternoon.

He dialed New York to see if there were any messages. There were none. Putting down the phone, he pushed aside the lace curtain and saw that rain was pelting down.

Five minutes later the doorbell rang. Claire had arrived with Eva and another child, who Sam assumed was Claire's son. Eva marched into the house wordless.

"Aren't you going to say goodbye to your friends?" Sam said.

"No," Eva announced.

Claire pushed the frizzled hair out of her eyes and then explained, "They're cross with one another."

"Cross or not, can't you at least say goodbye?" Sam asked the child.

Eva turned around and murmured something unintelligible.

"I'm sorry, but I can't hear you," Sam said. "Otherwise, it's rude."

Eva now looked up at him and her huge eyes were full of rancor. "How do you know?" she challenged.

"I know some things."

Eva finally turned to Claire and Alex and said "Goodbye" with great exaggeration.

Once they were alone together, Sam asked what she'd like to do.

"Well, first we could make Ribena," she said gleefully, her whole mood changing in an instant.

Eva went to the refrigerator and took out the bottle of blackberry syrup and a bottle of seltzer and mixed her own beverage. She offered some to Sam, who winced at the cloying taste. While Eva sat there swilling her drink and making loud kissing sounds, Sam fixed himself a cup of instant coffee.

He went and opened the glass door that led to the garden. A sharp wind invaded the kitchen, making the outdoors seem less inviting. Looking out, Sam was amazed at how tidy and varied the shrubs and flowers were. He suddenly wished he'd come directly from the airport to Jessie's, for then there would have been no disappointment and they could have had their ritual of tea-upon-arrival. When he was sexually obsessed, he began treating his friends shabbily, he knew. He turned to Eva. "When does your mom ever have time to garden?"

Eva frowned and said she didn't know. "Can we watch videos?" she asked instead.

"Is that what you do in the afternoons?" Sam felt utterly at a loss. Would he make a good father? Was parenting instinctive? Hormonal?

"Yes, we have lots." Eva led Sam upstairs to the stack of videos in the living room. From among them, she selected the same Barney video that he'd taken over to Claire's the night he got into the fight with Rudy.

"This?" he said, hoping not.

She nodded emphatically. "Will you watch with me?" she asked.

So Sam sat down on the sofa next to Eva and began watching the horrid purple dinosaur traveling effortlessly around the globe. Not ten minutes after the video started, her head flopped to the side; she'd conked out, her mouth wide open. Soon, her small body was inadvertently listing against him. He thought of Bobby, wondering where he might be—hopefully not with another man. When he got the note, would he call?

18 Bobby sat alone in Garland's living room, looking at a large nineteenth-century painting of the poet Sappho orating her verse to a gathering of disciples—an unusual work that he'd once urged Garland to buy. Over the last few days, both at the funeral and at the apartment, he'd been obliged to entertain people he hadn't seen in years. Certain friends of Garland's deliberately kept their distance, scorching him with supercilious stares, as if to blame him for the untimely death. Others were more gracious and made a point to approach Bobby and remind him of things he'd said or done, much of which he didn't even remember. Everyone wanted to reminisce about Garland.

Including Bobby, who was thinking about the first time he met Garland, in New Orleans. He counted back: England for five years, and before that, in New York for five years, three of which he'd spent with Garland. Ten years ago—he'd only been twenty-five.

One morning Bobby had been walking home from his job as a night bellboy at the Maison de Ville, in the French Quarter, and passed the small storefront of a modest gallery that advertised "Original Art of the Bayou." He'd heard about the place. On a whim he went inside to a studio loft whose enormous mullioned windows overlooked a Gothic cemetery where Marie Laveau, the voodoo queen of New Orleans, happened to be buried. There he found a man named Mr. Deshoteles.

Deshoteles was a wiry Cajun who later admitted that he'd taken one look at Bobby's eyes and knew that he was also of Cajun ancestry. That day Deshoteles was exceptionally harried because he'd just lost sales help in the store at the front of the gallery, where he displayed his Cajun artists. "Can I help you?" he had asked.

"I was just wondering if you ever needed help?"

Mr. Deshoteles face brightened. "Have you had any retail experience?"

"No, I mean in restoration?" Bobby had quickly glanced toward the back of the space and spied various surfaces cluttered with knives and razor blades, as well as spatulas and a vacuum pump—all of which confirmed something he'd heard: that the gallery owner was also a conservator of paintings.

Deshoteles was taken aback. It wouldn't exactly be clear to anyone that this, indeed, was a place where paintings were restored. "Well, I haven't really thought about *that*," he said. "Why, do *you* restore?"

"I know something about it," Bobby said. "May I look?"

"This is not the best time," Deshoteles said, though he seemed to be softening.

Bobby somehow knew that Deshoteles wouldn't mind and without another word ventured deeper into the work space. He soon could see the scattered leaves of gelatin, several glass jars filled with mineral spirits, the inpainting brushes made of sable, which were lying in a shallow basin filled with water and which he knew had to remain there in order to prevent the delicate paintbrush hair from bending. There was a box filled with huge cubes of beeswax and dammar resin, paraffin and gum elemi. Thick pieces of rag paper, shreds of linen. At the far side of the studio, which faced a huge, square floor-to-ceiling window in the old New Orleans style, was a jar that held sun-thickened linseed oil and Venetian turpentine. This, he would eventually learn, was glaze curing.

When he returned from his little tour, Deshoteles said, "Now, did someone actually tell you that I was looking?"

Bobby said that he passed by the store every day on his way to the bus stop. Then he lied and said that when he'd been a student at the renowned local art high school, he had seen Mr. Deshoteles's name and heard him spoken of.

"Oh, so you're a student at NOCCA?" Deshoteles said, referring to New Orleans's creative arts school.

"Was." Bobby then explained about having to turn down the scholarship to the School of Visual Arts in Atlanta on account of his father's death. And how since then he'd been working odd jobs and doing his own painting.

"So you've had no experience in restoration?"

Bobby's comeback: "Even if I did, wouldn't you want to train whomever you took on?"

The man was intrigued and decided to hire Bobby on a trial basis.

Because Mr. Deshoteles couldn't pay him much at first, Bobby maintained his night porter job at the Maison de Ville. He'd go home and sleep for four hours and then return to Mr. Deshoteles to do apprentice restoration, and then catch another few hours of sleep before showing up at the hotel where Tennessee Williams had holed up and written several of his plays. At first his mother thought he was crazy for burdening himself with such a hectic schedule, but she never tried to discourage him; she felt so guilty that he'd given up his SVA scholarship.

Deshoteles taught Bobby how to clean, how to remove yellowed varnish and later overpaint with various tinctures of spirits and cleaners. He taught him how to prepare impastos and cloth to fill holes, to make a ground mix of linseed oil with chalk and white pigments—either white lead or zinc or titanium—and to spread the gesso that resulted from the mix over the surface of the damaged areas of canvas to level the surface for delicate inpainting. From Deshoteles Bobby learned to use retouch varnish to eradicate dull areas and to bring out sunken-in colors as well as to protect against dirt. For the actual inpainting itself, following the line or the technical mood of the artists, Bobby needed no instruction. He was an excellent copyist. And knew how to mix glazes from his own experience.

After only two weeks it was apparent to both master and apprentice that Bobby possessed a rare gift. *"Vraiment étonnant!"* Deshoteles said. He had affectionately adopted speaking French with Bobby. Restoration, a highly technical practice, whose mastery added up to centuries of cumulative trial and error, came almost by instinct to Bobby, who knew without knowing how to relieve shadows and showed an expert hand in taking on the unstable areas of a painting and lifting flakes of paint. This was a laborious task that included softening the support with turpentine and pressing a hot iron through waxed paper. Bobby seemed to have an innate sense for how to treat an exposed ground of a canvas that was having trouble accepting new paint, adding the appropriate amounts of pumice and chalk and gypsum. And most of all, he had the knack of reading the true line of an artist's original intention through a heavy-handed restoration. *"Jamais je n'ai vu quelqu'un si doué,"* Deshoteles said on a day Christine happened to call and, forgetting herself, asked for "Wing." *"Parfait pour toi,"* Deshoteles said of the nickname. "You flew before you ever walked."

And then, one day two years later, Elliot Garland walked into the gallery, holding a very damaged painting, which he thought might be a Géricault. Deshoteles was not there to greet his old friend from New York, who already had been informed of Bobby's talent. Garland had decided to see if he might be able to use the promising young man and save himself some money on what he knew would probably be a very costly restoration.

And Bobby would never forget the impact of Garland's shrewd, slightly insolent gaze as he introduced himself and explained why he had come.

"May I see the painting?" Bobby had asked.

"Of course."

Garland took his package over to one of the worktables.

At first glance the female subject seemed to Bobby to be part of a portrait series of the incurably insane that Géricault did at a Paris asylum. The impassive, middle-aged face had a wanton curl in the lips, a lusty flickering in her eyes. However, the white ruffle at her throat and her black bodice suggested an otherwise prim and morally zealous character. The canvas's support had clearly suffered from water damage. Flocs of paint on the woman's face were gone, and her simple puritanical housedress had sustained some kind of gash—probably from being transported. The frame itself was riddled with wormholes. Bobby rubbed his index finger against the grimy surface. "The paint is too thick here," he remarked to Garland. "Not the technique of his late period—has to be either the restoration or another artist. In Géricault's late period he painted more translucently, less fashionably. He removed himself from the influence of Vernet."

Garland seemed surprised that Bobby knew so much about the artist but wouldn't let on at first. "So this could conceivably be in the restoration?"

Bobby grabbed a tiny knife as sharp as a razor blade. He thought there was a rather slim chance the painting was by Géricault, but it gave him a thrill nevertheless to scrape at one edge of the darkened, yellowed surface. He scored through several layers and said, "This paint seems original, though I couldn't tell you for sure. And as it shows substantial ruin, I'd wager there has been only light restoration, if any at all. Lots of water damage. Misuse. Probably was in someone's basement or attic for fifty years." He squinted at the canvas. "This might even be by Champmartin."

Garland edged next to Bobby to look at the painting's problematic surface. "How would you know? Champmartin is almost completely unknown!"

"I went to Paris on a student tour. I saw a few of his works there. It'll be easy to find out when I clean it. I'll see if there's a signature, if it's been painted over. As you probably know, Géricault hardly ever signed his name."

Garland shifted his gaze to Bobby, who couldn't help noticing the light in it wasn't all that different from the refraction in the reproachful eyes of the painting's subject. And yet Garland had this odd cherubic-looking face. "So you don't think there's any chance that this could be one of the monomaniacs?"

Bobby pondered this for a moment. "Well, there's the Delusional Militarist. The Kleptomaniac. Let me see, the Gambler, the Jealously Obsessed, and the Kidnapper. Five monomaniacs in all." He put down the painting for a moment.

Garland exclaimed, "My God, you really know this painter, don't you?"

Bobby said he figured that was why Garland had come, that Deshoteles had told him how much he loved Géricault.

"No . . . I mean, he said you were very good at restoring, but he never mentioned that you loved Géricault. Which I have to say I find strange, because *I* love Géricault. That's why I came here to New Orleans. Expressly to buy this painting. I'm in decorative arts. I don't normally deal in paintings."

"So you got this in New Orleans?"

Garland nodded.

"Really, in New Orleans," Bobby said. "That's wild. And they claimed it was by Géricault?"

"They weren't sure. I recognized the style and the subject matter."

"Well, I don't recognize the technique."

"What have you seen by Géricault?" Garland challenged.

Bobby had seen the *Raft of the Medusa* in Paris. He'd subsequently pored over all the artist's studies for the masterwork, the dramatizations of various scenes of the shipwreck from which Géricault made his final choice to depict the moment when the survivors on the raft finally sight the *Argus,* the vessel that rescued them after thirteen grueling days on the high seas. But he was also intrigued by Géricault's life, his reckless sportsmanship, his scandalous and tragic affair with his uncle's wife, the fact that he had ended up so alone.

"But you hardly could have examined all five of the monomaniac series," Garland said. "As far as I know, in this country there is only—"

"I've seen the one in Massachusetts." From Boston, where he'd once gone to look at colleges, Bobby had driven to Springfield specifically to see *The Kleptomaniac.*

"Well, then you know there are five more in that series of paintings that supposedly have disappeared."

"Much as it would pad your bank account, I don't think this is one of the missing monomaniacs," Bobby said, "although it does seem to be a portrait of a madwoman."

Garland considered this for a moment and then asked Bobby how long it would take to restore the painting.

"Two months. Three, max. We'll give you a good price. Including shipping."

"I have other business interests here in New Orleans. I could pick it up myself."

The very night of this first meeting, Bobby found himself telling his mother about the man from New York. It was hardly something he'd do normally, speak to her about clients who came into the studio, but there was something unsettling about the art dealer, something about his rapacious gaze that made Bobby want to talk about him. He wondered if Garland could actually be planning to sell the painting as a Géricault. Bobby was sure any expert would easily be able to tell it was not by the renowned French artist. However, he assumed that Garland probably knew private parties who might be willing to pay a fair price for a painting whose attribution was never clear—and there were certainly many paintings attributed to Géricault, whose unsigned canvases created confusion among scholars.

"Well, I hope you're not going to help him deceive anyone," his mother said, serving up the usual New Orleans Monday-night dinner of red beans and rice.

"Of course not. And, anyway, I worked on it all afternoon. The first thing I did was remove the paint over the signature."

"So it *was* signed?"

"By the man I figured, a guy by the name of Charles-Émile Champmartin. He was a disciple of Géricault's."

His mother sat down and served herself a minuscule amount. She was going through one of her rail-thin phases; though she was then only in her mid-fifties, her sunken cheeks gave the appearance of an older woman. She fretted about money, about her children; she tended to internalize everything and lost her appetite. In a curious reversal of the parent/child role, Bobby always had to cajole her into eating. In the family he'd been the more reticent of the two children—and the peacemaker. His sister was the wild one, used to cursing out their father on a whim.

"A friend of mine in the Quarter who knows Mr. Deshoteles told me that he's telling people that you're the best apprentice he's ever had."

Bobby laughed as he helped himself to more food. "That's not saying much. He's had no others as far as I know. Too much of a tightwad."

"Well, he said that you took to it—"

"Mother, I'd rather not make my living restoring other people's art."

"Wing, honey, this is something that has come your way and you should be thankful for it."

"I know, and I *am* grateful."

After they finished dinner, in order to prepare himself for the restoration of Garland's painting, Bobby went and got out his various books on Géricault, volumes he'd borrowed from the library before his father's death and, in the aftermath of grieving, had never bothered to return. Ironically, his last significant conversation with his father was about the nineteenth-century French painter. One day early in December, a week before his father died, Bobby was sitting in the family room that he and his father had built on to the ranch-style house with their own hands. He was looking at the preparatory studies for the *Raft of the Medusa*, many of them of severed human limbs, when his father lumbered in wearing a sleeveless undershirt and spoke to him, half in Cajun, half in English. "What is dat, *cher, qu'est-ce-c'est?*" And Bobby explained how Géricault procured the limbs from a nearby hospital, brought them to his studio, and arranged them in provocative attitudes, drawing them, painting them as they decomposed, living day in, day out with an ever-increasing stench of decay. Among all the studies, Bobby showed his father what he considered to be the best of them: an arm severed at the shoulder and made, at the crook of the elbow, to drape itself over a foot dismembered at the ankle. It was a touching pose, like bedfellows sleeping head to foot, and you could almost imagine that they were two conjugal souls rather than two disembodied appendages. *"Dommage,"* his father said, towering over Bobby. "Dat he want to draw dat kind of thing. *Dommage.*"

His father was deliberately sounding obtuse, a redneck guise he liked to take on when he hung out with his river pilot cronies, and Bobby wished he could tell them how his father would listen to opera and cry, that his father was the first person who ever took him to the New Orleans Museum of Art.

He looked up at his father, at his hairless, sagging chest, at a man who used to be so fit when he worked as a hydraulic engineer before becoming a river pilot. "So why you looking at dese pictures?" his father asked.

Bobby tried to explain that these real-life studies were Géricault's method of reimagining the horror of a raft of men floating on the high seas, slowly dying from thirst and starvation. That from them he was trying to learn about composition. His father flipped through the pages of severed limbs, until he got to the colored plate of the *Raft*. "Oh, so dat's the painting he did from all dat, huh? Well, I mus' say, *c'est très beau* dat paintin'. I seen odder pictures of it. *Incroyable.*" Bobby told his father how huge the painting was.

"But, Wing," his father had said. "Why a man would be *obséder avec cette histoire?*"

The painting had been based on a real incident, Bobby instructed his father, the result of an outcry among the French people over an atrocity involving an irresponsible captain commanding a frigate. Bobby told him the story of how the *Medusa* ran aground off the coast of Morocco and how, before escaping in a lifeboat, the captain ordered the lesser members of the crew to build themselves a raft from the masts and mainsail, thereby forcing 115 people to drift aimlessly on the high seas with dwindling rations of food and water and wine, and how those who died first ended up being cannibalized by the survivors.

His father took this in for a moment. "*Vraiment*, dey ate each odder?"

"They were forced to."

"Why do you want to *t'asseyer* on a nice summer's day and look at dead limbs and heads and tink about *ça?*"

"Well, look how beautiful they are. How well drawn."

"No, I tink you goin' to make yourself *fou*." His father glanced at his watch. "Well, I got a boat to drive. Got to go now. Wing. You got to find *travail*, a job for yourself now, you hear?"

During the months following his father's accident, Bobby would sit in his room for hours on end, sketching the tankers bearing down the Mississippi into port; the factories in Chalmette with their poisons vaporizing into the sultry air. He drew the hands of a drowning man flailing from the water, onlookers gaping at his mishap; then a death mask of his father, as if his father were Géricault himself. Bobby's self-imposed solitude alarmed both his mother and his sister.

Then again, hadn't Géricault spent eight solid months locked away in his studio, painting this great masterwork? Known for his beautiful head of curls, hadn't the artist hired a barber to come and shave his head, so there would be less incentive to leave? Delacroix claimed Géricault spoke little while he was working— even when his painter friends came to visit. Apparently, the smallest noises in the studio disturbed him.

"Remarkable, simply remarkable," Garland had said when he came back two months later to retrieve the painting. He ran his fingers along the flesh tones on the woman's face, then down her bodice. "Careful, the varnish is still wet," admonished Deshoteles, who had made it a point to be there when the painting was handed back to Garland.

"It looks even more like Géricault now, I think," Garland remarked.

"You're right about that," Bobby said. "Géricault's strokes were bolder, more confident that Champmartin's."

At this, Deshoteles clucked like a proud father.

Garland's glance, in the meantime, had turned quizzical. Almost immediately after the painting had been left in New Orleans, Bobby had called him in New York to say he'd found Champmartin's signature.

"Why did you make it seem more like Géricault, then? Why didn't you try and restore Champmartin's signature?"

"It's there. Look, it's just a bit faint," Bobby said, pointing to the name.

A clattering at the front of the shop announced the arrival of a potential customer and Deshoteles was obliged to leave the other two alone.

The moment he walked out the door, Garland whispered, "You're wasting your talents here. You know that?"

Bobby looked at him skeptically. "That's a strong statement."

"Restoration in the hands of someone such as yourself is a fine art."

"No, this is art," Bobby said, indicating the painting. "Even though it's discounted because it isn't by *him*."

Bobby told Garland that he sympathized with Champmartin, a talented artist who had remained relatively obscure. He'd first heard the painter's name, in fact, when a painting of a severed head that hung in the Chicago Art Institute, and which for years had been attributed to Géricault, was discovered during the course of a cleaning to bear Champmartin's signature—scratched into the wet paint.

"There are the greater artists and the lesser artists who flock to them. Often because the lesser artists don't believe in themselves," said Garland.

Bobby had agreed that it was as much about ego as it was about talent. Géricault came from money. He didn't have to worry about finding a patron or subject matter until late in his life, when his finances dwindled.

"Don't underestimate this gift you have," Garland had said. "It's a remarkable ability."

"To enhance, to clean, to *re*-create, but not to create," Bobby amended.

"Sometimes that can be valuable," Garland reasoned. "Because you'll bring something into relief, the light that might otherwise remain obscure."

Bobby smiled grimly. "You make it sound so romantic."

"You sound pretty jaded for a twenty-five-year-old."

"Some people live longer lives in shorter periods of time."

Garland looked toward the front of the store where Mr. Deshoteles was having a spirited conversation with what looked to be a Garden District matron with a chignon and pearls. "I can get you working with the best restorers. You can make a lot more money. Wouldn't you like to work on the most important paintings in the world?"

Bobby told Garland this was not what he had planned to do with his life. He wanted to be a painter. But Garland had his own idea of what Bobby should do.

A while later he and Garland went out to dinner, and then Bobby escorted the art dealer back to the Maison de Ville, the French city-style hotel where, ironically, Bobby had worked until Deshoteles could pay him enough money to quit his job. It was a building lit by flickering gas lamps and a tropical garden in the back, shaded by leafy banana plants, overlooked by bungalows, one of which Garland was occupying. Bobby was invited to his suite of rooms, champagne was promptly ordered, and then the art dealer began to apply layer after layer of temptation, detailing all the opportunities that New York had to offer. He told Bobby he kept a spare bedroom that was rented out to young painters or other men on the ascent in the art world. How there was somebody in the guest room at present who would be leaving in a few weeks (in fact, when Bobby finally agreed to move, Garland simply ordered the occupant to leave). And although Garland hadn't yet spoken to Jacopo Della Scorta, he said he was certain his friend, the famous art restorer, would want to have Bobby working in his studio.

Bobby sensed that the art dealer was angling for something to happen. He told himself he didn't really care, and his sexual doubts had diminished as they sipped the bottle of champagne. Besides, he was already intoxicated by descriptions of New York, so he didn't discourage Garland's advances when they were finally made.

Garland was somewhat awkwardly built, overweight, with an uneven pattern of hair on his chest, and at the first sight of him, Bobby was turned off. But whatever he lacked in physical attributes, Garland made up for in his passionate attention. Bobby actually began to enjoy himself—at least while it lasted.

Now, sitting in Garland's living room so many years later, Bobby remembered every detail of those first ungainly moments of intimacy. After all, it had established the pattern for a relationship in which he would come to love Garland with a great, dutiful tenderness.

19 Three days went by without any response to the note that Sam left under Bobby LaCour's door. He kept calling New York to get his messages, but there was no word from the artist. He stopped in at King's Gym, under the pretense of working out in order to solicit information from the proprietor. But Bobby had not come in for his usual workout. As it turned out, however, the proprietor remembered Bobby having said something about being away for at least a fortnight.

Terribly dejected, Sam arrived back at Jessie's shortly before five o'clock to find her making a very elaborate dinner, taking small sips from a glass of white wine that was resting on the counter tiles. Hair piled up on top of her head, she was wearing a bright turquoise Mexican smock fastidiously embroidered with vermilion threads. She showed him what she was preparing: fresh salmon, dressed in chives and brushed with olive oil. She was also cooking a pot of jasmine rice with coriander and steaming some white asparagus.

"Isn't it early for you to be home?" Sam asked.

"I took the afternoon off." Jessie was pouring soy sauce into a measuring spoon.

"But you've been so swamped lately."

"Today I told them I needed to get out of there for my sanity."

Sam put his hand on her shoulder and could feel how tense Jessie was. She leaned her head against his hand and sighed. "Did you find out anything at the gym?"

"Yeah, he went away for two weeks."

Jessie shook her head. "I'm sorry, luvie."

"It's a bitch." He sighed. "I don't know what to do now."

Jessie put down her chopping and wiped her hands on her apron. "Well, you could stay with us until he gets back."

There certainly was no overriding reason for Sam to return to New York. The publisher was paying him promptly and he had calculated that after attending to his outstanding bills, he would have around five thousand dollars left. It wasn't a fortune, but it certainly would last a few months. Jessie took a pair of reading glasses hanging on an elegantly beaded chain around her neck, put them on, adjusted them halfway down her nose, and then peered at a dog-eared cookbook that was open on the counter. Her eyes still on the fine print, she said, "Do you find it strange that the moment Garland dies, Bobby LaCour skips town?"

"That's presuming he knows."

"He may. And wouldn't he have gone back to the States?" Jessie now looked at Sam.

"I got the distinct impression that he couldn't go back—for legal reasons."

"Garland told you that. But did Bobby corroborate it?"

Sam felt stunned at the thought. "He was evasive the first time I asked him and . . . you know, I never got a chance to ask him again. "However, he recalled how Bobby had said that he hadn't been back to America for five years. "I would've thought that if he could've gone back, he would have—at the very least, to see his mother."

"Maybe he couldn't afford it," Jessie said.

"He's gone to Corsica several times."

"They have very cheap flights to Corsica. London/New Orleans must be a fortune."

And yet Sam felt that for Bobby, having to visit his mother would be a compelling reason to return to America on a somewhat regular basis.

Jessie served dinner early enough so that they could eat together with Eva, who'd seemed sullen and barely touched her food. "When do kids ever eat?" Sam wondered aloud as he watched Eva pick at her meal. Every time he was around children at mealtimes, it seemed that they never ate what was put before them and always clamored for sweets. And any small children he knew who cleaned their plates usually seemed to be overweight for their size and their age. Jessie explained that children often fell into two categories: those who thought about food and were constantly importuning for snacks and such, and children who were so preoccupied with their own inner life that they often forgot about eating. Eva fell into the latter category.

"But when *does* she eat?" Sam asked.

"Eva, darling, when do you like to eat?" Jessie asked.

Eva appraised both of their faces before answering diffidently, "When I get home from school."

"Does Raymonda feed you?"

"Who's Raymonda?" Sam asked.

"The child-minder."

"Sometimes we make sandwiches," Eva said.

"Such a weird expression, *child-minder*."

"No worse than '*baby-sitter*.'"

"I'm not a baby," Eva insisted and dug at the tablecloth with her fork.

"Don't do that, darling. It's my best linen," Jessie scolded plaintively.

Sam suggested he tuck Eva into bed and, as he did so, he said, "I have a secret to tell you."

Sleepy and heavy-lidded by now, she said, "Bring me home."

"What?"

She struggled to keep her eyes open but couldn't. He realized she was speaking the gibberish of a child half-asleep. But then she said, "What's the secret?"

"I'm going to get us a set of plastic golf clubs and teach you how to play."

When she asked, "Where is it?" and started to sit up, he knew he'd made a mistake to mention it.

Eva scolded him by lying back and saying, "Golf's weird." Then her breathing slowed and grew heavy with slumber.

When Sam and Jessie were finally alone, sipping brandy in the sitting room, he mentioned that Eva had seemed a bit withdrawn at dinner.

"Do you really think so?"

"Don't you?"

"It's hard to say. I'm around her all the time. I know she loves having you here. But sometimes children get very inward."

"Meaning preoccupied?" Sam amended.

"Yes."

"Do you have any idea what might preoccupy her?"

Jessie hesitated for a moment, as though reluctant to say what was on her mind. "Well, she was on a play date today at the house of a friend whose father is home a lot."

"Yeah, so?"

"Well, this particular friend's mother called me once to say that when Eva comes to visit she'll just want to spend time with the father rather than the daughter."

"But that must happen all the time with kids. I mean, adults are the source of everything. Aren't they?"

Jessie took a sip of her brandy and shrugged.

"Oh, I see." Sam set down his after dinner-drink. "Has this been going on for a long time?" He was afraid Jessie was going to tell him that his being with Eva was making her long for a father.

"It seems to get more intense as she gets older." Jessie was deliberately avoiding meeting his gaze.

"What can you do about it?"

"I don't know." There was a drawn-out silence. "Kind of ironic, isn't it, that you once offered to have a child with me?"

"You said it. I didn't."

"Well, I say it because I know you're thinking it."

Sam took a hefty swig of her drink. "Water under the bridge," he forced himself to say.

"Yeah, right." Jessie looked at her almost-empty glass. They were both silent. "A funny thing happened today," she said after a while.

"What?"

She tilted her head and looked at him, as though not quite resigned to what she was about to say. "Well, I had lunch in Soho. And I happened to spot Rudy and his wife, Carolyn, shopping together in a linen store."

"Really?"

"Carolyn was noticeably pregnant. She must be at least six months along."

Sam considered this for a moment. "So he's put off telling you for as long as he possibly could," he extrapolated.

"Yes, it would seem."

"Doesn't that upset you?"

"I don't give a toss about that so much." Jessie took a moment as if to compose herself before continuing. "But there they were talking and shopping and I thought to myself: My God, I've come between them. And not only that, she knows about *me*, she knows about my affair with her husband."

Sam was moved. "Yeah?"

"And I felt horrible, absolutely horrible."

"This is the first time you've felt horrible about having an affair with a married man?"

"Come on, Sam, don't be so judgmental."

"All right. I'm sorry. So what happened? Did you go up to them?"

"No! Of course not. I made sure they didn't see me."

"You just watched."

"Yeah, I watched and felt incredibly—" She looked at him. "I won't say the word."

He saw she had tears in her eyes.

20 Night after night at Garland's empty apartment, Bobby found himself wide awake and blinking at four in the morning, his heart jangling and arrhythmic. Jet lag lingering longer than it should? Could it be a sign that he would never be able to feel at home in New York? Though he kept the windows closed, he was amazed at the levels of street noise that came through garbles of conversation, screeching cars with faulty shock absorbers careering down Fifth Avenue, tires bouncing over potholes. Even his rough, heavily nocturnal neighborhood in Dalston fell completely silent during the wee hours. He had to remind himself that New York was a twenty-four-hour city in which, at any given time, hundreds of thousands of people were either working a graveyard shift or out carousing, or, he imagined, weathering the ravages of insomnia.

Both dogs had taken to climbing up on the bed and sleeping at his feet, no doubt their pattern while Garland was alive. Bobby had gladly assumed the responsibility of walking and feeding them. It occurred to him that Garland never had much interest in dogs; in fact, whenever they'd spend the weekend at a country house where there were dogs, Elliot would always gripe about the presence of animals. Bobby couldn't help wondering what had persuaded his former lover to acquire such a motley pair. Perhaps it had simply been loneliness: as far as he knew, after their breakup Garland was never truly involved with anyone else, and at some point, probably when his health began deteriorating, must've decided there would never be another lover in his life.

Lying there, Bobby remembered waking up like this during the last year of his relationship with Garland—seven years ago, two years before he left for England. When his sexual feelings for the man had all but died. To sustain his sanity, to get the erotic fixes he thought he craved, he would arrange for late-night trysts downtown. Telling Garland that he wanted to sleep alone in another room, Bobby would bolt awake at 3:00 A.M., an anxious rankling in his gut. Dress for the encounter in jeans and pale T-shirts that showed off his natural *V*, and scuffed cowboy boots. He'd stride through the lobby past bleary-eyed doormen, who, he was sure, knew what he was up to. In the eye of his memory, it was always summer, always a multitude of empty cabs swarming down Fifth Avenue, vying for his attention. He would coax the cabdriver into staying abreast with the synchronized green lights, feeling as if he'd finally become a true New Yorker, ordering a cab around at 3:00 A.M. En route to pleasure, the ride never was fast enough. He remembered going out one night with Garland and a bunch of socialites after an opera gala, climbing into a limousine and hearing one of the tuxedoed men, a wealthy foreigner, say to the chauffeur, "Driver, go faster, we are very impatient people."

Seven years ago, when he took those late-night cab rides, Bobby was still in his twenties, at the peak of his attractiveness, his ardor. Exhilarated by the idea of a man awake and freshly showered and waiting for him, he would tell himself that the best part of living was the anticipation of making love to a stranger. Flying past dark brownstones, scantily lighted office towers, he would picture himself climbing flights of stairs to the man whose face he could barely remember after the brevity of their first meeting—in a bookstore, a department store, strolling along the street—an angle of light slanted out from the apartment into the vestibule, illuminating the stranger's anxious, anticipatory smile. The sound of the apartment door shutting softly, the first light kiss on the lips, stretching his arms around the man's wide back, the rush of feeling a tight torso. Bobby had this habit after the first kiss of letting his head fall against the chest of his partner and sighing. Most people never asked him what that sigh meant; only a few dared. Of course, he'd lie and say the sigh was for pure pleasure, when in reality he was reckoning what was to come in the morning.

Once Bobby arrived home from one of these nights out to find Elliot standing in the midst of a flock of screeching spice finches, Amazonian parrots, macaws, putting out ground carrot to some, special mash to others, and mealworms to the carnivores. Garland was clutching his morning mug of coffee and, with a look of terror on his face, saying to his birds, "So look who the wind blew in." Bobby managed to avoid his lover's eyes. "He's been out all night, breaking hearts, again."

"Well, you said . . . you said I should."

"I know. But what choice do I have?" Garland still would not look at him. He dipped into a white plastic jug and pulled out several mealworms, which he placed into the cage of an aggressive, piebald jay that needed to be cordoned away from the spice finches, which he would otherwise prey upon. "If I tried to restrict you, I'd drive you away. But don't think I'm having a picnic here at home." Garland situated the writhing worms as though tastefully arranging a plate of food.

"That's why I should go, Elliot. I should go so you don't have to see this. I should go so you can just get used to the fact that I'm not here." For it was chipping away at Garland's self-confidence, decimating his morale. "You've got to see how miserable I'm making you."

Garland took a dropper, stuck it into a bowl of water and put several squirts into the dish belonging to the jay, which suddenly swooped down and pecked his hand. Garland jerked away and yelped and then took a half-hearted swipe at the bird. He slammed the cage shut. "I tell myself I have to endure it," he said in a measured tone. "Some of these guys"—he indicated the birds—"are ornery, and I manage to put up with their shenanigans."

Bobby said, "By the way, Elliot, you've got shit on each shoulder."

Garland regarded each of the bird turds and remarked, "Epaulets. I always say if you're going to shit for the world to see, let it have symmetry."

Bobby laughed. "Such a scat."

"I'll be a miserable scat if you leave," Garland said. "No matter what I say, even if I give my consent, don't go, okay?" His voice was small and meek.

To hear him importune like that was shattering. Their lives together had shrunk—couldn't Garland feel that? Bobby went out, Elliot would wait for him to get home. Bobby would feel as though he'd misbehaved, Elliot forgave him, and Bobby wished it would be the last time, even though he knew it wouldn't be. "You deserve a lot better than this," he tried to say. "You should not be waiting up for somebody who might not come home."

"Sometimes there are great old flicks on television and—"

"Stop making light of it."

"Okay." Garland ceased feeding the birds and finally faced him. The pained look on his face almost made Bobby beg his forgiveness. "Although I know you have to go on with your life, I still think your life should be here. So, it's kind of a Catch Twenty-two. I'm not that much older than you are. There are plenty of young guys who adore older men."

"That's what I keep telling you."

"So why can't *you?*"

They'd been through this so many times. "Obviously, I thought I could. But I want to be with somebody my own age. I'm being made to feel like it's some kind of crime."

"We"—and Garland had meant "we" as a subculture—"don't have enough rules to live by. If only we did," he theorized. "Maybe there are supposed to be these kinds of connections between people like us, extremely close but just not sexual. Maybe I should be content in the role of the father figure. I know plenty of men who are. But I don't want to be, that's the thing. I want to be lusted over, I want to be hungered for, I want to be craved—like anyone does. On the other hand I want not to care about who you sleep with, to be able to ask you if it was fun, but the idea of knowing anything makes me totally insane."

"I wouldn't want to know, either," Bobby admitted. "But I wouldn't stand in your way."

"Well, then, I'll tell you this: I hired a beautiful man last week."

Despite everything, the news of Garland's infidelity hurt. "I'm sorry you feel it necessary—"

"You've driven me to it!" Garland cried out, his eyes sparking.

Bobby turned away to look at one of his favorite paintings: the one of the ice trawler breasting the Neva; lost for a moment in the bleak tableau of a solitary vessel braving the great Russian river, perhaps on some kind of dire mission, breaking ice as it traveled. They had planned to visit Russia in a few months' time. And Bobby wanted so much to see the paintings in the Hermitage, but not when things were like this; it wasn't fair to either of them.

He knew that Garland had relished playing the role of the one who was losing something. But Bobby also felt as though he were losing something: a career as a painter. Once Bobby had arrived in New York, Garland had never encouraged him to pursue a career in painting, but rather kept driving him to work in restoration in order to become renowned and wealthy. Clearly, Garland never really believed in Bobby's talent. The proof of this was that he'd always introduce Bobby to other painters and gallery owners as an up-and-coming restorer, never as an artist in his own right.

Now, from behind him, Garland asked mournfully, "So do you think you'll ever see this guy again?"

Bobby felt he had no choice but to lie. "Probably not."

Bobby finally fell asleep and woke up with only a half hour to spare before his meeting with Garland's lawyer. And even though he rushed to get dressed, he ended up arriving fifteen minutes late for his appointment. The receptionist asked him to wait while she called the office of Jennifer Lassiter, a woman Bobby had spoken to many times over the telephone during the Géricault fiasco but had never actually met. Bobby couldn't help noticing that the law firm's hallways were lined with canvases by art world household names. Red Grooms, David Salle, Julian Schnabel, a few artists Bobby recognized who were big in Europe, less well known in America. No doubt a part-time curator had been paid to advise on these acquisitions, many of them numbered lithographs or monoprints. The sad part was that none of the works by these notables was particularly great; the law firm's walls were dripping with mediocrity. Bobby reminded himself how in New York, ambitious, unschooled wealth will spend thousands of dollars on a Name because somebody of repute says they should. Never would they consider relying on their own aesthetic sense—on their own eye.

"Mr. LaCour." The receptionist disturbed his reverie. "Somebody will be coming to take you to Ms. Lassiter's office in a moment."

"Robert LaCour."

He looked up into the face of a rather wan-looking man with auburn hair wearing a beautifully tailored gaberdine suit. The man's eyes give him the familiar once-over, and Bobby felt the vibration of a sexual prowl. With a cordial smile, the fellow said, "I'm going to show you to Jennifer Lassiter's office, if you'll follow me."

"Sure."

As they walked in tandem down the hallway, Bobby was trying to think of something to say. Usually men in corporate dress turned him on; however, this fellow, though well formed, was unfortunately drab-looking.

"I'm Matthew Calais," the man said at one point, and Bobby asked him if he worked with Lassiter.

Matthew shook his head. "No, I'm an associate. Her secretary got tied up.

"Well, here we are," Matthew said finally. "Jennifer is right inside."

Bobby glanced into a large room and could see a partial view of a woman with blunt-cut pale-blond hair. He shook Matthew's hand, thanking him. Strange encounter that, thought Bobby as he walked into the office and finally made eye contact with Jennifer Lassiter, who looked to be around forty.

She got up from her desk, strode around it, approaching Bobby with an outstretched hand. "I feel like I know you after all our conversations," she said, giving a single, exaggerated shake. "It's been a while. Have a seat, please."

Bobby sat down in a chair opposite her desk and waited for the lawyer to settle herself behind a monolith of lacquered wood. She was deeply tanned and the effects of premature aging were already apparent in a slackness of skin on her cheeks and chin and tiny fans of deep lines on either side of her small, pebble-colored eyes. On the wall behind her was an Art Deco poster of a high-kicking dancer that Bobby judged downright ugly. "So, I gather you've been in New York for a while?"

"A week altogether."

There was an uncomfortable lull. "Mr. Garland is a great loss—and we're very sad here. He was wonderful to work with."

"Yeah," Bobby said, anxious to get on with the interview.

"Are you comfortable at the apartment?"

"Sure, but I used to live there, if you remember."

Lassiter held his gaze for an uncomfortably long time before she picked up the conversation again. "Anyway, you've probably guessed the reason why I've called you here is . . . well, you are named in Mr. Garland's will, a copy of which I'll give you in a moment."

"Elliot did mention something."

Lassiter looked at him appraisingly. "How old are you now, Bobby?"

"Thirty-six."

"So you were thirty-one when all this business happened with the Géricault?"

"Yeah."

"I didn't realize you were *that* young. And Garland was fifty-six, so there's twenty years' difference between you."

"He was forty-nine when the relationship ended," Bobby pointed out, remembering how Garland had deliberately made it seem as if there was no hope he would ever find somebody else. "But what difference does it make?"

Lassiter's expression turned thoughtful. "Just cross-referencing . . . May I begin now?"

"Please."

She looked down at her papers and then at him. "The bequest is basically very simple. The contents of the apartment have been left to you. And that is all. All his money, except for a few small gift bequests, is left to and being divided among several charities for incurable diseases."

Bobby remained poker-faced. "That's as it should be," he commented. Lassiter appeared to have more to say, but seemed to be hesitating. Finally, he said, "And what about the apartment?"

"The apartment?" the lawyer said with a blank expression that Bobby distrusted. "What about it?"

"Who did he leave the apartment to?"

"The apartment was not owned by Mr. Garland. It was a rental."

Bobby was stunned. "What? How can that be? He led me and everybody else to believe he owned it."

"Well, he probably felt as though he *did* own it. After all, he held the lease for twenty years." In fact, Lassiter said, Garland had paid some pretty hefty key money to procure the rental rights. "Which brings me to my next remark, which is actually a caveat," the lawyer said. "You're going to have to move everything out of that apartment within two months. The building wants to take it back, refurbish and rerent it."

Bobby still couldn't quite accept what he was hearing. "Do you realize how much work I put into that apartment?" he told the lawyer. "I slaved over every single door, I painted everything in *faux bois.*" He inwardly cringed at how precious this sounded.

"I saw the doors, Mr. LaCour. I thought they were beautiful. But the doors are fixtures. Fixtures go with the apartment."

"Could I at least take them and replace them with new ones?"

"I'll call the landlord and ask. But I can't guarantee anything."

"Maybe you shouldn't say anything. Maybe I should just take them out right away and have them replaced."

"The doormen will see you do it. And then we'll have problems."

"I'll pay them off."

"I see you've spent some time in New York," the lawyer said sarcastically.

Bobby was now having difficulty remaining calm. "You don't understand. Those doors are really valuable."

"Mr. LaCour, so is a lot of Mr. Garland's artwork. If I were you, I'd focus on what you're going to do with that."

He lowered his eyes "I guess I'm too afraid to even consider it."

"Well, I suggest you do. You also should understand that the moment you sell any of it, you'll have to pay hefty estate taxes."

Bobby explained to Lassiter that due to his precarious financial situation, as well as his meager living space, he would probably have to sell many of the treasured objects—much against his will. And then it occurred to him that this is exactly what Garland had wanted: to give him objects he loved and then to force him to part with some of them. What better way to have remained involved with Bobby, postmortem in the same push-and-pull way they'd been involved during Garland's life.

Lassiter turned momentarily sympathetic. "I have the name of somebody at Sotheby's."

"That's not necessary. I know whom to contact."

"So many beautiful works of art," Lassiter said, as it occurred to Bobby the calculated brilliance behind Garland's remark, "*Almost* everything in the apartment will belong to you." Almost everything *except* the apartment.

"Can't you ship it all to England?" the lawyer asked. "And sell some of it there if need be?"

Bobby barely heard her and she had to repeat the question. "I'm sure I can't afford to. I told you, I have very little money."

"Then perhaps I can talk to the other executors."

He would now remain Garland's captive in death and well as in life—the idea was overwhelming. Bobby made a peremptory move to get up and leave.

Lassiter said quickly, "Before you go, Mr. LaCour, there are a few things I would like to ask you."

Bobby gestured to her to ask but said nothing.

"Questions I would ask purely for my own understanding of what happened. This part of our discussion will be off the record."

Bobby waited.

"First, why have you stayed in England so long after we settled the lawsuit?"

He hated being asked this question and his face must've shown it because Lassiter suddenly sat back in her chair, looking momentarily unnerved. "It was Garland's idea," he finally began to explain. That they should be away from each other for a while, that neither of them were getting on with their lives. "You must have known this."

"I had a sense it *was* something of that nature. But then . . ." The lawyer twirled her pencil. "Nobody was holding you there."

Bobby suddenly realized there was no need to be on the defensive. After all, now he knew where he stood as far as Garland's will was concerned. There was nothing left to wonder about, nothing left to fear. Ambivalent though it might be, his legacy had been quite clearly spelled out. Yes, it was true, five years ago he'd relied upon this woman to extricate him from a legal mess in which he had once been implicated, but that matter was now settled. And he'd paid for the settlement by giving up a lucrative career in art conservation. For once it became known that he had refurbished a painting without an autograph, worked on a painting with the purpose of making it appear attributable to Géricault, he lost all his credibility as a professional restorer. Whether or not he had ambivalent feelings about restoring, it had still been a good way to make a living.

And so he told Lassiter that he had remained in England knowing that the moment he returned to America, once again, he'd be in Garland's thrall. And back in America he would have been unable to live his own life without the sense of somebody watching, judging, commenting, and, ultimately, disapproving of him. He told her that living in England had allowed him to earn money from his own work, even if it meant supplying kitschy paintings to various museum shops. Whereas New York was such a competitive town, London was a more forgiving environment in which he could pursue his own painting and not feel he had to be successful in order to justify his existence.

And when Bobby refused to return to America, Garland, affronted by his obstinacy, circulated a rumor among their professional as well as private friends and acquaintances: Garland told everyone the lawsuit over the false attribution was still being fought out and that, in America, Bobby still stood accused of forgery, and for this reason had to remain abroad.

The lawyer reached for a pitcher of water on a small table next to her desk and poured it into a Styrofoam cup. She casually offered some to Bobby, who declined, and then drank half the cup before setting it down carefully on her desk.

"But, as I understand from people close to Mr. Garland, you actually corroborated, if you will, his apocryphal reasons for why you had to stay in England."

"Yes, I did."

"For what purpose?"

Again, there was no reason for her to know the *entire* truth. And so he told her, "When he finally asked me to come back and I refused, I felt so guilty about disappointing him, I figured the least I could do was help him save face by allowing other people to believe that I still couldn't return for legal reasons."

Lassiter nodded, and Bobby could tell that she didn't entirely believe him. Then, rotating her pencil between her thumb and forefinger, she said, "And on the painting in dispute, the falsely attributed Géricault. The trace of a signature they found with infrared, Champmartin, why did you deliberately remove it?"

Fighting to control his suddenly quavering voice, Bobby glanced down at the drab, industrial carpeting. Finally, he looked up at the lawyer's impassive face. "I'm sorry, but I don't feel that I have to answer that question. I will say, however, that he asked me to do it once before, for another picture, and I refused. It was his idea. And I can say that now because *now* no one can charge him with it."

21 It was a beautiful Indian-summer day, and Sam was strolling around in Hampstead with Eva, who gripped his hand tightly, as though afraid of being separated from him. She was wearing a very grown-up-looking outfit of black leggings and a yellow knit sweater. As they meandered along the rows of shops, he searched for things that might interest her. In a way he was trying to recapture her world. They stopped at a pet store, wandered among the tropical fish tanks and the reptile terrariums. Sam put his hand under an ultraviolet tube and showed her how it made his skin look riddled with white specs. A mynah bird heckled them. Later on, he bought her a chocolate hare, an orange crush, and then they shared a bag of vinegar potato chips.

"Can we go to the Heath now?" she asked when they had bought nearly everything on Jessie's shopping list but the red mullet for dinner.

"Now we have all these packages."

"The fishmonger lets Mummy leave her packages there. Sometimes," Eva said hopefully.

"However, he may not let *me*."

"I'll tell him you're my daddy and then he will."

The words jabbed their meaning. "I don't know if that's such a good idea."

Eva nevertheless insisted upon enacting her little ruse and made Sam wait outside the store while she went in and dealt with the fishmonger, standing dutifully at the end of a short line of customers who kept turning to smile. When the fishmonger finally noticed her waiting, he bade her circumvent the line and come to the counter, bending his head down to hear what she had to say. He nodded toward Sam.

"You think your mom will mind that we fibbed?" Sam tested Eva once the fishmonger had relieved them of their packages.

Eva glanced up at him, but said nothing. It was as though she somehow knew he was fishing, as it were, for reassurance.

They took a short bus ride to Hampstead Heath. Moments after leaving the sidewalk, they left all traces of urban life behind to wander through a pathway beneath arches of butterfly bushes. They followed a narrow bridle path that led past the men's and women's swimming ponds. Sam was amazed at how rural parts of the park appeared: wide, gently sloping hills, covered with golden grass that reminded him of country plains. They climbed a winding lane to a large yellow Georgian building, Kenwood House, where Sam and Jessie had once gone ten years ago to hear an outdoor summer concert. Adjacent to the concert hall was a café with large outdoor patio where people sat drinking tea and eating pastries and swatting at the hovering wasps.

"You've had enough for one day," he told Eva when she asked him to buy her a poppy seed cake.

"Just one," she begged.

"Your mom would not let you keep stuffing yourself like this."

This remark was unexpectedly devastating to Eva, who bunched up her lips and seemed to be verging on tears.

"Please don't cry," Sam found himself imploring her.

"Why not?" she said.

"Because . . . " He didn't want to tell her how upset she'd make him. To make things easier, he bought her the cake.

By the time Jessie's key turned in the front door, they were stretched out on the floor of Eva's bedroom, working on a coloring book of the planets in the solar system. Sam had explained that the various gases in the atmosphere were different colors and they had to try and create the special effect. So, choosing the brightest, most audacious colors they could find, they tinted the rings of Saturn and the moons of Jupiter. Eva insisted they play musical crayons, which meant switching colors at intervals that she controlled by ringing an imaginary bell.

Jessie didn't come in to see them directly. Sam heard her listening to the answering machine. Finally, she appeared. "Sam, there's a message from Matthew. Says to call him at the office."

"Okay."

"Now, could I have a word with you?"

Excusing himself from Eva, Sam told her to keep coloring and that he'd soon return. As he followed Jessie down the stairs, he noticed that she kept her head down as though to avoid meeting his eyes. She led the way toward the kitchen and then turned to face him just outside it. "I have a bit of disturbing news."

Everything stopped. Searching her expression for signals of disaster, his first thought was something had happened to Bobby— that was why there were no messages from him in New York! Seeing how she'd alarmed him, Jessie assured him, "No, don't worry, nobody is dead, nobody is sick. Somebody in my office saw the *Vanitas*."

"What do you mean, they 'saw the *Vanitas*'?"

"A guy who works with me, a gay man, went to a group exhibition at a gallery at lunchtime. He came back describing a drawing. Obviously, you're not the only one who thinks that *Vanitas* is beautiful."

Sam just stared at her. Finally, he said, "How do you know it was Bobby's *Vanitas*?"

Intrigued, her colleague had noted the name of the artist signed at the bottom of the drawing. The name, he said was LaCour. He also said the picture frame was "gold and flaking."

"I can't believe this!" Sam raged. How could Bobby, knowing how much he wanted the drawing, attempt to sell it without even offering it to him?

Jessie went on. "My colleague also said he would've bought it but it was way too expensive."

Sam shut his eyes and asked how much the gallery was asking.

"Two thousand pounds."

"Two thousand pounds? I can't afford that!"

"Mummy, what's wrong?" Startled by Sam's loud exclamations, Eva was now hanging over the banister.

"Darling, just a second," Jessie said. "Everything is fine." She turned to Sam. "Maybe he needed the money and figured you couldn't afford it and didn't want to be awkward about it."

"He said to me several times that he wouldn't sell it without consulting me."

She shrugged.

"I have to go and see it, Jessie," Sam said.

Looking overwhelmed, she warily eyed her watch and said it was nearly five-thirty.

"Are we going to finish, Sam?" Eva called from upstairs.

Jessie walked out of the kitchen and climbed to the next floor. Sam heard her say, "Darling, there's a bit of a crisis now."

"What's wrong, Mummy?"

"A friend of Sam's did something to upset him."

"Is he going out now?"

"I don't know. You'll have to ask him."

"Sam, are you going out?" Eva called down the stairs.

"If I do, you can come with me," Sam yelled back.

Jessie returned downstairs and tossed her handbag on the dining room table. "Thanks a lot," she said, half-amused. She went into her study to get the *London Business Directory* and, flipping through the listings, said softly, "Somebody is becoming quite possessive of you."

"That's not bad, is it?"

"She hasn't registered that you'll have to go back to America."

"Well, hold off. Don't tell her anything."

Jessie said plaintively, "Sam, it isn't so easy. You have to be as honest as you can. Children don't like surprises." She began leafing through the directory. She found the gallery, called to learn that it was still open, and put down the phone. "Now, can you wait until tomorrow?" she requested. "Because after all this I'd like to see the drawing. But it's rush hour. The Tube will be horrendous, packed to the gills, and Eva gets upset in crowded trains. And the traffic . . . God it wouldn't even be worth getting a minicab."

Sam listened to all the good reasons against going to the gallery. Then said, "I've got to go there right now. That's all."

Without another word, he went back upstairs to where Eva was standing outside her room, impatiently awaiting his return. Her face lit up when she saw him. "There is something I have to do near Covent Garden," he told her. "Would you and your mom like to come?"

Eva frowned as though she didn't really want to but nevertheless agreed.

Jessie was right: Eva got frightened of the crowds on the Tube and began sobbing. Sam tried to hold her, but in such an inconsolable state, she would only be comforted by her mother. As he watched the child weeping on Jessie's shoulder, he realized how selfish it was to insist on going to the gallery during rush hour. What was the matter with him, anyway? He was suddenly afraid that he'd let them down in some fundamental way. He felt even worse when he realized that though Eva had been affectionate and allowed him to take on the role of the father/protector, she didn't really see him that way, particularly in situations such as this one.

"Nudes of the Plague" was a collection of gouache, charcoal, and pastel drawings, all figurative, of male nudes in various stages of illness. The moment Jessie identified the subject matter, she worried that Eva would ask pointed questions about the paintings, the answers to which would give her nightmares.

"Let's just hope she doesn't require too much explanation," Jessie whispered to Sam.

Wandering through the gallery, their footsteps softly echoing between the hardwood floors and the vaulted ceilings, they quickly viewed the exhibition. One study was of a man covered with the telltale purple lesions facing his own pitiful image in a mirror; another man stood behind him, hands resting gingerly on the first man's bruised shoulder. The expression in the sick man's eyes was somehow both alarmed and resigned. Another was of an emaciated patient lying on a hospital gurney that had been turned upright. There were great details of his inner organs, which, on closer scrutiny, turned out to be a collection of test tubes and pots marked with a skull and crossbones and the green cross, the European pharmaceutical insignia. Fortunately, Eva was so distracted by the traffic of all the people in the gallery that she didn't look at any one picture too carefully.

In contrast to many of the other works, Bobby's *Vanitas* was simple and elegantly forceful. Sam didn't even have to show Jessie which one it was; she knew at once. And, yet, looking at the *Vanitas* once again, he felt there was something changed about it but couldn't quite express what that difference was. If pressed, he might have said it seemed a bit more crude than he remembered, not quite as meticulously drawn. He was puzzled by the fact that the drawing seemed less . . . *potent* was the only word he could think of. "This is quite good," Jessie said, leaning toward the drawing, examining the minutiae of its technique. "I see what you mean." She had a fine and discerning eye, and hearing her appreciation ironically filled Sam with despair. "The figure is well done," she went on. "You actually can't see the face the way he's got it shaded, but I feel I know exactly what the man's expression is."

"What do you think it is?"

"It's rapture. The rapture of someone who makes love to the dead. The rapture of someone resigned to dying."

Sam tried to remember what Bobby had said about his drawing—was it something about the fascination with which the living regard the dead? He supposed it was the same idea. Jessie traced her finger against the glass. "The texture of the charcoal is so velvety. Has he done a lot more like this?"

"Nothing more, as far as I know."

"Shame, that." Jessie once again looked at the figure. "He's quite stunning. . . ." Then she peered at Sam. "And you said that he died as well?"

Sam said quite some time ago, that this particular man was one of the first to go.

"So what is Bobby's other work like?" Jessie asked when they finally moved beyond the *Vanitas* and were looking at the gallery's other offerings.

Sam said the only other work that he'd seen were tourist watercolors that Bobby painted on order. Very predictable. However, he had done a few on a trip to Corsica. "Those were gorgeous."

"Well, judging by this drawing, I'd say he could have some kind of career."

"He's very self-deprecating about his talent."

Jessie said that was a sign of serious creativity. Sam suddenly felt a sharp tug on his hand. "Can we go now?" Eva asked, looking up at him with a face full of boredom.

"Can we just have a few more minutes?" Sam asked her.

"I want to go home *now*."

They were interrupted by a silkily handsome dark-skinned man dressed entirely in black. "May I be of any assistance?" he said with a very cultured accent that wasn't quite British. Eva glared resentfully at the person who was now obstructing their leaving the gallery.

Jessie responded that they were just browsing through.

"I saw you admiring that nude over there." The man pointed in the direction of Bobby's drawing.

"The *Vanitas*, you mean?" Jessie said. "Yes, we have. Somebody told me it was two thousand pounds."

The man confirmed the price.

"The price seems a bit high," Jessie pointed out.

The dealer explained that half the proceeds of the show were being donated to a local London AIDS charity. "But that's a moot point, really, as one of our regular clients has already asked us to put the drawing on hold."

Sam froze, his world withering. This could not happen to him. He would think of something to prevent the drawing from being sold.

Jessie didn't waste the opportunity. "We know the artist who did it. We've actually been trying to get hold of him—unsuccessfully."

"Because he promised it to me," Sam blurted out. "I'm supposed to buy it."

Though Jessie looked amused, the man was startled by Sam's news.

And Sam went on, shamelessly, "Bobby and I even agreed on a price. He's not in England right now. So somebody must've—"

"Well, he brought it here himself," the man interjected. "Before he went to America."

Sam shut his eyes and willed himself across the ocean. He'd checked his answering machine every other day and there'd been no message from Bobby. Why?

"Well, we need to sort this out," he heard Jessie saying through his panic and bafflement. "Can you possibly wait until we speak to him?" she asked the man.

Given the fact that the drawing had been consigned, this would be quite irregular, the man said.

"Do you happen to know where he is in America?" she pressed him.

"It's not our policy to give out—"

"This is dire," Sam insisted. "We know this man. And we need to get hold of him."

A silver-haired gentleman dressed in a double-breasted herringbone suit now approached them. "I'm Sebastian Kemble," he said in what sounded to Sam like an Oxbridge accent. "I own the gallery. How can *I* help you?"

The matter was explained and the gallery owner said, "I happen to know Bobby LaCour. Who *are* you?" he asked Sam.

Sam explained that he'd been hired to write the memoirs of a man named Garland.

"Oh," said the owner. "Elliot Garland. You should have mentioned that before."

Sam herded Jessie and Eva together and quickly left the gallery. As they strolled along Neal Street, passing the fashionable shops that Sam, in a normal frame of mind, would've eyed eagerly, Jessie kept telling him to calm down. His eyes were riveted to the pavement, his mind grinding away with the fury of the betrayed. Eva skipped along on Jessie's right.

"Well, maybe there's a reason you don't know about," Jessie suggested after a long interval. "Why he consigned it."

"Like what?"

"Sam, you don't know this man. It could be anything."

Eva interrupted, wanting to look in a store that sold handmade wooden toys. Jessie asked Sam if he minded, and he said no. Then, without waiting for either of them, Eva ran off into the shop. Sam said, "I'll go get her."

"No, let me. She loves this store. I know what's coming."

A moment later Sam heard a shrieking protest, and then saw Jessie leading a wailing child. "What's happened?"

"She touched something she wasn't supposed to," Jessie cried above Eva's weeping. "She refused to listen to me."

"Did you hit her?"

"No, I never hit her. I just dragged her."

Sam couldn't help but laugh. Eva allowed him to put his arm around her and kiss the top of her head until she recovered. They managed to reach the Covent Garden Tube station without further incident.

"I mean, if you think about it, the man in that drawing is the reason why Garland is dead," Jessie continued once they were inside the station. "It's no wonder Bobby wants to get rid of it. In order not to have somebody he knows own it. If it were me, I certainly would feel superstitious."

"He did say he was afraid it might bring bad luck. I don't believe in bad luck. But I do believe in coincidence."

"I still don't understand why you're so fixated on that drawing."

"It's incredibly sexy. I want to hang it in my apartment and look at it every day. It gives me a charge, what can I tell you."

The elevator arrived, the metal doors rumbled open, and they got in with a half dozen other passengers. Guarding the privacy of their conversation, they didn't speak again until they were standing on the train platform.

"But you certainly couldn't long to be this young man," Jessie pointed out. "He probably died a horrible death."

Their train rocketed around the corner. When it finally came to a stop and the doors parted, Jessie remarked, "Thank God it's not crowded!" Feeling guilty about what had happened on the Tube on their way to the gallery, Sam reached for Eva's hand to escort her inside. They found two seats together. Sam lifted Eva up onto his lap and she immediately laid her head against his shoulder. He remembered that Bobby had once done the same thing and how the gesture had touched him, while making him nervous about displaying his sexuality in public. To think that he'd nearly asked Bobby to sit up straight, but he didn't in the end, reluctant to hamper one of Bobby's first spontaneous gestures of affection. Thinking back on that exhilarating afternoon, Sam felt incredibly depressed. Who would have thought things would end up like this and that, on top of everything else, he'd lose the drawing, too.

"I'm not letting you off the hook yet." Jessie disturbed his sad reverie. "This is a portrait of a beautiful man before he declined. That's the definition of nearly every portrait that captures some person at the height of their lives—before their lives begin to buckle. In that regard, every painting is ageless. There has to be some other reason why it means so much to you."

Sam knew Jessie was right. "It's hard to explain. I have to think about it."

And then he wondered, could it have to do with his encounter with the man he called "the angel," the man he'd never been able to forget? Not because he was beautiful. Not because he quite possibly could have been Sam's great love. But for another reason entirely.

Eyeing the other passengers, Jessie leaned toward Sam. "You don't think you're obsessed with owning the drawing the way you're obsessed with Bobby LaCour?"

Sam shook his head and said that it had nothing at all to do with Bobby LaCour.

22 When Bobby returned to Garland's after seeing the lawyer, the two dogs were absent, which gave him an uneasy feeling. Sure enough, when he went into the kitchen, their food and water bowls were gone: while he'd been out of the apartment, Gus and Diane had been ferried to new homes. Their departure actually left him feeling bereft, but he didn't have time to dwell on their absence. The doorbell rang and a Hispanic woman wearing a pink uniform announced herself as the maid. Bobby asked how often she came and she replied, Twice a week. With one person living there, this frequency seemed rather extravagant.

He went and sat down on one of the Louis XVI gold-leaf settees in the living room. Then, in what Garland would certainly have viewed as an irreverent act, he lay down, resting his street shoes on the brocaded fabric. He dreaded what lay before him: going through the apartment, cataloguing everything, figuring out what to sell and what to save. What if he just walked out and left everything? That would certainly create a scramble. In the worst way he just wanted to pack his bags and flee the apartment for New Orleans, to tear himself from the lair that Garland had so artfully laid down for him. And yet, Bobby knew—and Garland probably also knew—that he would be emotionally unable to part with some of the paintings; and despite the heavy taxes, there was money to be made from selling the furniture. With careful planning, Bobby might end up ahead. And of course, there was the disputed Géricault that had also been bequeathed to him.

Garland had left Bobby another envelope with a key to the bank vault in which the falsely attributed Géricault had been stored. The painting now leaned against the living room wall. Bobby got up off the divan, reached for the canvas, brought it into Garland's bedroom, and placed it carefully on the bed. No matter who was the author of the painting, to him, it would always be magnificent. The subject matter—a dying youth lying on a wooden pallet, head thrown back, eyes rheumy with the agony of starvation—was itself clear and resonant, all because of Bobby's careful restoration. Perhaps this *was* his most sublime work, his greatest accomplishment. Perhaps Garland had been right all along: Bobby could have left his mark on the world by reversing the damage done to great works of art.

The first time he had ever seen the painting was here at the Fifth Avenue apartment, ironically, shortly after Bobby, to his own great amazement, had discovered his own *Vanitas* drawing. In those days it was hanging in Garland's bedroom. In fact, when Sam had arrived in London that first time and said he was carrying a piece of artwork, Bobby naturally thought that it would be *not* the *Vanitas* but rather this nineteenth-century depiction of yet another dying youth, a *painting,* which, when he was deposed by lawyers in London, he described as falling between the cracks of various possible attributions. A painting that he'd restored to the best of his ability in the direction of Géricault.

He remembered his first impression of it: the suggestion of a rocky shore, the field of water that vanished toward the edge, the doming suggestion of a sky at the top of the canvas gave it the appearance of a partially completed picture, though Bobby knew immediately it was only a study. The nude figure of the dying youth lying on his back was meant to be taken for the left corner of the raft itself. Both of his knees were bowed out, the foot of the right leg crossed under the calf of the left, the left hip slightly turned in, the left foot pointed like a dancer's. The stomach was taut and concave, the head, framed with soft curls and long sideburns, was thrown back in limp, dislocated abandonment.

The darkness of the palette, the heavy use of bituminous paints, made it look as though it were done at the very end of the eighteen months Géricault had worked on the *Raft.* It certainly could've been one of the many studies done for the intricately choreographed coupling of the dead son and the grieving father, except that the position was reversed: the young man was lying in the opposite direction. So it probably was an oil study for the final figure that was added to the painting after it had been removed from the artist's studio and placed in the foyer of the Théâtre Italien, where it waited to be hung in the hall of the Salon of 1819. For it was there that Géricault realized that the group of figures that swept across the canvas toward the rescue ship in the upper right was too top-heavy and needed to be widened somehow. Which he accomplished by adding two more figures on either side of the raft—all this in the eleventh hour before the exhibition.

The face of the boy was in the worst condition, a state of partial and potentially total ruin from water damage. When the water stains finally dried, whole sections of the paint seemed to have flaked off. The dark curls, the sideburns, were in better shape. Because Bobby had trouble making out the features in the face, it was difficult for him to tell whether the original model had been dead or alive. Alive would have meant that it had been drawn from one of Géricault's friends, most likely another artist such as Delacroix, who often dropped by Géricault's studio during the period when the final painting was being created and had served as a life model for the figures on the raft. But Géricault also visited the Hôpital Beaujon, to study and sketch patients in varying degrees of mortal agony, as well as fresh corpses and severed limbs.

Bobby and Elliot took the painting downtown to Bobby's studio. With a few exploratory swipes, Bobby could peer through the scrim of the finishing varnish and spy the sagging quality of the young man's skin, the paleness painted to an eerie gloss. As he removed more varnish, he noticed that the brushstrokes were longer, somehow tentative, unlike the small, closely blended strokes that marked the technique of the master. The contours of the limbs were not created with the same kind of relentless intensity that marked each of Géricault's master strokes, the shadows were not deep or tenebrous enough, and the skin itself did not have the true feeling of flesh or matter. All in all, the study was not marked by the searching compulsion of a man who shut himself away in his studio, plagued by the failure of a love affair, by guilt over the fact that he had fallen in love with the wife of his uncle, a man who when he painted was observed to be in a highly strung yet relentless state of concentration.

It basically came down to this: If the figure had been modeled on a living subject, then it was probably by Géricault, for it would have been executed in his studio. And it would have been painted sometime in the eighteen-month period during which he prepared and finally realized his masterwork. Although many of Géricault's friends lent him a hand at certain strategic moments during his rendering of the *Raft,* no one came into his studio to paint his living models. Géricault was disturbed by the slightest motions, the hint of any noise, and could never have tolerated the distraction of another artist working alongside him. However, if the painted study was of a dead youth, than it conceivably could have been done by any of several acolytes who accompanied Géricault to the Hôpital Beaujon to paint and sketch corpses (Géricault was allowed to bring severed limbs back to his studio, but *never* an entire cadaver). If the painting was of a dead youth, it certainly could have been done by Champmartin, the author of the severed head owned by the Art Institute of Chicago, the painting that was once thought to have been by Géricault. And if the painting was of a dead youth, the attribution would probably always be inconclusive. Bobby's gut told him the painting was *not* by Géricault.

Bobby turned to Garland, who had been standing there next to him, waiting for his verdict. "How did you get your hands on this?"

"Why does it matter?"

Bobby ran his fingers over the upper part of the canvas, where the sky was unfinished. "I will say, however, that whoever was painting this was forced to stop or stopped because something else took precedence. A lot of Géricault's painted studies, especially the ones he did toward the end of painting the *Raft,* were intense but unfinished like this."

"So then it could be by him," Garland said.

Bobby shrugged, but then said, "I really don't think so."

"One expert I showed it to thought it very likely could be."

"Who was that?" Bobby asked, and Garland mentioned a former Christie's vice president who was now a private dealer.

"I guess nobody has tried to find out if there's a signature," Bobby said.

Garland did not respond.

With that, Bobby took a bottle of acetone and a piece of cotton, saturated it, and began rubbing at the bottom right corner, over an area depicting rock that seemed slightly raised. Whenever he did something so daring, dug his way through the layers of inpainting and varnish, he felt as though he were excavating ruins, X-raying through the rubble of nearly two centuries of life that the painting had silently witnessed from a wall, going back to its creation, to the first moment of fervor and intent. But as he rubbed, he realized by the way the grime and the varnish came away so easily that somebody else had also tried to find a signature. For this reason, it only took him a few moments for him to see the faint name, Champmartin: yet another work by the same artist of the painting that Garland had brought to Bobby years ago in New Orleans.

He turned to Garland. "That was too easy. You've already tampered with this painting, haven't you? You already knew it wasn't by Géricault."

"Let's put it this way. I had my doubts it was by Géricault."

Bobby said, "I have the strangest feeling that when I was working for Deshoteles and you brought me that painting of the insane woman, you already had this one in your possession."

"Maybe I did."

"I'm willing to wager that you bought the two paintings together from the same individual—in New Orleans."

Garland avoided responding to this. "Just think," he said exuberantly, "if you turn back the time machine just another notch, then you'll be at the day before Champmartin put his name to it. The day when the body of this boy was still alive, still dying in that hospital. With that in mind, if you take him and restore his face with just a hint of life, just like you did when you were executing your *Vanitas*, then we would have ourselves a Géricault."

Were it that simple, Bobby had thought then, as simple as looking at the dying man who had commissioned him to do the *Vanitas* and drawing him to look as fresh-faced and lovely as the day he left Idaho, his mind full of expectations, of encounters with men like Garland or even like Bobby, who would change his life forever. And then Bobby pictured a great wide swath of water, the black hull of the tanker in the river, the calamitous fall of his father. He imagined the frigate *Medusa,* manned by an incompetent captain, taking dangerous shortcuts to overtake the rest of the French fleet and running aground, the selfish captain escaping with his command crew in a lifeboat, while ordering the rank and file to cobble together a raft on which they rode the seas until nearly everyone died a slow, pitiful death.

And now he saw a man, infected with a fatal virus, asking him to gloss over and enhance a small corner of history.

"Was this restoration part of your original plan for me?" he asked.

"No," Garland said. "You know I would've done anything to get you to New York."

Bobby turned back to the severely damaged painting. "So what do you want me to do, Elliot?"

Garland hesitated a moment and then he said. "Restore it as one of his lost oil studies for the *Raft of the Medusa.* And I know somebody who will pay seven hundred fifty thousand dollars for it."

"A private collector?" Bobby asked.

Garland nodded and said it was a German industrialist who collected nineteenth-century French paintings and already owned two oil studies of the *Raft.*

Bobby turned back to the canvas. "This one is actually very much like the one at the Museum at Alençon."

"Also an oil?"

Bobby nodded.

Garland pressed on. "If you make this a living study, then you're pushing the probability that Géricault did it."

Bobby remembered looking from the damaged painting over at his *Vanitas* hanging on Garland's bedroom wall, his own drawing that seemed wan in comparison. He remembered the first time he'd seen the *Vanitas* hanging in Garland's bedroom and suspecting immediately the reason why it might be there. He remembered turning to Garland and recognizing his expression of dread. "So how did you end up with *this*, Elliot?" he'd asked.

"A little birdie brought it to me."

"Who?"

"A dying little birdie," Garland had said, and then Bobby realized who it was.

"But why would he ask *you* to buy it?"

"Because I'm dying, too," Garland admitted. "I'm dying because he gave *it* to *me*."

And so Bobby had blamed himself for not being honest earlier, for not just moving out and sparing Garland the pain of knowing he was openly looking for someone else. He blamed himself for not telling Garland that the man in the *Vanitas* was HIV-positive when Garland first saw the picture at his studio. He blamed himself for saying too little about the fellow, suspiciously little because at that very insecure time, when he was trying to make it on his own, Garland's jealousy, though it made him feel trapped, also made him feel loved.

And so he had agreed to undertake the restoration.

For the next month Bobby remained cloistered in his studio, had food delivered in, let his garbage pile up in bulging plastic bags. A rancid odor invaded his apartment, and he told himself that he would live as Géricault lived, amidst the stench of decay. In so doing, he made the restoration a ritual. He worked by candlelight, taking his time, the procedure itself, like a slow, transatlantic crossing, the painstaking removal of the yellowed varnish, inpainting the lifeless, sagging corpse to look hued with life. The face turned out to be so damaged as to be nearly a tabula rasa. Garland managed to get a transparency from the museum in Alençon of the similar study, and Bobby re-created a facsimile of the face. He overlaid it with a cast of daylight, the same daylight that falls across the figures on the *Raft*, light Géricault added to illuminate the drama of the shipwreck, because the natural light in the morning sky at the top of his canvas was not strong enough to illuminate on its own. At the very end of the restoration, Bobby went out to the Robert Moses State Park on Long Island and watched the waves rolling in off the Atlantic the way Géricault did at Le Havre. Bobby then returned to his studio and invigorated the presence of the sea in which the body of the dying young man would be submerged once it was discovered that his life was gone.

Garland was amazed by the transformation, by the sense of living spirit so subtly conveyed in the figure originally intended to be deceased. He took the painting to another expert, who felt strongly that it was one of the final oil studies of the *Raft of the Medusa*. Garland was subsequently able to sell it to the private collector for $850,000.

However, soon after the painting was shipped to Germany, the buyer, who was by nature skeptical, had it seen by yet another— a German—scholar. The scholar felt that the painstaking restoration, particularly the heavy inpainting, was a dubious condition that made attribution difficult. The collector suddenly decided he'd paid far too much money for something that could not absolutely be sanctified as a work by Géricault. He called Garland, who reminded him that the painting had been purchased with the understanding that it had recently undergone substantial restoration. The collector turned a deaf ear and insisted that Garland take back the painting and return his money. Garland flatly refused, claiming that the painting had been sold "as is."

The phone suddenly rang, startling Bobby. He picked up.

"Bobby, is that you, Bobby?"

"Hello, Sam," he said.

"What the hell is going on, Bobby?" Sam asked.

The other man's state of anxiety was all too palpable to him. Bobby chose to play it down—for the time being. "Well . . . I was . . . actually just looking at a painting I really love."

"You know what I mean. Why haven't you called me?"

"I tried calling you, Sam, a few times, as a matter of fact—but your machine says 'out of town.'"

"You should've left a message," Sam insisted.

"You're right, I should have. And I'm sorry. How did you find out I was even here?"

Sam explained that his friend Matthew was the man who showed Bobby the way to Lassiter's office.

"So where are you?"

"London," Sam said.

Bobby was taken aback. "London?"

"I came here to find *you*. I came here to tell you that Garland died. Because I didn't know how you'd find out otherwise."

Bobby's eyes abandoned the painting. "Well, obviously, that wasn't necessary." He kicked off his shoes and lay back on Garland's bed. "I was already in America."

"You sound so cold, Bobby," Sam said. "You sound as though if I hadn't called you, it hardly would have made a difference."

"No, I'm glad you called, Sam. But I've been . . . I'm sure you can understand that this death has been hard. For many reasons other than the fact that I barely got to see him."

Bobby briefly explained the nature of Garland's bequest and its implications. Sam told him the book was off and Bobby said he'd already heard that from Pablo. "Elliot never wanted to publish that book," he told Sam.

"I know. It took me a while, but I finally figured that out." There was an uncomfortable silence and then Sam said, "Do you know when you're coming back? To England."

Bobby said it wouldn't be for a few more weeks. After all, he still had to spend some time with his mother.

Sam told him that he was planning to remain in London for a while longer. "If I'm still here, can we see each other when you return?"

Bobby tried to gauge how he felt, but there was only a sense of bewilderment and loss inside him. He'd given everything he had to someone who ironically believed it still wasn't enough. How could he possibly explain this? He had to say something. "Sure," he began, "but seeing Elliot as ill as he was, then having him die and not being here, then having to deal with people, and now having to figure out what I've got to do with all these objects—it's left me kind of wasted. Try not to take it too personally."

There was static silence on the other end.

"I just have one more thing to ask before I sign off," Sam said, now sounding angry. "Why would you put the *Vanitas* up for sale when you promised you'd sell it to *me?*"

Just then Bobby noticed a flaw in his blending of color on one of the thighs of the youth in the disputed painting. This disturbed him. "I didn't put the *Vanitas* up for sale," he said distractedly. "I'm actually going to give it to you. I know how much you've wanted it."

"Bobby, that's really cruel! That gallery has already sold it!"

"Wait a minute, wait a minute, the gallery? Oh, Sam . . . you went *there?* But did you really look at that drawing?"

There was no response.

"You didn't look at it very closely, did you?"

"Bobby, what are you telling me?"

"It's only a copy, Sam. Not nearly as well executed as the original. I made two drawings. I made one for the man who was dying and I made one for myself. And I put mine up for sale because . . . well, I thought I'd need the money to fly back to New York. To see Elliot. As it turned out, I didn't need to. He kindly paid for my ticket."

There was appalled silence at the other end of the line. Finally, Sam spoke. "I knew there was something different about it. I just didn't register what."

"If you stood them next to each other, you could easily tell," Bobby explained as his eyes rested once again on the limbs of the dying youth in the falsely authenticated painting. He could just picture Sam roaring into the gallery, so ready to believe that he had been betrayed. "I still have Garland's drawing," he said sadly. "The one you fell in love with. I kept it for *you*. And it's yours as soon as I get back to England."

23 The two of them were lying naked on Bobby's bed.

"And so both Elliot and I made people think I couldn't come back for legal reasons, but the real reason I couldn't come back was I just couldn't face him dying, knowing why and how." Once he had learned about Garland having been infected, Bobby felt so appalled and guilty, that when the opportunity rose to leave America, he fled, knowing he was fleeing the consequences of Garland's fatal illness.

"And yet," Sam said, "you must've realized you'd have to come back at some point."

"Sure, but I didn't let myself think about it. I figured he'd contact me when he wanted to see me."

"But how? You didn't have a phone."

"I know," Bobby said—guiltily, thought Sam, who assumed that Bobby's fearing bad news might have something to do with why he eventually turned off his telephone.

"So, your living in England really was unrelated to having committed fraud."

"No, in fact, the dispute over the Géricault was settled fairly quickly."

Bobby explained further. Since the sale was transacted in New York, the dispute was in the jurisdiction of the American courts. The problem, of course, was that both sides agreed that the painting was completed at approximately the same time Géricault was completing the *Raft of the Medusa*. Which basically meant that even if his restoration was inspired by wanting the painting to seem more like a Géricault, it would have still been difficult to prove that Bobby had willfully attempted to do that. Knowing this, the collector finally settled by accepting a pretty large payback of what he'd originally paid to Garland.

"But why did Garland pay him back if it would've been so hard to prove your intent?"

Bobby thought about this for several moments. "I think that he was afraid. Not of losing the case, but of it actually going to trial. For then, under oath, I might have explained why I'd agreed to do the restoration to begin with."

"And why did you?" Sam asked. "Wasn't it for money?"

Bobby laughed bitterly and looked away. "Hardly. On Garland's part it was. Purely financial. And he was willing to take the risk because he felt he didn't have long to live. So, obviously, for me the risk of being ruined was far greater. And yet I agreed to do it—for him. I did it to make up for everything that I'd done to hurt him. I did it because I felt as though I had . . . destroyed his life."

Sam was moved to silence. After a while, he looked over at the *Vanitas* drawing that Bobby had brought out to give to him. It now leaned against the mound of paperbacks that piled up against his bedroom wall. On a whim, Sam reached for it and rested the frame against his pubic bone. "You're really not wild about this drawing, are you?"

"I can't be objective—I told you, there's too much associated with it. Why do *you* love it so much?"

Jessie had asked the same question, and Sam had been unable to tell her the truth. "Because it reminds me of my own *Vanitas.*"

"Regarding?"

"The same kind of reckless behavior that killed the two men who loved the drawing too."

"Wait just one second," Bobby interjected. "Just to set the record straight, Garland never *loved* this drawing."

"He told me he did."

"I think you're imagining he did because you do. But the truth is, he never liked it. He never really liked my work. He didn't think I was very talented." After a short silence Bobby asked, "So what do you mean by 'reckless behavior'?"

And so Sam told him about the angel.

It was someone who used to live in his building, one half of a couple, a magnificent man, but wasn't it always somebody magnificent? This one wore his blond hair long, and his eyes were so pale that sometimes they looked completely limpid. Many times over the years, Sam and this man would find themselves riding alone together in the elevator. The man would sometimes smile at him, guilelessly, but no words were ever exchanged. Sam never could say anything, because the intensity of his desire left him tongue-tied. Because of the silence fraught with their mutual admiration, because the man was so arresting and yet so unreachable, Sam ended up nicknaming him "the angel." For years they continued their moratorium on conversation until one day the angel addressed him in a soft, easy manner, as though they'd been on speaking terms for all that time.

"We're moving to California," he said matter-of-factly. "To Los Angeles."

"When?"

"Around three weeks."

This fact possessed a terrible urgency and all Sam could think to say was "I wish I'd known." This sounded silly, obviously, and the man laughed and said in a slightly sarcastic tone, "Why?"

Sam met the man's gaze and said, "Because . . . I think you know why."

"Oh, well," the man said as he got off the car.

A few hours later there was a knock on the door. There he was, dressed in an overcoat as though on his way out somewhere. "I have some time now," he said. "Do you?"

"What was under the coat?" Bobby asked, unable to suppress a smile.

Remembering this now, reminding himself that the encounter occurred only six months after Jessie had ended it with him, Sam shook his head and looked down at his naked legs, on either of which were red runners made by the press of the picture frame. "Not what you think. He wasn't naked, he wasn't wearing a jockstrap or torn shorts or jeans or underwear. He was wearing a wool suit."

"Really?"

The man was unemployed, whereas his lover, a freelance photographer, was often home. And so in order to leave without arousing suspicion, the man lied to his lover and said he had suddenly gotten a job interview with a Los Angeles–based company whose New York office was located down on Wall Street. He dressed for a business meeting and then took the elevator six flights down to Sam's apartment.

The sex itself had the charge of years of anticipation and the abandon of two people who completely and instantly opened themselves to each other. And when it came time for Sam to fuck the angel, as he liked to perversely describe it, he reached for a packet of rubbers and the man grabbed his hand as though he were falling off a building ledge and said, "No, from you, I want it raw. I have to have it. I have to have *you* raw."

There it was, the great taboo of the *fin de siècle*: raw sex. Up until 1980, the idea of two men fucking raw had been humdrum and routine. But this had changed—for obvious reasons. Though it was hard for Sam to admit it, "I want you raw" was probably the single most thrilling moment of his erotic life. A dangerous and primal moment that resonated with the idea of original sin.

Skin to skin—it had been years since you could do this without inviting fatal consequences. There was nothing like it. And it left Sam plagued with a terrible longing that he couldn't understand, a longing that soon turned into a marathon depression. A depression over the fact that he'd deliberately danced with disaster, with death, a depression over the fact that he and the man had touched one another as deeply as they could—the man even said "I love you" to Sam as he came—the perfect act of lust you dream about your whole life. But then the partner disappears, and it begins to seem as if the whole experience itself has been some kind of withering delusion.

For the man came into Sam's life and left without even uttering his name and then moved away from New York. The lobby mailbox listed only the lover and, for some reason, the building superintendent couldn't remember anything more. Sam felt he'd been incarcerated in a dangerous act of love with someone about whom he not only knew nothing but whose name he couldn't even hold on to as a keepsake.

Sure, he knew he could get in touch with the guy by calling LA information for the number of the photographer. Sure, he could hear the angel's voice again. But what would Sam say? The man would probably consider it an intrusion. For him, clearly, once the act was over, it was out of his mind. He'd probably gone on to other things, probably was the sort of person who could make love with every cell of his body and then slough off the experience, like a satisfying meal.

But Sam was different. That torrid afternoon lived on in him; he thought about it all too frequently, about a stranger at the height of pleasure saying "I love you," never understanding why this was at once so confusing and so profound. And whenever he visited Los Angeles, he'd stroll down Santa Monica Boulevard, hoping, praying, to somehow run into the guy, who, of course, would now be single and available. But Sam never managed to find him again.

Several years after the fact, on a winter Sunday, Sam was having brunch with a few friends when somebody mentioned the blond man's lover, who had, in Los Angeles, miraculously metamorphosed into a famous photographer. "And what about the guy he's with?" Sam asked. "That beautiful angel."

The man speaking quite visibly flinched and narrowed his eyes at Sam. "You mean Peter?"

"I never knew his name. When I knew him he had long blond hair and very light eyes."

"Yeah, that's Peter. Peter Croce."

"How did you know them?" somebody else asked, and Sam explained that they'd lived in his building.

"What a beautiful name," Sam had said. "An Italian name." He explained to the table that in Italian, Croce meant cross, as in Christ on the cross. The man who had originally mentioned the couple chuckled nervously. "Well, I guess you might say the name was appropriate, all right. Because he died. In fact, they moved out to California more for his sake. Because Peter always wanted to die where it was warm."

No, it couldn't be! Sam remembered that face, blessed unmistakably with a sheen of health and youth; how could there always have been this shadow on his chimera? How could he not have known? Then, again, it made sense. It was hardly dangerous for Peter Croce to ask for it raw. The light in the restaurant had bristled into fierce pinpoints that dug into Sam's eyeballs. All his friends suddenly looked so far away. His hair was damp—

how had it gotten so wet? "What is wrong with you?" somebody asked, irritated. "You look like you've seen a ghost."

"I was in love with that guy," he told the gathering. "I was in love with Peter Croce."

His friends looked shocked. "What do you mean, you were in love with him?" demanded a man who considered himself one of Sam's closest friends, his confidant. "You never said anything about a Peter Croce."

"I know . . . but I was. We got together once, just once, and it was amazing. And I always thought I'd somehow end up with him."

After Sam finished telling his story, Bobby remained quiet for a while, clearly distressed. "As you've probably figured out, I'm not like that," he said finally. "I would never, ever take such a risk."

Sam felt foolish. "I know. I know you wouldn't."

Obviously, upset, Bobby went on. "It's just what Elliot did. Except he knew, that's the thing, he knew. The guy told him he was sick and yet he stumbled ahead. Blind."

"Do you ever think maybe he wanted to die?"

Bobby whirled on Sam and roared, "Did you?"

"I didn't know."

"But you knew the chances, how many barrels might have bullets in them. Come on, Sam!"

"No, it's not the same. Because you look at somebody you've dreamed about, who's lying there breathing in your ear that he wants you, inside him, and you want him just as much, and of course you tell yourself he's okay."

"So, in the heat of the moment, when he was whispering to you that he wanted you to fuck him raw, if he told you he was infected, would you have stopped right there? Would you have stopped and protected yourself?"

Sam considered this, although it was terribly difficult to do so. Finally, he answered. "I think that if he'd told me he was infected, I might have stopped completely."

"That's exactly why he *didn't* tell you!"

"Yes, that's right," Sam agreed.

Bobby canted backward against the pillows and got lost in his own ruminations. "I just want you to remember one thing about *me*. That the greatest relationship of my life has and probably will always be with somebody I was not really attracted to."

Sam hated hearing this. "How do you know it was your greatest relationship? You have a lot of life left."

Bobby was moved almost to tears. "I don't think so," he said. "I may have half my life left, but I feel like I gave someone the best I ever had and it still wasn't enough. Not nearly enough."

With that, Bobby tried to grab the drawing from Sam. But Sam was a lot stronger and managed to hold on to it. "What are you doing?" he cried.

"I want to get rid of this."

Incredulous, Sam tightened his hold. "You can't do that. You just gave it to me!"

"I know, but I'm tired of stumbling over it. If it were still mine, I'd destroy it." Bobby finally let go of the painting.

"What, do you think it's evil?"

"Evil?" Bobby said sarcastically. "Hardly." It would just mean having to see it hanging on Sam's wall as he'd once had to see it hanging on Garland's wall. "It's the kind of work that I don't do anymore. I know you like it, but I find it melodramatic and obvious."

Sam gently swept a streak of dust away from the picture glass. "You don't like looking at it because it reminds you of too much. The story it tells. But the story isn't just about somebody beautiful dying. The story celebrates life, too."

Bobby shook his head. "Sam, you don't understand art. A true artist never believes a work of art has meaning. A work of art merely invites you to invest it with meaning."

2 4 Eva seemed to appreciate any twist on the mundane. She loved the plastic glow-in-the-dark golf clubs that Sam bought her and would spend hours in her darkened bedroom, swinging fairway irons like the magic fluorescent swords of space avengers. Whenever Sam played with her in the upstairs parlor, she gripped her club with both hands, fully concentrating, Sam bent over her protectively, his hands over hers, guiding her through the arcing motion of the swing, loving the sight of her wispy hair fanning out to the sides and the ball skittering along the carpeting.

The day after Sam saw Bobby, Jessie went to have a final lunch with Rudy and came home complaining of a migraine. Encouraging her to lie down, promising to make dinner, Sam left her in the bedroom and went downstairs to the sitting room, where Eva had put on a video of *The Nutcracker*. For a moment he watched a variation involving the Sugar Plum Fairy and a bunch of dancers in Asian costume and then glanced at his watch. "I thought there were no videos allowed until five. Your mother's rules."

"Except the ones for school," Eva said.

"This is the first I've heard of that."

"No," Eva insisted. "The ones I learn from."

"So you got this at school?"

"It's on the school list."

"Should I go check with your mom and see?"

Defiant, Eva shrugged.

Sam grunted. "Hmm. I thought so. Anyway, I'm making dinner tonight. What would you like?"

Eva tilted her head to the side, pondering his request for a moment and then said, "Turkey burgers?"

"Are there any?"

Eva didn't answer; she'd reentered the video dream. "Hello," he said. "Are there any turkey burgers?"

She looked at him. "In the fridge. Mummy bought some."

"You better turn that down."

Eva crunched her bony shoulders together, in a gesture that was exactly like her mother's. "Don't worry, I won't tell," she said.

"You won't have to." He pointed to the ceiling, indicating upstairs. "She'll hear."

Eva picked at her turkey burger sitting at the wooden trestle table in the kitchen with Sam next to her, leaning on an elbow. She turned to him at one point and, pointing to his biceps, said, "How come your arms are so big?"

"Peer pressure," he said.

"What's that?"

"That's what you're supposed to do if you're a man. Make your arms as big as you can so people think you're strong. I suppose it's kind of silly."

Eva looked at each of her arms. "Mine are small."

"Well, mine were small once, too, and they'll get smaller again. Arms get smaller as you get older."

"Oh," said Eva.

After dinner, she wanted to play another game of parlor golf. Sam made her wait fifteen minutes while he washed dishes and then they went upstairs for another round. He soon began to notice that every time Eva failed to connect with the plastic golf ball, she'd hang her head and whine. At one point, obeying an instinct, he picked her up and held her to his chest. Her first response was resistance. She tried to push him away, but then she softened and allowed herself to be carried off to bed.

The moment Sam laid her down gently on top of her down comforter, she stared at him with glassy eyes.

"Why don't you put on your pajamas?" he suggested.

"Don't want to."

"Come on. I'll let you get away with not brushing your teeth, because your mom is not feeling well, but you can't go to sleep in your clothes."

Eva shrugged, dutifully sat up, and, without a second murmur, undressed down to her underwear and laid her clothing carefully on a white wicker chair. Every movement she made seemed delightful to him. From a small chest of drawers, she fished out a white flannel nightgown with fringe on the bottom. She put on the nightgown as neatly as a woman would, then came back to bed. Sam pulled back the sheets and the comforter and she climbed in. He sat down next to her and kissed her. She smelled sweet, like bath powder. "Would you like me to read to you?" he asked.

Eva whispered, "No, thank you. Just leave the light on in the hallway."

Leaving her door ajar, Sam climbed the flight of stairs to Jessie's bedroom, where Jessie lay in the dark, a cool washcloth on her forehead. She was staring at the ceiling.

"How are you feeling now?" he asked, thinking she looked like a zombie.

She stirred and didn't answer right away. "My head is still pounding," she answered finally. "But it's a bit better. I just took something for it."

"Why don't you try and sleep it off? Then maybe when you wake up in the morning, it'll be gone."

Jessie nodded. "By the way, you mustn't let her watch television until after five no matter what she says."

"It was *The Nutcracker*. She claimed it was educational. That she was allowed to watch it."

Jessie slowly shook her head back and forth on the pillow. "That was ballsy of her. She knows it's an iron rule. And there are no exceptions."

"She's like anybody, I guess," Sam said. "If you give her an inch she'll try to take a mile." Then, feeling he'd somehow earned the right to question Jessie's parenting style, he said, "Anyway, what's the big deal about five o'clock? Is it like a cocktail hour?"

Jessie managed to smile.

Sam sat close to her and began massaging her forehead and her temples. "Is that better?"

"Wonderful."

Thus encouraged, he gently lifted her and settled her head and shoulders onto his lap and kept up his ministrations. Purring at first, she suddenly burst into racking sobs. Not alarmed, Sam simply leaned down and hugged her. She positively quaked in his arms. Instinct told him to say nothing, to wait for her to speak. A while later, somewhat more calm, she referred to Rudy, saying, "I haven't seen him in weeks. And it wasn't as though I were used to being with him very much, anyway. I mean, I have a whole life apart. As upset as I am, I know it's mostly my ego, my pride. Still, the whole thing makes me feel wretched." She fell silent for a few seconds and then, "I think part of the wretchedness is realizing that I mustn't let myself have any more relationships like this. It's like desperately missing a bad habit that you know you have to give up."

"But you won't," he said. "That's just it. You won't give it up."

"What do you mean?" She sounded almost offended.

"You won't give up these relationships any more than I will. We both have to have them."

Jessie considered this for a moment. "You, too . . . I suppose you're right. I suppose we do."

Sam was thinking of his reunion with Bobby LaCour as he said, "Absolutely."

Then Jessie flopped on her side in order to look at him through squinting eyes. As if reading his mind, she said, "You still haven't told me how it went. Seeing Bobby again."

"It went okay. I guess we'll probably keep seeing each other."

"There's something you're not saying."

Sam was at first reluctant to divulge what was on his mind. "He's insisting I get the test."

Jessie took this in for a moment. "Well, it's understandable, isn't it? So did I, once upon a time."

"Yeah, but it's a different situation now. I mean, when you and I were together, I knew I couldn't think twice, couldn't look back. I had to go ahead and do it." Sam hesitated. "And I had nothing specific to be afraid of."

"You're saying you do now?"

The lace curtains draping Jessie's window ignited for a moment as car headlights in the driveway of a house opposite them began to move forward. Sam looked directly into the light, as if to stun himself like a deer jacklighted into a stationary pose.

Jessie repeated more gravely, "You do now?"

He shrugged. "I guess I do. Yes, I do."

"What specifically?" Jessie had rolled away from him. She was lying on her back and peering at him from a slightly greater distance.

And he confessed about his reckless act of love with the angel. Not in any graphic detail, just in fact. She wanted to know when it had happened and he told her, "Six months after you and I broke up. When I was in my funk."

"And you haven't gotten the test again since I asked you to, have you?"

Sam shook his head.

"Because you've been afraid it might be positive?"

"That and— Probably more because it would negate an important event in my life, a crowning moment, in fact."

Jessie had a remote look in her eyes, and Sam wondered what she was thinking. She said only, "Oh, I see." Was she struggling with the notion of his having had such a powerful response toward another man? "So you've basically been living in fear for ten years," she said finally.

"Well, not constantly. From time to time I get a little worried whenever I get a bad cold or the flu or some weird-looking rash."

"You know," Jessie said after a moment, "I often wonder if any of the 'crowning moments,' as you just called them, in *my* life have actually been sexual. I wonder if other moments, obviously less intense, have been more important."

"I'm talking about sexual pleasure, Jessie, only that. I'm not talking about boat trips down the Nile."

"But the phrase 'crowning moment'—"

"I don't mean to say we haven't—you and I—"

She laughed. "No, don't worry. It's a pun for me, Sam. A woman who's had a child has definitely had a 'crowning moment.'"

They both chuckled, and then she suggested, "Have you ever considered that you might have blown the *angel experience* out of proportion?"

"How so?"

"Once you found out that he was dead, you obviously began to worry. But if you'd done something to find out that you were okay, would it have remained in your mind as so significant?"

"Maybe not. I really can't say."

She told him that up until forty or fifty years ago, people lived more comfortably with the idea that they could die at any moment. "Nowadays, we kid ourselves into believing there's guaranteed longevity."

He noticed that her eyes were still glistening from having wept earlier.

"But it wouldn't be such a bad idea," she said.

"What wouldn't be?"

"Your getting tested again."

Sam sighed. "If I could only just bring myself to do it. But knowing there's a chance I'm positive, I can't."

If he were infected, the knowledge would suddenly make his life seem so incredibly unlucky, the result of a gamble taken once and lost. How could he live with that? Especially while he was still well? It would almost be better to live in ignorant bliss until something happened, he explained.

"Only once? So would you really be that unlucky?"

"It's possible."

"These days there are such good treatments for it."

Sam agreed there were. And yet, life would become all about managing a chronic illness. About taking scores of pills every day, constantly going to the doctor to get blood counts taken.

"Better than dying."

"I know it is. And I know I've been stupid waiting as long as I have. But Jessie"—he gripped her hand tightly—"I've been really afraid to get bad news. I'm afraid of how I'll react."

Tears were now rolling from her eyes, and Sam, feeling she was doing his crying for him, cradled her close to him again. "Don't you think I'll be afraid, too?" She wept, looking up at him. "To lose you, my best friend? Who in the world cares for you more than I do?"

"I don't know." Sam stifled his own urge to cry.

Jessie stanched her tears, sat up fully in his embrace and placed both of her bony hands on his knees. "I have to admit something to you, Sam," she said. "That I've made a mistake."

He waited.

"I made a mistake by not letting you be the father of my child. I've known that for some time now. It's no longer hard for me to tell you."

He was moved and silent. All he could do was blink at her. Finally, he was able to say, "Your telling me helps."

Jessie nodded. "I've been afraid of losing you to this terrible illness. And that was the reason I was unable to face the idea of having a child with you. Because if you were to get sick, then it would be more than just devastating to *me*. It would be devastating to our child. I guess what I'm trying to say is that I've been as scared as you, as scared of something that neither of us could predict."

"I think I always knew that."

It suddenly occurred to Sam that anyone able to peer through the window and see them holding one another like this would instantly assume that they were a pair of lovers having an intimate conversation.

"You know," she said after an interlude of thought. "If you decide to get tested, I'll come with you to the clinic."

"That's really not necessary."

"But I'd want to."

"Well, we'll see."

He gently relinquished Jessie from his embrace and lay back on the bed and listened to the sounds of residential London, the passing cars, the bawling street cats, the distant clamor of buses and trains. "I love being here," he murmured, "in this house. I've always found it soothing."

"I love having you here," she said. "And you know you're more than welcome to stay."

Relieved, Sam suddenly felt drowsy and lay there next to Jessie in a kind of stupor. After a while, he said, "But maybe I should ask Eva's permission first. What do you think?"

Waiting for the answer, hoping she didn't think he was wavering, Sam looked over at Jessie and realized that she was asleep. He knew that securing the child's permission would merely be a formality and that Eva would be delighted to have him remain in London. To think that fatherhood so recently had seemed like an impossibility.

Then there was a rumbling outside the window. He wasn't sure how much time had passed, if it had been minutes or even hours. The sound of tires braking to a halt, the telltale idling diesel sound of a black cab, a door opening and closing and then a voice, noticeably Oxbridge, saying goodnight made him wonder: Was it goodbye to the cabby or to someone in the cab? Good Lord, he thought, why did he even care? And in that instant Sam knew he would stay. He had spent far too much time listening for subtle messages beneath words.

A NOTE ON THE AUTHOR

Joseph Olshan is the award-winning author of six novels,
one of which – *Clara's Heart* – was made into a film
starring Whoopi Goldberg. He lives in Vermont and
New York City.